LUCK BE FATAL TONIGHT
A ROXY HORNE NOVEL

VANESSA M. KNIGHT

Luck be Fatal Tonight

Copyright © 2025 by Vanessa M. Knight

Published by Inked Publishing

Cover Art © 2025 by Qamber Designs & Media

Edited by Nancy Canu

All rights reserved. No part of this book may be reproduced or transmitted in any form or by any means, electronic or mechanical, including photocopying, recording, or by any information storage and retrieval system, without permission in writing from the publisher.

The characters and events portrayed in this book are fictitious. Any similarity to real persons, living or dead, or events, is coincidental and not intended by the author.

ISBN: 978-1-963575-03-3

To Sofia. Your dedication to the music you love keeps me motivated and inspired. Love you always.

CHAPTER 1

ANYONE UP FOR A LITTLE BREAKING AND ENTERING? ~ MATTHEW CODY, POWERLESS

THE OFF-HOURS SECURITY lights inside the building blinked while the alarm squawked like an air raid siren, thumping death metal in Roxanna Horne's ear drums. She ignored all of that and concentrated on picking the lock.

"Hurry up, Roxy. Security will be here any second." Sarina was her bouncing, yapping lookout. And bossy. Her best friend was bossy. Not that any of that was needed in a lookout.

Yet. Here they were.

The knob didn't budge. It was too damn early in the morning to be dealing with this. She slapped the inner office door with Manager etched on the glass. *Ouch*. Not smart.

Roxy rubbed her stinging hand and got back to work.

Nothing. Not one click. How had her boyfriend Rafe made this look so easy?

Roxy unclenched her fingers from the lockpicks

and wiped at her forehead. Sweat built and slid down into her eyes. Footsteps echoed in the distance. They were getting louder. Any second they'd get to the hallway door that Sarina was guarding.

"Did you lock the door?" Roxy asked her.

"Of course I did, but they probably have keys. And they have boots. They kick in doors." Sarina leaned toward the dimpled glass window at the top of the door separating them from security outside. "I've seen *Law and Order*. This is so illegal."

"Not illegal." Much. "Only unlawful. Now stay down," Roxy hissed as quietly as she could. "It will take them longer to find us if they don't know which room we're in."

Voices rose in the hall and a key jiggled in the door from the hallway. *Shit*.

They'd run out of time.

Roxy pulled the lockpicks out and slid them in her back pocket as the door flew open. She stood up and jiggled the handle before she looked behind her at the new visitor.

A burly mountain of a man engulfed the doorway to the accounting firm. "Who are you?" he bellowed over the blaring alarm.

Sarina turned to Roxy like she somehow had the magic answer to the question. The magic answer that would not lead to them getting arrested. But since they were mid-B&E, the magic required was some Gandalf-level shit.

"I'm trying to open this door." Roxy jiggled the

doorhandle, hoping she looked innocent and confused instead of guilty and sneaky.

None of this would have happened if the wife who'd hired them to "borrow" the receipts from her husband's infidelities—yes, that was with an s—had both a key for the front door of the office where she'd worked as the front desk clerk and the key to her husband's office.

Turns out Fred Gromme wasn't just hiding his keys. Apparently, the wife didn't know he'd invested in motion sensors. Motion sensors meant there was something to hide. It also meant loud noise when Roxy entered the room. Hence the ongoing screeching.

And then it stopped. Heavenly silence echoed in her ears.

"Why are you trying to open this door?" huge mountain guy asked.

Crap. She needed a story. "I'm so sorry." She bobbed her head, ditzy-mistress style.

Ditzy mistresses all thought the guy would leave his wife. The guy never did. Unless said wife called Roxy to get proof that he was a slimy, cheating whore-bag and the wife was planning on taking every last penny he had. Taking down the slimy ones was always fun.

Her voice tipped up an octave. "Oh my God. My boyfriend Fred told me to get a folder so he can work from home."

"If he sent you to get something from his office, why didn't he give you a key?"

Good question... She bit her lip and hoped a sexy, innocent look was splayed across her face.

"Are you sick?"

So—not sexy. She sighed. "I forgot the key at home. He's going to be so mad."

The guy looked at Roxy, and not in the *you sexy thing* kinda way. It was more like *are you off your meds*.

Sarina knocked a stapler off the desk in the main office. "Shoot." She leaned over. Gorgeous long blond hair set against bronzed skin. Long legs covered in skinny jeans. A tight T-shirt barely containing the ample curves at the top. Too bad she didn't know how to use them.

Sarina picked up the stapler from the floor, and impressive cleavage kept the guard's eyes transfixed. But instead of taking things slow and letting her girls linger under his stare, she bounced up. "I dropped this. I'm sorry." She put the stapler on the desk and fixed her top so the jiggly bits were covered.

If Roxy didn't love her so much, she was sure she'd hate her. Of course, right now, those curves were hypnotizing the burly mountain at the door.

"Are you okay, miss?" Mountain-man stared at Sarina as she ran a hand through her hair.

"I'm fine." She smiled, but it was stilted. How did someone so gorgeous miss the class on seduction?

Mountain-man grinned as he looked at Sarina. He was buying the whole subdued hot-chick thing. Roxy needed to cash in. "Can you help us? We just need one file. We'll snatch it up—and let you get back to securing this big building."

"I'm not sure..."

Roxy slipped her lip between her teeth. "Please?"

His eyes locked back on Sarina before turning to Roxy. "One thing?"

"Absolutely."

He sifted through the keys in his hands. "One thing."

"I promise."

He unlocked the door, then held it open so the Roxy and Sarina could slip inside.

"We'll just be a minute." Roxy smiled and hoped he'd wait outside till they were done. Not likely. He stood at the door with his arms crossed, watching her move around the desk positioned in the center of the office.

Roxy headed for the wall of file cabinets in the back. Hopefully they weren't locked, or this was all for nothing.

Sarina leaned into Roxy. "What are we looking for?"

"The folder labeled Robinson." Roxy pulled on the top drawer and it slid open. A through D.

"Robinson. Are you kidding?" Sarina muttered.

"No." Roxy was not kidding. The slimy, cheating husband was not only dumb enough to keep receipts from his philandering ways, but he kept the mementos in a folder named after the infamous Mrs. Robinson from *The Graduate* movie. She pulled open the lowest drawer. Q through Z.

She found Robinson and pulled out the file. Receipts for everything from jewelry to hotel rooms spilled from the folder. "This is it." She shoved everything back inside and held it close to her chest.

"Thank you. Fred will be so pleased." Roxy sidestepped past mountain man and tried not to run out of the next room and into the hall. Sarina followed, leaving the mountain in the office to lock up. "Let's get the hell out of here."

Roxy headed down the hall and to the stairs, Sarina a few steps behind. Their gym shoes thwapped on the steps. So far, the security guard wasn't following.

They burst through the stairwell door and into the main atrium. Fifty feet separated them from the glass doors of freedom.

"Stop!" A different security guard stood in their way.

Darn. Roxy squashed the urge to put her hands over head. The guard didn't appear to be armed, and as far as he was concerned, they were just grabbing something for Roxy's boyfriend. Although, this guard hadn't been upstairs for the show.

"My boyfriend works upstairs." Roxy inched toward the front door. "Just stopping by."

"Why?" First-floor guard was crankier than the man mountain.

Roxy leaned into the guard, pushing her chest out. "He needed me to grab something for him."

The guard glanced at her chest and shook his head. "Put those away. You're shaking up the wrong tree."

"Fine." Roxy pouted. Even if it wasn't the right tree, he didn't have to be dismissive of her assets.

The guard stared her up and down. "Who's your boyfriend?"

"Fred Gromme."

"Isn't he seeing a dancer with giant..." The guard cupped his hands in front of his chest. "...never mind."

"Yes. That's me." She could pass for a dancer. She was thin-adjacent. Her boobs didn't exactly stop traffic, but they were an adequate flotation device.

"I've never seen you in this building."

"I've never been here before." Roxy slowly moved toward the exit, dragging Sarina by the hand. "We like to be discreet."

"Then why would he send you here to grab something?"

Good question, darn it. "He's sick."

"He's sick? Or maybe he doesn't know you're here."

Well, that too.

He reached for his cellphone. "I should call Metro."

"You don't want to do that." Roxy did not need another run-in with Las Vegas's finest. With her luck, they would show up and not just throw the book at her —they'd throw the whole damn set of police procedurals. Her and cops didn't exactly mix. Although maybe her boyfriend Rafe Amato could get her off—the charges.

Get your mind out of the gutter.

"I think I do." He pulled out his phone.

The mountain of a guard came up behind them. "What are you doing?"

"Calling Metro."

"This is his girlfriend."

"How do you know?" The smaller guard held his phone up in the air like a confused Statue of Liberty.

"How do you not know?" Mountain man shook his head and turned to Roxy. "I'm in charge."

Roxy edged toward the front door, still towing Sarina. She didn't care what sort of power thing was going on here. She only cared about getting out of the building and far, far away. Not only would a run-in with the cops be uncomfortable, she'd never get her PI license with the smudge on her record. And that PI license was why she did all these ridiculous things. Without the hours of training and random tasks a licensed PI threw at her, she'd be stuck in the process-serving department until she died of failure.

"No, it's my turn." The shorter man yanked his arm down and started scrolling on his phone. "I have the email."

The mountain slid his phone from his pocket and started to scroll. "No. I have the email."

Roxy tugged on Sarina's arm and whispered, "Run."

"Hold on!" one of the guards yelled. But she wasn't stopping. Odds were, someone was going to call the cops and she didn't want to be anywhere near the building when they got here.

Roxy slammed the door open as the guards' voices grew closer. "Get back here."

Not a chance. Roxy flew across the empty lot toward the only car, parked in the center—Sarina's awaiting pink Jeep. She scrambled into the passenger side at the same time Sarina got behind the wheel. "Drive before they catch us."

Sarina slid on her seatbelt and started the car. She

drove toward the lot exit without one tire screech. Her speed hovered at tortoise.

"Vertical pedal on the right." Roxy watched the front door open, and then the two guards barreled outside.

"What?" Sarina's blinker ticked a slow rhythm as she braked for the stop light at the exit. The red light scrawled across Sarina's face in the early morning darkness. The roads were mostly empty. The city a hollowed-out shell, on the verge of the bustle of the morning.

Roxy's fingers drummed along her thigh as the men ran closer. "We're in a hurry." This was obvious, right?

The light turned green and Sarina took the right-hand turn. "We're getting away."

"Getting away implies urgency. Fred Flintstone could move faster courtesy of his two feet. And you have an engine."

Sarina sighed. "My engine is moving just fine. There are no sirens."

"Maybe they're being stealthy." Roxy folded her arms across her chest.

"Next time you should drive." It was like Sarina could read Roxy's mind. "Oh wait, you can't drive because your car is in the shop from hitting that pothole at fifty miles per hour."

Very true.

Sarina briefly glanced at Roxy. "So beggars can't be choosers."

Roxy did not sigh. Or roll her eyes. "I can Uber."

"Go ahead." Sarina drove across town, still barely

reaching the speed limit. "Maybe then I won't be stuck doing illegal things."

"Not illegal, unlawful."

"What's the difference?"

"Does it matter?"

"Yes." Sarina turned toward M&J Private Investigations, where they both worked. "I need to know what I should tell my lawyer if we get caught."

"You won't have to tell them anything if you hit the gas."

"If I hit the gas, we'll get pulled over."

Roxy leaned her head back against the seat and prayed that she wouldn't hear sirens or feel the cold steel of handcuffs. Her breath slowly sputtered in and out. Calm. She couldn't control Sarina's driving, and getting mad wasn't going to help.

"Oh no. Flashing lights behind us."

Roxy's eyes flew open. The one thing they didn't need were flashing lights. They were so screwed.

CHAPTER 2
HAVE YOU EVER NOTICED WHEN YOU'RE DRIVING THAT ANYBODY DRIVING SLOWER THAN YOU IS AN IDIOT? AND ANYONE GOING FASTER THAN YOU IS A MANIAC! ~ GEORGE CARLIN

THE SEAT BELT pulled on Roxy's shoulder as she turned to look. Yellow and white flashing lights. Hovering behind the car. Disembodied. She turned back around to look at Sarina. "Those aren't Metro lights."

"How can you tell?" Sarina gripped the wheel like it was threatening to run. Her eyes were manically cutting from the sideview mirror to the road in front.

"Metro cars have red, blue and white."

"Well, it's something."

"Unless random lights are just twirling, it probably is something." Roxy tried to be casual, but she was freaking out. She'd spent the past three months being bossed around by one of her PI coworkers. All that would be for nothing if they got caught. "Speed up!"

"Maybe it's a UFO. I was reading about the UFO that touched down outside of Rachel, Nevada. People said they saw white lights blinking and moving across the sky."

"Watch the road." Roxy wanted to look at the lights, but Sarina was watching them hard enough that Roxy was afraid her eyes would cross. The lights reflected off the rearview mirror, and they were getting closer. "We might be getting abducted." Roxy could only hope. It was better than the alternative.

"Don't joke." Sarina swerved. Thank goodness they were a good twenty minutes from a June sunrise, and the streets were still mostly empty, because Sarina was veering back and forth to avoid little green men with cattle prods.

"I won't joke, but let's keep the car on this side of the street, okay?"

Sarina stopped for a red light and a large garbage truck pulled alongside them, the flashing lights slowly disappearing when the truck turned right and went down a side street. She breathed in a sigh when darkness surrounded them. "I was so mad."

"About what?" Roxy couldn't remember anything in the last few minutes that would make her mad. Sarina thought she saw a UFO, which was huge in her world of Alien Hunters. "Are you mad it wasn't a UFO? You've seen them before."

That was the whole reason Sarina had joined the Alien Hunters. She wanted to see UFOs and, apparently, she had a few years back.

Roxy might be a good friend, but listening to hours of alien folklore was about as enticing as a children's party—which had children, balloons and clowns. Three things Roxy could live without.

Aliens made four.

Sarina shook her head. "I'm not mad at that. I really wanted to do the road trip to Rachel, but Cliff was too busy. He said he was working on his demo. He's always working on that stupid demo tape."

Oh. And Cliff Foster. Five things Roxy could live without.

Kid gloves were needed here. Cliff and his assholism had to be handled gently. He'd do something hideous— like cheat on Sarina— and she'd break down. Roxy would say something about him being the antichrist, Sarina would agree, and two days later they'd make up. Roxy would be accused of being heartless and not understanding. Which was true. She didn't understand. "Maybe Cliff has been working a lot."

"Bull. He's not working. He's a horrible DJ. His transitions are awkward, random backspins with no sense of timing. He's not working because no one wants him."

Roxy could feel her mouth hanging open. Not a pretty sight, she was sure. Sarina rarely talked bad about Cliff—if at all.

"I'm so tired of it. I wanted to go to the landing site. I don't ask for much from him. I've forgiven a lot." Sarina didn't say anything else. She seemed to be lost in thought. Lost in all the things Cliff had done—hopefully. She deserved someone so much better.

Sarina took a left away from work, away from their destination.

"Where are we going?"

"I thought we'd drive around a bit, before we have to go into the office."

That was fine by her. Roxy was in no hurry to get to work. The thought of dealing with the private instigator that was training her was enough to make her eye twitch. Random driving sounded so much better.

They drove in silence for a while. Roxy was good with it. She'd stayed up too late with her boyfriend, so the soft purr of the engine clung to her eyelids and pulled them down.

"Sometimes I think of ways to kill him." Sarina's voice cut through the quiet.

Roxy eyes popped open, because she didn't believe what she just heard. Maybe the words would be different with her eyes open. "What?"

Sarina stared out the front window, her voice barely above a whisper. "I just think of ways to kill Cliff."

"Like really kill him?" This went dark fast. Cliff was a terrible boyfriend but killing him seemed extreme. Maybe break up with him first?

"Like I come home and find him in bed with a sex worker and I pick up his turntable and bash it over his head. Then I burn his beloved demo into ash."

"Wait. You smash the turntable over his head. Not hers?" It was like Roxy didn't know her best friend at all.

"It's not her fault he loves that turntable more than me and sleeps with anything that isn't nailed down."

"Well, he does like to nail the things not nailed down." Roxy laughed.

Sarina did not. She seemed to be lost in murderous

thoughts. "He makes me so mad I don't know what to do. So I dream of ways to kill him."

"You don't see anything wrong with this?" Roxy said slowly.

"What? I can't have a little fantasy."

"A fantasy is Thor naked and giving you the best orgasm of your life—maybe while you eat a stack of pumpkin pancakes and drink a bottle of moscato. That's a fantasy. Not... killing a boyfriend. Why don't you just leave him?"

"I love him." Sarina sniffled. "And you're supposed to be my friend, not telling me what my fantasy should be."

"No, honey." Roxy laid a hand on Sarina's knee. "I am not judging your fantasy. I'm just disappointed I didn't get to say it out loud first."

Now Sarina laughed. "You've always hated him."

"You can't blame me." Roxy leaned against the seat. "My fantasy about Cliff would include some sort of venereal disease with splotchy red spots on his penis and a giant case of testiculitis."

"Is that a thing?" Sarina turned into the parking lot of M&J Private Investigations just as the sun made its way over the horizon. Their home away from home.

"Not sure, but it sounds good and there'd be no cure. He'd have to walk around with giant balls attached to a mini dill. And he'd pick up chicks on the reg, but he couldn't sleep with them, because they'd be too afraid to get near his junk-funk."

"Junk-funk." Sarina wiped her eyes as she laughed. "Thank you for that." She pulled her car into an empty spot near a Dodge Charger. Not any Charger. An orange Charger with the plates 2Koolio. The owner leaned against the car, her cell phone haloing her face. Which was ironic since halos were generally associated with angels, not minions of Satan.

Karan Kafatos didn't dress like a private investigator. She wore a red silk shirt with black skinny jeans and heels. Some might think she was good-looking, but that just meant they hadn't heard her speak.

She sauntered to the passenger side of Sarina's car. Her wavy dark brown hair and her boobs bounced, but the rest of her was eerily still. Roxy was pretty sure it was Botox. Roxy opened the door and braced herself.

"Did you get it?" Karan snapped.

"Good morning to you, too." Roxy stepped out of the car. "It's going to be a lovely day today."

"Really?" Karan's phone lit up, and she stared at it while her manicured nails tapped on the screen. She stopped typing and stared at Roxy with her hand out. "Where's the folder?"

"Folder?"

"Dammit, Roxy." Karan's eyes narrowed. "How are you shadowing me, if you can't handle a simple task?"

"Shadowing implies your involvement."

"Don't start. It's bad enough I have to train you, I can't do that and do these meaningless tasks."

Meaningless tasks? "Your job?"

"Maybe I should tell John that I don't have the time to train you."

John Sherwood, their boss. The man who was

helping Roxy get her PI license by forcing Karan to work with her to get the required hours of PI training.

Karan held a taloned hand out. "Did you get it, or did you screw it up?"

"Don't talk to John. I got it." Roxy got the file from the floor of the front seat and handed it over.

Karan flipped the folder open and receipts tumbled to the ground. "This is good. But we need more."

"More?" There were enough receipts to track him from Vegas to New York and back. Maybe she'd be happy with a receipt for a blow job. Although Roxy didn't think working girls carried around a point-of-sale printer. Or maybe they did.

"Why are you still here?" Karan glared at Sarina, who hit the alarm on her car and scurried for the front door.

Roxy almost begged her to stay so she didn't have to be alone with Karan. But that just felt pathetic.

Sarina waved and unlocked the door to the office. The wave said many things—the biggest thing being Sarina was deathly afraid of Karan. Maybe she was afraid Karan's head would spin around and vomit pea soup or that Karan's fangs would protrude from her gums. Either way, Sarina ran whenever Karan spoke to her.

Roxy was so jealous. She wanted to run too.

"You have work to do," Karan said. "Follow him, and call me if anything happens."

Follow him? "And where will you be?"

"I have a few errands, then I'm getting a manicure."

Roxy looked at the ice blue nails with sparkly crystals in the centers. Her nails looked awfully manicured.

Karan must have noticed the direction of Roxy's eyes. "I need a new color. You watch him."

"Isn't there supposed to be a shadow?"

Karan headed to her car and slid inside. "Do you want me to sign your form?"

Blackmail. Not just for breakfast anymore.

John had a form to document Roxy's hours, so when it came time to provide the information to the state of Nevada they'd have everything documented. He was a stickler like that. Too bad he hired morons.

Roxy and Sarina being the exception, naturally.

CHAPTER 3
MARRIED MEN GET SO THEY MAKE A ROUTINE EVEN OF KEEPING A MISTRESS. ~ ERLE STANLEY GARDNER, THE KNIFE SLIPPED

ROXY WALKED in the front door of M&J before Karan even made it out of the parking lot. Sarina was already at the front desk, pressing buttons on the phone, headset in place.

"Can I use your car?" Roxy asked.

"Why? Aren't you working with Karan today?" Sarina clicked the mouse next to her PC.

"I'm working *in lieu of* Karan. So I need to provide my own transportation."

"Sorry. I have to run errands, or it would be all yours." Sarina pressed the messages button. It was the first thing she did every morning

Roxy couldn't compete with Sarina's job, but she had to talk her into lending the car before she picked up the message. "Can't you run them tomorrow?"

"We're out of coffee and toilet paper. I'm not explaining to everyone that there's no caffeine. Or toilet paper. Can't you take an Uber?"

Of course she could take an Uber. That was always

an option. But just try to get the driver to park in front of a stranger's house for hours on end. And not get paid for their time. That wasn't an option. Roxy didn't have the money to buy a companion for the day.

Although that sounded less Uber-y and more hooker-y.

"Why don't you take the bike?" Sarina had finished documenting the message while Roxy contemplated word choices.

"The bike?" Roxy was hoping and praying that Sarina was talking about something else. Maybe a nice Harley or a moped. Not *the* bike.

"Yeah. The one in the back hall."

Oh, *the* bike. Roxy nodded and headed through the empty office. Desks sat cluttered but lonely under fluorescent lights. Soon the place would be hopping with PIs, process servers, and skip tracers, but not yet. It was too darn early for the skip tracers to be making calls and the PIs tended to work from home until lunch. Of course that didn't apply to Sarina and Roxy. Not when Roxy was under the thumb of Karan.

Roxy entered the darkened back hall. There it was. Bright pink— even in the dark she could see it. She pulled the clunky mode of transport from against the wall. It probably didn't even work.

She could always dream.

She lifted the bike a few inches and let it bounce. The scuffed whitewall tires didn't explode.

Not that it was embarrassing to be without a car because it was in the shop. But she was a grown woman who couldn't afford a rental and currently contemplating using a clunky retro bicycle. She pushed the bike out the back door—don't judge.

She put her purse strap over her head, onto one shoulder, and swung the bag behind her. There wasn't a basket or even a tasket. Not that she knew what a tasket was, nor how it would help her carry her bag while she pedaled. She sat on the wide, mostly padded seat and put her feet on the pedals. Right. Left. The bike wobbled forward. She made it down the back alley of the building and turned toward Fred Gromme's house. Thankfully, he lived in the same area of Summerlin. Less than a mile away.

The wind whipped through her hair as she pumped the pedals. Up and down. Through the side streets, past retail stores and the elementary school till she rode into the edge of the Pioneer Park neighborhood and the postage-stamp yards in front of modest suburban homes.

She made her way down the street to a white stucco two-story. Rounded blue edging surrounded the windows and a garage door stood open. No greenery in the yard, just rock, except for two yellow boxes filled with red and purple coneflowers.

There weren't a lot of places to hide in this neighborhood. All houses in tiny rows. She stopped her bike across the street and partway down the block. She just needed a place to hide her bike and herself so she could watch the house.

Of course, if he went anywhere, she couldn't follow him—which kind of defeated the purpose of watching him at all. But if he did move, she'd just call Karan.

Maybe he'd wait to move until after Karan's fingers were perfectly bejeweled.

She rolled her bike up to the side of a garage across the street. The house had a realtor's sign in the front yard and looked empty. She leaned it against the stucco siding, took her purse and hung it on the handlebars. Which meant she couldn't just leave the bike. She kept one hand on the seat—in case she needed to make a quick getaway. She waited for at least twenty minutes, watching the house stand there in the early morning sun.

Bored. Out of her mind. This was going to be a long day.

She stared off to the right-hand side. The garage hung open, but no one came outside. The streets were relatively quiet with the occasional whir of cars from the main road the only sound.

"What are you doing?" A little girl appeared to her left. Dark brown pigtails with rainbow ribbons hung from her head. She was adorable in her pink leggings and sequined-heart top. Well, she would be adorable if she was leaving Roxy alone. "Why are you standing there?"

Why? She didn't think telling the kid she was staking out the neighborhood would go over really well. That was a surefire way to get the girl's parents involved. Nobody wanted that.

"I'm taking a break from my ride."

"Is that your bike?" The girl pointed at the bike and tilted her head to the side. A grown woman with a bright pink bike probably wasn't normal.

"Yep."

"Aren't you too old to ride a bike?"

Too old to ride a bike. Was that a thing? "How old do I look?"

The girl tilted her head from one side to the other as she watched Roxy. She put her little finger to her chin. Adorable. "Fifty-two." Less adorable.

Roxy's heart hurt. Her mother was in her fifties. Not her. She needed to look into buying a face cream or something. One of those anti-aging kinds that kept children from spurting out that she looked in her fifties. "How old are you?" Children under five didn't know anything. She was probably a confused five-year-old.

"Six."

Dammit. Maybe it was six. Six-year-old children were confused and didn't know anything. "Six? I thought you looked twenty-six." Catty, yes. But it was only fair. The kid added twenty years to Roxy's age, so turnabout was fair.

"Silly." The girl laughed. She didn't appear as affronted by the additional twenty years. "I'm only six."

"Well, you should go home *only-six*. I think I hear your mom." Roxy put a hand to her ear like she'd actually been listening.

The girl glanced down the block and back to Roxy like she was torn between going home and staying here. "Are you going to ride away?"

"Soon. My fifty-two-year-old legs need more rest."

"That's a lot of rest." The girl scrunched her lips.

"It's for all the years."

"Oh. Yeah."

Roxy was almost offended—again, since the kid bought the story without even one question.

Out of the corner of her eye, she saw movement. Fred Gromme walked out of his front door and Roxy nonchalantly switched her attention to across the street. He had a pitcher of water and poured the contents over the flowers in the flower boxes. Apparently, her chalant was not non, because a little voice said, "That's Tyler's dad."

"Really."

"My mom said he has lots of friends." She looked Roxy up and down. "Are you one of his friends?"

Roxy never thought to ask the five-feet-and-under club about a case. Maybe this little age-estimation-impaired person could offer some good stuff. "I am a friend."

Only-six scrunched her nose again. "Oh. Are you seeing him on Tuesday like the others?"

"He's seeing one of the women on Tuesday?" Apparently, the kindergarten crowd was where the info was.

"Yep." The little girl's chest puffed out. She must know how incredibly helpful she was being. Roxy would offer to buy the kid some candy, but that felt like the beginning of an after-school special. She didn't want to encourage her to talk to more strangers.

"My mommy said that his women are all see you next Tuesdays."

They are all *see you next Tuesdays*? What did that even mean? He didn't seem like the type of guy to gather his conquests around a table on a random

Tuesday. She'd have to make sure she came back tomorrow.

"I wouldn't go near him. My mom says he has crabs. But when I play with Tyler, I've never seen them. I'm going home now." *Only-six* waved as she pedaled away.

But that didn't matter, Roxy had a clue. *His women are all see you next Tuesdays.* That's weird wording. Almost like... she closed her eyes and stuffed down the urge to slap her palm to her head. He wasn't going to see them on Tuesday. Her mother obviously was talking in code in front of a six-year-old. All the women he cheated with were C-U-Next-Tuesdays.

This was why you never heard of a six-year-old informant. Totally useless information.

Gromme finished his watering and walked back in the house at the same time a black pickup truck pulled up to the curb in front of Roxy. The passenger window slid down, and a deep, smooth voice came from inside. "Hey, Horne. Busy?" Rafe Amato sat at the wheel. All six-foot-two Italian bits of him. He had dark brown hair that he cut monthly to rest just above his shoulders. His brown eyes and light brown skin made her insides melt —not to mention the silk that used to be on her lady bits.

"Extremely." She walked over to the truck and leaned her crossed arms on the open window. "You should have contacted my assistant for an appointment."

"I was hoping you could fit me in."

Fit him in. So many naughty things passed through

her mind. All of them would lead to her naked. And she didn't have time for naked. She was working, and he'd be heading back to the Pura Vida hotel and casino to run his security team.

He actually ran the security for the Sonutoso Group of hotels in the Vegas area, which translated to three or four properties. But lately he'd been spending more time at Pura Vida. Roxy didn't mind since his condo was in the same building and having him nearby meant she got to see him during the day on occasion.

"Shouldn't you be at work?" she asked.

"I have a lot of time off and things were slow. I thought I'd see if you wanted to grab breakfast."

"I always want breakfast." She dropped her chin to her forearms. "But I'm on a stakeout. How did you find me?"

"Sarina told me where to find you." He looked so disappointed. But that might just be Roxy projecting her own feelings. She hated turning down time with him. And food.

"Are you off for the day? Why don't you stay here with me?" Two birds, one stone. She'd get to hang out with this gorgeous man and do her job in an automobile —like a normal person.

"How about, I'll stay here and hang for a while if you come with me to grab some pancakes first."

"Sounds good." Another win-win for her. He'd said the magic word, pancakes. "Let me grab my bag."

She ran to the bike and slid her purse off the handlebars. Part of her wanted to leave the stupid bike here. But if it got stolen, she'd have to replace it. And she barely had the money to cover her car repairs, let alone buy the office a bike they'd never use.

She walked the bike to the passenger door. "Can I throw this in back?"

"Where's your car?" Rafe whipped open the driver's door and jumped out. He went around to the back of the truck and popped open the tailgate.

Roxy met him there and handed off the bike. "It's still in the shop. I'm using this."

"How is it still in the shop? I thought Romeo said he was going to have it done yesterday."

"He called and said he was still waiting on the part. When he's not waiting on a part, he's trying to shake me down." Did she say that out loud? Romeo was an old friend—well, friend-adjacent. He liked to overcharge her while telling her he was taking care of her, while he eyed her like dinner and flirted. But he was a good mechanic and didn't ask questions.

"What do you mean?"

"Nothing." She didn't need to invite him to the pity-party she would be throwing once she got the final bill. She'd be selling blood or other body parts to get it back.

He lifted the bike like it was Barbie-sized and slid it along the pebbled plastic bedliner. "How are you on a stakeout without a car?"

"I was just roaming the neighborhood and watching my guy."

"And what if he left his house?" He closed the tailgate.

"He did leave. To water his plants. It was handled."

"And what if he drove away?"

She shook her head. She'd gone over all of this earlier. In her head, but still. She knew there were minor kinks in her plan. But when your car was in the shop and you had to do the job of the woman you work for, you improvised. "I would have called Karan."

"Is she around the corner? Why didn't she just let you sit with her?"

"She's getting a manicure."

Rafe shook his head and walked to the passenger side. Opened the door. So fricking chivalrous, her girly bits sighed. She slid in the truck and moved over as he closed her door.

As soon as he got behind the wheel, Rafe said, "She does know that she's supposed to train you and then watch to make sure you do everything according to regulations."

"She might know it, but she does not care."

He pushed the ignition button and the car sparked to life. That's how cars worked. Hopefully, when Romeo was done with her car, it would work like that, too. Except for the button part, because her car was ancient. "So you have no one watching your back."

"Sarina came with me this morning when I went to get a folder for the case." The disastrous lockpick episode passed through her mind. "I need you to show me how to use the lockpicks again."

"You need to make sure you're listening for the click."

"Yeah. I did that, but it wasn't as easy as I thought."

"You and Sarina doing B&E in the dark of morning. Sounds safe." He pulled away from the curb.

"The building had lights." It's not like she was outside in the dark. "And what would Karan offer that Sarina can't."

"Sarina wouldn't hurt her own shadow." Rafe knew Sarina—mostly from what Roxy told him. But he'd met both of them when they were in their very early twenties, partying after a football game. Not that she had cared about football back then. Just the cute little pants and what they did to accentuate cute male butts.

Rafe shrugged. "I get the impression Karan has hidden a few bodies in the desert."

She probably had. Which was why Roxy didn't want to cross her. "We can't be gone too long. I need to keep my eye on Fred Gromme."

"What did he do?"

"His assistants."

"Oh. The usual." He headed down the block. He passed homes and residential areas and block after block of turns that would lead to food. A quick stack of pancakes swimming in syrup, and then back to the Gromme house before Fred headed off to commit adultery again.

CHAPTER 4

FRIENDS HELP YOU MOVE. REAL FRIENDS HELP YOU MOVE BODIES. ~ JEFF MACH, THERE AND NEVER, EVER BACK AGAIN: DIARY OF A DARK LORD

EIGHT VERY LONG HOURS LATER, Roxy pedaled her bike through the park toward her office. The outside air slapped against her cheeks. Most of the people were finishing their day in the office or heading home from work. She swore it hadn't taken this long to get to Gromme's house.

Of course, on the way there, there was a promise of the excursion being successful. Now she knew it was a waste of time. Fred never left. He'd played catch with his son, for heaven's sake.

She should be glad the man had spent the day being Dad of the Year, but since he'd already spent three nights at the local crab motel, where they sold their rooms by the hour and it was a good idea to splurge on the fifteen-dollar fee to "upgrade" to clean sheets, she wanted to get this over with. She needed a money shot and maybe the name of his playdate.

The guy lived in a nice part of the town with a good job. Why he was slumming it at roach motels was the fifty-dollar question. Although there was no way he'd run into his wife there. Between the questionable neighborhood and the stains on the walls, she'd never set foot in the place.

Luckily, his wife was smart enough to hire Roxy— well, actually Karan. But Roxy wasn't afraid of the stains. She wasn't too fond of the bed bugs, but she stayed outside so her body never went near the bedspread and what was crawling on it.

The streets were quiet as she crossed to the M&J parking lot. Sarina's car sat alone. Most of the offices had closed. Besides M&J, the ice cream joint was the only business all lit up. They'd probably be busy when people were done with dinner.

Roxy opened the front door of the office, propping it open as she pushed the bike inside. "Honey, I'm home."

"You're late."

"I was busy at the office, little lady." Roxy leaned the bike against her desk. "What's for dinner?"

"I don't know."

"You don't know? I've been out slaving away, working to put a roof over your head."

"You don't put any roof over my head." Sarina got her purse from the drawer. "And you haven't slaved a day in your life."

"Saucy. I like it." Roxy headed for the door. When Sarina didn't follow her, she turned around. "Are you going out with Cliff?"

"He's still not answering his phone." Sarina looked at her phone with such longing in her eyes.

Maybe that was a sign—not that she'd say that to Sarina. "Then you can hang out with me. I'm thinking Shake Shack to-go and *Aquaman*."

"The first one or the second one?"

"Do we have to choose?" Roxy put an arm around Sarina's shoulders. "We can watch them both."

"That works." Sarina looked back at her phone.

Roxy took it from her hands. "No more of this." She dropped it in her purse.

"But..."

"No but. No phone. Only hot guys with bare chests."

"And shakes." Sarina smiled as they walked outside. She locked the door and turned to Roxy. "I feel better. Thanks."

"Good."

An hour later, they pulled down the Roxy's street. The windows of the two-story dingy gray stucco building were lit up with TVs. They were late. People were already home and watching their streaming channel of choice. Which meant the parking lot was full. Only two spots were available, and of course they were next to the dumpster. She always had to park by the monstrosity. The only way to get the good spots was to not work, and she needed her job.

"I think something died back here." Sarina's nose scrunched as she parked the car and double checked the windows were rolled up to the top.

Roxy slid out of the car. "It always smells like this lately."

"Maybe you should have management look into that."

"I will." Probably not. Telling management would mean talking to the landlord. Which wasn't the worst thing. Ms. Potter was a wonderful woman. But Roxy had promised her she'd help clean out the building's storage unit. It hadn't been done in years. The things they would find... alive and dead. No. She needed to push that nightmare off for as long as possible.

They walked across the lot and up the brown metal stairs to the second floor. She opened the door and dodged the clothes on the living room floor, dropping fast food bags on the kitchen table.

"How can you live like this?" Sarina used wooden tongs from the floor to pick up a bra. Yes. There were wooden tongs on her floor. But the wire behind the TV got loose and Roxy had needed to reach it.

Still Roxy asked, "Live like what?"

"This place is a mess."

It was. There were clothes everywhere. She'd like to say it was because she had a hot date and did some mating-preparation fashion show. But it was more that she'd been too lazy to do laundry and needed to differentiate between clothes that were clean, semi-clean and so filthy they were walking around the apartment on their own.

How clothes could walk around, she had no idea. It was the threat her mom always used to get Roxy to clean her room. Honestly, when her underwear started an uprising, she'd burn the joint down before they escaped.

"I just needed to figure out what needs to be washed." She lifted a t-shirt and brought it to her nose. Ripe like moldy sweat.

"It all needs to be washed." Sarina walked down the back hall to Roxy's bedroom and came out with an empty basket. "How did it get like this?"

"I've been staying at Rafe's a lot." Which was true. They'd been basically cohabitating—not with like a drawer or anything, but she'd spent at least four nights a week with him. And if they were going to part-time-cohabitate, might as well be at Rafe's gorgeous downtown apartment instead of her apartment where the closet spewed clothes.

Sarina picked up a pile of clothes with the tongs and dropped them in the basket. "I would hope so. This can't be healthy unless you like creepy crawlies."

Crap. She did not like creepies or crawlies. "If there is anything alive in this apartment besides us, I'm moving." She did not do bugs. Ever.

Roxy picked up a stack of clothes and dumped them in the basket at the same time someone knocked on the door.

"Expecting someone?" Sarina produced the TV remote from under a pile of clothes.

"There it is." Roxy took the remote and put it on the end table. Well, she pushed the clothes off the end table and then put the remote there. "I was looking for that."

Another knock.

"You should get that." Sarina kept piling clothes in the basket. Well, more like on the basket. The thing was full. And they'd barely made a dent in the clutter.

Roxy walked to the door, praying it wasn't Rafe. He didn't need to see this. She looked through the peephole. Dammit. She somehow wished it was Rafe. At least Rafe didn't ask for overdue rent or ask her to do random tasks around the building.

She edged open the door for her favorite— albeit only— landlord. "Hi, Ms. Potter."

"Sorry to interrupt your girl time." Ms. Potter's black and gray Annie hair bobbed as she peeked around Roxy like she was looking for illegal activity. "I found these two pratting about. Figured I'd bring them on up."

Two of Metro's finest stood behind her. Two detectives Roxy had gotten to know very well a few months ago. And those experiences were not exactly pleasant.

Detective Geary and Detective MacAuley stepped out from behind Ms. Potter. Not that they were exactly hiding. They were each about six feet tall and Ms. Potter was barely over five feet.

"You're not getting nicked again?" Ms. Potter clucked her tongue.

"I didn't get nicked the first time, Ms. Potter. I was innocent." And she had been. Find one dead body and suddenly a girl was the prime suspect. Thank goodness all that craziness was over.

"Hmm." Ms. Potter's dark skin crinkled. Almost like she didn't believe Roxy. Then again, neither had Detective Geary.

Speaking of whom... "Detective Geary." Her least favorite detective. Not that she had anything against him.

"Miss Horne." He just disliked her. She had a hard time liking people who couldn't see her charm.

"Roxy, we're looking for Sarina West." Detective MacAuley wasn't smiling, but he didn't have the disgust in his eyes like Geary. Roxy and MacAuley had a friendly relationship—although he didn't like her boyfriend much. But that was a story for another day. Like when detectives weren't at her door looking for Sarina.

"I'm right here." Sarina came into view. She wasn't even trying to play hard to get.

"Ms. West, we need to talk to you for a moment." The detectives waited at the door, using Sarina's last name like they hadn't met her before. Like something was wrong.

"Come on in. Is everything okay?" Sarina was inviting people into Roxy's house now. Not that it mattered. Sarina spent as much time here as Roxy spent at her house. Although lately they'd spent less time doing the sleep-over thing, with Roxy staying at Rafe's.

"You might want to sit down." MacAuley still hadn't smiled. That wasn't like him. Then again, he didn't stop at Roxy's very often. Unless there was a problem. "Are you still dating Cliff Foster?"

"Yes." Sarina's eyes widened as she looked at Roxy. Her eyes said, what the heck? Roxy's eyes didn't have an answer.

"When was the last time you saw him?" MacAuley sat in a chair next to the couch.

Sarina thought about it for a moment. "Last Wednesday."

Detective Geary wasn't getting as cozy. He stood over the Sarina like an angry high school teacher. "You haven't seen him in almost a week?"

"No. We were supposed to go out of town on Friday, but he never showed."

"Where was he supposed to meet you?" Detective Geary pulled out a little book.

"He was picking me up at my place. Why?"

Detective Geary shook his pen and then started writing. "So, when he didn't pick you up, did you go to his house?"

"No, I called Roxy and came here."

"At what time?"

"Ten or eleven."

Roxy was tired of watching the tennis match of questions. She wanted to join. "What is this about?" Mostly she wanted to ask that.

"Cliff Foster was found dead this morning."

"Wait, dead?" Yeah that was Roxy again, but Sarina's mouth just hung open. And someone had to make sure this wasn't some kind of joke.

"Yes."

"What happened?" The conversation from this morning played on a loop in her mind. Cliff getting bashed with a turntable. "As long as his turntable didn't jump up and knock him out."

Sarina didn't laugh. The detectives didn't find it funny either.

MacAuley's eyes went wide. "How did you know that?"

Oh dear goodness. There's no way that's what happened. "You're messing with me."

"This is an active murder investigation." Detective Geary sneered. "We don't mess with anyone."

"Murder?"

"Yes, we're pretty sure he didn't hit himself with the turntable."

Well, at least there was no sex worker. But a turntable to the head. How does one unsee that? Roxy tried to hold the gulp that was building in her throat. She didn't need the cops to think she was a suspect again. She had motive.

It was Cliff. She had lots and lots of motives.

And Sarina—that was her fantasy. Why the hell hadn't her fantasy included Thor and pumpkin pancakes?

"Did anyone have a grudge against Cliff?" Detective Geary asked.

"I don't think so." Sarina shook her head, probably to shake the fact that both Roxy and she had something against him from her mind. Sarina didn't like that he was a no-calling cheating dirtbag. And Roxy didn't like that he breathed—which was probably something she shouldn't tell the nice police officers since he no longer did.

"Did you have a grudge against Cliff?" Detective Geary glared at Sarina.

Oh crap. Lie, Sarina. Lots of lying.

"No." Sarina gulped that lie down her throat. Hopefully the detectives didn't notice.

Detective Geary's eyes narrowed, so he probably noticed. "So, you didn't mind that he was last seen dropping off a prostitute on Fremont Street?"

Sarina's mouth hung open. The Fremont Street playdate was obviously not something she'd known about. "I didn't know."

"Sorry to be the ones to break that to you." MacAuley did actually look sorry. Which was more than Detective Geary was offering. He just kept scowling. "Can you think of anything else that might be pertinent to this investigation?"

Roxy shook her head as Sarina said, "No."

"If you think of anything, please call." MacAuley nodded to Sarina and then Roxy as he stood. They both had his number after the last murder investigation Roxy had been a part of.

There were so many things wrong with that last statement. But Roxy didn't have time to think about that. She was too busy thinking about Cliff and how many horrible stories she could share—from deadbeat friends and drug use to overall assholeness. They'd need to block out an all-day conference call to get through it all.

"And this should go without saying, but don't leave town." Detective Geary walked out the door behind MacAuley.

Well, damn. And they were just about to go on a

hot air balloon ride through the Rockies. That's out now.

Not. They weren't going anywhere. They had burgers and shakes and *Aquaman*. Although the look on Sarina's face said aqua didn't have enough man to take her mind off of her dead deadbeat boyfriend. It was probably too soon for Roxy to mention any of that, though.

"How about a drink?" Roxy had a feeling it wasn't too soon for that.

CHAPTER 5
EARTHQUAKES JUST HAPPEN. TORNADOES JUST HAPPEN. YOUR TONGUE DOES NOT JUST HAPPEN TO FALL INTO SOME OTHER GIRL'S MOUTH! ~ GEMMA HALLIDAY, KILLER IN HIGH HEELS

IT HAD BEEN two hours since the detectives left. Sarina and Roxy had watched *Aquaman*, or at least tried. It felt more like background noise to the drama swimming in both of their heads. Sarina didn't want to talk. About any of it. Roxy wanted to talk. Lots. But it wasn't Roxy's story and it wasn't her heartbreak.

"I should go home." Sarina sat on the blue suede-like couch, her legs curled beneath her as she watched the bourbon swirling in her glass. She also didn't appear to want to drink.

Another difference between Sarina and Roxy right now. Ever since Rafe got her hooked on bourbon, she'd been enjoying a glass here and there. Ever since she found out Cliff was dead, she'd been downing the glass here in her hand— she was tempted to take the glass from Sarina's hand and finish that one off, too.

Roxy kneeled on the carpet and put on her best pout. "You can't go home. We've been drinking."

"You've been drinking." Sarina dumped the

contents of her glass in Roxy's. It was like Sarina read her mind.

"Do you really want to leave?" Roxy tried to hide her hurt, but she had a feeling it wasn't working.

"I don't know. I'm just not very good company."

"What are you talking about? You're always good company." Roxy pushed at Sarina's knee. "If it wasn't for your company no one would hang out with us."

"No one does hang out with us."

Good point. They were more of a two-woman show. "I don't want you to go. You can have my bed."

"Really?"

"Yeah, I'm sleeping in it too, but you don't have to sleep on the couch."

"Fine." Sarina picked at the shaggy blue strings coming from the old furniture. "This couch is terrible."

"It was apparently very comfortable when I was a child." But over the years, osteoporosis and wrinkles had made the couch ornery as hell. She should retire the damn thing, but it was paid for, so it stayed on the payroll.

Sarina tipped her glass from side to side. A small drop slid around the bottom. Back and forth. She just stared. Her gaze said she was lost in her thoughts. The frown said those thoughts were not good ones. "He dropped off a sex worker."

"Maybe she just needed a ride home. You know, cars for call-girls. Like a service. Chivalry and all."

Sarina looked at Roxy like she'd just said unicorns could fly. To be fair, Roxy used the word "chivalry" in reference to Cliff, so maybe the horned bastards had grown wings.

"He wasn't an Uber."

True, he wasn't an Uber, but he also wasn't chivalrous. And Sarina knew that. She had to know he had someone on the side. He always had. That was the one thing she could count on him for.

"Why didn't you tell the detectives you stopped at Cliff's before you came here?"

"He wasn't home."

"Wasn't he?" Roxy didn't like the path her thoughts were taking. But the whole turntable smashed into his temple thing was a large coincidence.

"Are you asking if I killed him?"

"Not really." That the thought even crossed Roxy's mind was ridiculous. Sarina had turtled her way from a B&E this morning. She couldn't even drive over the speed limit. She wasn't exactly the bashing kind. "Do you know who it could have been?"

Sarina popped off the couch like an angry jack-in-the-box and paced the room. "I don't know. I keep going back and forth. This is murder. How could anyone do that? And now he's gone." She swiped at her damp cheeks.

"I'm so sorry." Roxy stood and enveloped her best friend in a hug. Pulling her close felt good, as she could practically feel Sarina's heart breaking.

Sarina's shoulders shook for so long, Roxy was afraid if she didn't hold on tight, Sarina would shake out the door. Roxy squeezed her a little tighter.

"He's not going to hold my hand and bring it to his

lips. He's not going kiss me ever again." The pain in her stuttered words was too much. Too much pain.

Roxy wanted to wrap her in a bubble and make it stop.

"I don't even know when the funeral will be." Sarina hiccupped and pulled away. She ran her arm over her wet cheeks. "I can't even say my goodbyes."

"Can't you call his mom?"

"Oh, my goodness." Sarina turned, the manic back in her step. "His mom must be a mess. She lost her only son. Oh my god. I have to call her."

"Should I get your phone?"

"No, I have it." Sarina dropped to the couch. "But I don't have her number."

"No worries." Roxy leaned across the table for her cell phone. "We can look her up. That's what Google's for."

"I can't call her."

"Why?"

"I've never met her."

Wait. "What?"

"I never had a reason to meet her."

"You didn't visit her on his birthday or on her birthday? What about holidays." Roxy hated to be a bitch, but they'd been dating for years. Yet she hadn't met his mother. How was that a thing? How was she still with him?

Sarina glared at Roxy. "We tried to set up a time to meet, but it just never worked out. Either we were fighting, or it got cancelled."

"What about his friends? Can you reach out to them?"

"I don't have any numbers."

"Not one."

"Wait." Sarina pulled her phone from her pocket. "I have one." She scrolled through her contacts. "Davis. He lived with Cliff's mom for a few weeks." She tapped the screen and waited, setting the phone on the coffee table and putting the call on speaker.

A male voice said, "Hello."

"Hey. Davis, I'm sorry to call so late."

Roxy checked the time. After ten. Yeah, it was a bit late for a cold call.

"I don't know if you remember me. This is Sarina."

"Who?" Davis said.

"Cliff's girlfriend."

"Kandi?"

Who the fuck was Kandi? And where did Davis get that name?

Sarina ignored the implication of a Kandi or maybe she didn't hear it. "No, Cliff's girlfriend, Sarina."

There was silence and then he said, "Oh yeah. Hey, Sarina. Blond straight hair, right?"

"Right." Sarina did have blond, straight hair. But the fact he had to identify her by it and not just the girlfriend title—so crappy.

Roxy had mentioned her hatred of Cliff and his douchey friends, right? She might not have thought about his friends in a while, but she hated them too. They covered for his bad decisions.

"Do you have his mom's number?"

"Uh, nope." Davis sounded sketchy, but maybe Roxy was reading too much into it. Not everyone had their friend's parents on speed dial. Just because Roxy and Sarina did, didn't mean it was normal.

"Didn't you live with her?"

"Yeah, but that was a while ago."

"Did you hear what happened to Cliff?" Sarina was playing strong, but Roxy had a feeling if she had to actually say the words out loud, the woman would be a mess of tears.

"Yeah, it sucks."

"Yeah. Do you know if they've planned anything, like a funeral or wake?"

"Nope."

"Could you contact me if they schedule something?"

"I don't think so. I don't think they'll have anything. And even if they did, I wouldn't go. We had a falling out. I haven't talked to him in forever."

"You both went clubbing last week."

"Oh that. We did." Davis squeaked, like a chipmunk without a hula hoop. "Look, it was with a group of guys. I barely even saw him."

"Fine." Sarina's face was a warzone. Sadness fought with anger, which fought with frustration.

Crap. Roxy hated Cliff's friends.

Davis was lying. Roxy could hear it in his cartoon voice. He was lying about last week, or he was lying about not being friends. He was at least lying about something. Roxy opened her mouth to speak her mind.

She might not have a lot of extra to give, but this jackass needed it more than she did.

Sarina rested a hand on Roxy's arm and brought a finger to her lips. She took a deep breath.

"I should go." Davis was dodging her now too.

Didn't Sarina see the red flag in that?

If she did, she ignored it. "Call me if you hear anything," Sarina whispered. The tears hadn't fallen again, yet. But given that conversation, she was about to let go any second. Rightfully so.

"See you." Davis clicked and ended the call.

Roxy wanted to reach inside the damn thing and throttle him. Although, saying that out loud might make it happen like with Cliff and the turntable. Visualizing and dreaming about assholes' deaths was one thing. Having it happen was an entirely different thing.

"Are you okay?" Roxy wanted to mention the lying and the throttling. But this wasn't her fight. If Sarina hadn't put two and two together, Roxy didn't want to be the one to burst her bubble. Not today. Today was for mourning. They'd talk about the reality of all that happened today when the sting of losing Cliff hurt less. "Do you want to talk about it?"

"Not really." Sarina stared at her phone before sliding it face-down on the table. "You know what I really want to do? Watch *Aquaman II*."

Roxy wasn't sure that was a good idea. Sarina shouldn't bottle up what was happening here. "Don't you want to let all the sadness out?"

"I will. But tonight I want abs."

Agreed. "It is impossible to be sad when he flexes those abs."

Sarina attempted a smile. It was a little flat on the edges. But she was trying. She grabbed Roxy's glass. "Do you mind if I take this?"

"Anything you want, honey." Roxy stood and kissed Sarina on the forehead. She started for the kitchen. "I'll grab another one. Want chips?"

"Yes to chips. And bring the bottle." Sarina tilted the glass back and the liquid was gone.

"Are you sure?" Roxy's tracks stopped dead. This wasn't like her friend. Sarina wasn't a big drinker. Neither woman was. They might drink a glass here or there, but they generally avoided the gulp.

"Yep. I'm never going to be able to sleep without a little help."

Roxy nodded and found an open bag of chips in a cabinet. She took one out and stuffed it in her mouth. Winced. Mildly stale. But given Sarina's determination to drink herself to oblivion, she'd never notice. And Sarina needed to eat to soak up all that determination.

Roxy grabbed the bottle of Maker's Mark and headed into the living room for a long night of denial and drink.

CHAPTER 6
IF YOU WANT TO BE A PRIVATE EYE, YOU HAVE TO GET USED TO SUCH THINGS AS HIDEOUS DEPRESSION AND ABJECT DESPAIR. ~ ARTHUR BYRON COVER, THE PLATYPUS OF DOOM AND OTHER NIHILISTS

THE NEXT MORNING, Roxy entered work with a very hungover Sarina, complete with bloodshot eyes. No orange Charger sat in the lot. Karan must have been getting a pedicure or something.

Roxy might not even need to borrow Sarina's car. She was happy about that. Not that she minded sitting on the Gromme house, but she didn't want to be away from Sarina.

A hollowness Roxy had never seen had taken hold of her best friend. Her sunglasses were firmly in place, since she couldn't even handle the word sunshine. And Vegas had all the sunshine today.

Sarina slunk to her desk and melted into the seat. She didn't put away her purse or move any of the paperwork from in front of her. She didn't take off the sunglasses. She just dropped her forehead to the desktop. She should have called in sick with a migraine. So what if it was a Maker's migraine—it was all the same.

"Why don't you let me take you home? We'll watch

Marvel movies and eat ice cream." Roxy had to try again.

"I need to keep busy." At least that's what it sounded like with Sarina's head snuffled into her arms.

"Ok." Roxy attempted a smile as she looked over at her desk. She had the perfect view of Sarina if anything went wrong. So it was good Karan wasn't here to pawn off her own work on Roxy. Even if she had to run out to serve a few papers, which was her day job with M&J—when she wasn't Karan's flunky—she'd only be away from the office in short bursts.

Of course, she could always tell the bosses she was helping out Karan and surf the web and try to find Cliff's mother, keep an eye on Sarina and find some information for her.

Even though the topic sucked, she was looking forward to all the surfing. She passed Sarina's desk and went to her own. A Post-it was stuck to the center of her computer screen. *Sit on Fred Gromme today*.

Crap.

Any surfing she wanted to do would have to be on her phone. Not nearly as useful, since the people-finder software was on her computer. Roxy wasn't sure if that software was available for the phone, but M&J was never going to spend that kind of money, even if it was.

Roxy pulled the note from her screen and watched her best friend. Sarina hadn't moved. Her forehead glued to the desktop. She should not be here. She should be bowing to the porcelain gods while swearing to never drink again—like a normal person.

Roxy walked over to her bestie and tossed the Post-it in the trash. "Let me take you home."

Sarina didn't lift her head. "No. You need my car to do Karan's bidding."

Oh so true. "But you don't need to be here. I'll drop you at home and take your car."

Sarina didn't offer any witty retorts. She didn't say anything all.

"Sarina?"

"I'm fine." Her voice came out muffled against the paperwork on the desk.

The phone on Sarina's desk chirped to life. Sarina did not chirp. There was very little life.

Another ring. Roxy lifted the handset. "M&J Private Investigations." Roxy had heard Sarina answer the phone enough to know what needed to be said.

"Can I talk to Mr. Sherwood?" the voice on the line asked.

"Of course, I'll transfer you now." Roxy looked at the multitude of buttons lining the phone cradle. *Shit.* She found John's name in all the blinking lights and hit the button for the J in M&J Private Investigations. She hit the transfer button on the phone and prayed that the call went to her boss. It wasn't like she transferred calls every day. Or ever.

Sarina looked up. "I'll be fine."

"You're not fine. Go home and sleep away the bourbon under your eyes."

"I need the money." She did need the money to pay her rent and normal bills, like everyone else. The difference was Sarina had parents who adored her and a father who could afford to bail her out. Not that Sarina would ever ask her parents for money. She was way too proud. And she didn't want their money.

"But that's why they give you paid time off. You can sleep it off and still get paid."

Sarina shook her head but then grabbed her temples and closed her eyes. Shaking the head is a bad idea when it's soaked in bourbon. Roxy knew this was true from bitter experience. "I can't sit at home and do nothing. At least here I have a purpose." The phone rang but Sarina's hands were too busy ensuring her head stayed attached to her neck.

"M&J Private Investigations." Roxy answered, hit some buttons and probably transferred another call. This job was harder than it looked, especially since Roxy was phone illiterate—at least with this phone and its gaggle of buttons. "You have to answer the phone or you'll get in trouble."

"I can handle it." Sarina tried to look tough, but she was tough as a baby deer—complete with the headlight look. The reminder of getting fired seemed to be what she needed to open her eyes.

"Maybe we should both go home." If Sarina needed a hooky companion, Roxy was all in.

"Don't you have a Post-it to follow?"

Apparently, Sarina *had* been paying attention while she stared at her desk. Sarina lifted a key fob and handed it to Roxy just as the phone rang. "Go. I've got this. I need to try to find Cliff's mom."

Cliff's mom. If they wanted to find her, they'd need the computer system here.

Sarina lifted the receiver and painted on a chipper tone. She almost sounded normal. If it wasn't for the edge in her voice and the fact that Roxy had known the woman her whole life, even Roxy would've been fooled. As it stood, Roxy knew better.

But she also knew Sarina long enough to know that she'd made up her mind. She was staying and working and researching Cliff's elusive mom.

Roxy swung the key fob and Sarina shooed her out the door. She turned and walked out into the sunlight.

CHAPTER 7

SOMETIMES YOU DEAL WITH THE DEVIL NOT BECAUSE YOU WANT TO, BUT BECAUSE IF YOU DON'T, SOMEONE ELSE WILL. ~ LAURELL K. HAMILTON, CERULEAN SINS

ROXY SAT across the street from Fred Gromme's house. The garage was closed. No one moving around the neighborhood. She slid the window down a smidge. The sun was still half asleep and peeking out from behind the mountains. The angry rays of light hadn't fully arrived yet. So it was mildly cool.

She leaned against the headrest and watched the house. This was so much better with a car. She had coffee and a breakfast sandwich. She also had a place to rest her head if she got bored. And so far, today was looking like another boring day at the Gromme house.

Her eyes slid shut and Rafe popped into her thoughts. He did that. And she did not mind. Especially like this. Roxy laid on the couch as Rafe held her hand. He smiled while he slowly placed a Cheeto in her mouth. He licked his finger of cheesy dust. Yummy. The Cheetos and the man.

A banging sound popped her eyes open. The sun had crawled higher in the sky. How long had she been asleep? It didn't look like anything had moved by the house, but who knew. The garage was still closed and there was no movement inside. So in other words, boring.

Another bang.

Roxy's heart jumped into her throat and stole the boring right out of her chest. She looked over and that damn six-year-old from yesterday stood outside the passenger window with her bike leaning against her hip.

The car dinged as she started the car so she could open the window. Roxy pushed the button, wishing it would transport her back in time before she decided to become a PI.

"You're back." This kid was unfortunately observant. "With a car."

"I am."

"Why?" And curious. An annoying combination for a kid talking to strangers.

Especially when Roxy had no good reason for sitting in this car. She'd come up with a good excuse on the bike thing. Taking a break, that was it. "I'm taking a break from driving."

The girl's eyes narrowed. "That doesn't make any sense." This kid had one hell of a brain between those two pigtails.

Fred's garage door opened. As his car pulled out of the garage, a little boy with brown hair ran up to the car waving a bag. Fred got out of the car and swung the boy in the air. Giggles were heard. Kisses were exchanged.

Eventually this daddy-son love fest had to end and

Roxy had to follow him. But she had a new BFF next to her car.

The girl looked over. "Are you in love with him?"

"With who?" Maybe the girl had seen Rafe.

"It's with *whom*." Four-foot-tall grammar tyrant even had the sneer down.

"With whom?" Roxy said the words so the little dictator would answer instead of just giving her a linguistics lesson.

"Tyler's dad."

Roxy in love with Gromme. She looked over at the car. He wasn't bad looking even with the dad-bod and receding hairline, but hell no. "Why do you think that?"

"Because you're staring at his house again."

Telling the kid she was a PI in training probably wouldn't go over well. She'd tell her friends and parents and they'd all talk about it at the PTA. Then Gromme would know they were onto him.

"Yep. I'm in love with him." She tried not to cringe at that outright lie. She needed to make a swoony face. But she had no idea what one would look like. Across the street, Gromme said his goodbyes and slipped into his car. "I gotta go."

The girl didn't move. And she was too close to the car for Roxy to just drive away. "He's not worth it."

Truer words were never spoken.

"You're right." Roxy had to give the kid props for that. "Just remember, never change to please a man. They're never worth it."

"Yep. That's what my mommy says."

"Smart woman." Roxy smiled. This kid was fun. "You must get your brains from her."

The girl actually preened. Her skin glowed with pride. Roxy almost didn't notice the car pulling down the street. Gromme. Crap.

"I need to go now. Watch your feet." She felt like she could leave now that she'd imparted feminine wisdom to the younger generation.

The girl waved and stepped back. "See you tomorrow." She kicked her leg over the bike and started to pedal away.

Tomorrow? Hopefully not. She had worn out her welcome if she was actually expected to appear. And she was expected. Nothing she could get would ever be good enough for Karan. So she'd probably be here until she retired or died—whichever came first.

Roxy pulled away from the curb and followed Gromme down Tenaya Way to Lake Mead Boulevard. They drove through the morning traffic. She'd say he was heading to work, but his office was the other way. So unless he was making accounting house calls, he wasn't going to work.

She rested her hand on the passenger seat. The camera Karan had loaned her sat in its case. She was ready for whatever shenanigans he had in store.

They drove for another twenty minutes toward North Las Vegas, turning into the parking lot of the Fancy Desert Motel. Deceptive name. Although it was in the desert, there was absolutely no fancy. The building was pink stucco with peeling green trim. A little run-down for a mid-morning delight, but maybe adulterers can't be choosers.

Gromme pulled behind the building and parked, away from the road. Probably making sure his car couldn't be found quickly. Luckily she'd followed him and didn't have to rely on searching. Thank goodness for Sarina's car.

Roxy parked behind the motel, too, but on the opposite side. Might as well be inconspicuous too. She pulled the camera out of its bag. She'd used her phone on her first stakeout, but Karan whined about picture quality, and finally gave her one of her old cameras.

The quality was still sad, but it silenced Karan. And wasn't that what ninety percent of Roxy's job was these days? Keeping Karan happy—or at least quiet.

Roxy inched the handle forward and opened the door. She slid out, keeping low as Fred swung his head back and forth. She leaned down behind a van and lifted the camera until she could see him on the tiny screen. *Click.* Not close enough. She angled down so she could sneak behind a Ford Taurus. She kneeled behind the front fender and watched Fred knock on room 105.

Click. She took a picture of his shifting eyes and guilty stance.

The door flew open, and a woman stood in the door in skin-tight black lace. Her breasts were uncovered and pointing at Fred.

Click. Click. Click. Roxy pressed the button again and again. She didn't care what she got. Something had to turn out.

Fred walked in and the door shut. Shading her hand over the screen, Roxy found thirty-two pictures. Nice. She sifted through them. A lot of the woman's front. A lot of Fred's back. Shit. His back. His back. She needed his face.

One with the side of his face. That was a start. She finished clicking through them all. Good pictures, but hardly the smoking gun.

She walked across the parking lot, in front of the window at room 105. The curtains were drawn. Dammit. She checked left side. Bingo. She plastered her face to the window, looking through the gap.

Ewww.

An eye wash of bleach wouldn't even wash away that image. The woman rode Fred like a pony. She jumped up and down on him screaming, "Giddy up." Her girls flopping up and down with a slap.

Yes, Roxy could hear it outside the room.

Talk about the money shot.

Roxy pushed the lens against the glass and hit the button.

FLASH!

Crap. She pulled the camera back as a yell came from inside. And not one of those sexy yells. It was angry. "What the fuck?"

She straightened up and turned from the window.

"Who are you?" Fred stood in the doorway, his pants around his ankles. Eye bleach would be needed. His naked girlfriend had pulled a robe around her shoulders. Thank god for small favors.

"Wrong number?" Roxy turned the camera on the

couple and shot a few pictures as she walked backward toward her car. Fred apparently figured out what she was up to, and pulled up his pants.

Run.

She spun on her heel and dodged a car hood as she heard him scream, "I'm calling Metro!"

"Go ahead." She was calling that bluff, because he wouldn't want today in the record books any more than Roxy wanted to see local law enforcement.

She ran to the car, pulling the key fob from her back pocket. Juggling the camera. She flipped the fob around with one hand till she got to the front. She clicked the locks and opened the door.

A few steps more and she was throwing the camera on the passenger seat. She hit the button for the ignition.

Gromme ran toward the car, holding his pants around his hips with one hand. The car started right up and she backed out of the space.

Gromme hit the back window and ran to the side, beating on the driver's window. "You bitch."

She'd been called worse. She threw it into drive and peeled out of the lot with a tire screech.

CHAPTER 8
WHEN NOTHING GOES RIGHT, GO TO SLEEP. ~ UNKNOWN

ROXY DROVE toward the office and hadn't hit one light. Which was good, since she was trying to get away from Gromme. But it was bad because she wanted to take a look at the pictures. Given she was moving when she took them, she couldn't be sure they wouldn't just be a blur.

Her phone rang and she hit the speaker. "Hello?"

"Hey, Rox. Your car is ready." Romeo sounded so happy.

Almost as happy as Roxy was to hear the news. "Great." Her baby was fixed.

"There were a few unforeseen problems."

"What kind of problems?"

"The impact bent the front struts."

"That sounds expensive." Too expensive for Roxy to afford without selling off unused parts of her body.

"The final bill is two thousand fifty-six." Romeo said the words with no inflection. Like he wasn't destroying her dreams of ever seeing her car again.

What. That couldn't be right. "Dollars?"

He ignored her question, of course it was dollars. She wasn't lucky enough for it to be in another, more friendly currency. "We're open till six."

"Okay, thank you." She said the words to a dial tone. Delightful customer service.

She turned into the M&J lot. Nothing out of the ordinary, except the squad cars with spinning lights.

Gromme had called the cops. Great. Not only was he a cheating horn-dog, he was also a narc. She should run. But in her experience, they always found her. And she wasn't sure Rafe would be on board hiding her again. He'd already been stuck doing that once this year.

So she had to stay and fight. And by fight, she meant face the music.

Roxy took the camera and slid it under the seat. She needed these pictures. She'd seen things that no one should have to see. And she better be able to keep the reward.

Taking a deep breath, she checked the rearview mirror. A little disheveled, but overall good. Not that it mattered. It's not like she had plans to woo the locals in Clark County Detention Center.

She opened the door and walked to the building. Each step felt like a mile. The door opened and Sarina walked out in front of two cops. Her arms were at her sides. Her eyes were wet. She'd been crying.

Detective MacAuley and Geary walked out behind them. They were talking to each other like nothing was going on—like they weren't giving Roxy's best friend the perp walk. At her place of employment.

Roxy steeled her spine and stormed up to MacAuley. The other cop already hated her. Why give him more ammunition. "What is going on?"

MacAuley stopped walking. "She's being brought in for questioning."

"We already were questioned." Uh, duh.

MacAuley ran a hand down the front of his face. "New evidence has come to light."

"What evidence?" She needed to know what she was up against. It had to be circumstantial. At best. Because there was no way she killed Cliff. If Roxy was the main suspect, then they might have more than circumstantial, but this was Sarina. She couldn't hurt anyone.

"We're not at liberty to say." Detective Geary stonewalled her. Of course. That was his main goal in life—stonewalling Roxy and trying to throw her in jail. Two goals.

"Are you kidding..."

"Look." MacAuley stepped in front of Roxy. His tone was calming. At least he sounded like he was going for calming. "We have a warrant for her work and house."

Roxy was not calm. "Why did you pull her out of work?"

"She's a murderer." Detective Geary walked over to his SUV and opened the back door, holding Sarina's head as she slid onto the back seat.

"Allegedly," Roxy yelled at his back, but he didn't

turn around. She asked MacAuley. "Why do you think she did this?"

"Someone said she was the last one to see him. We need her in a lineup and we have some questions."

"Can I follow?"

"Don't worry. She'll be fine." MacAuley had his calm voice out again. Like she was somehow crazy. "I'll make sure of it."

"It's Sarina." Roxy tried to hide the wobble in her voice, but the sympathy on MacAuley's face ratcheted up a notch.

"Fine. But you have to stay out of the way."

Roxy would take all the sympathy if she got her way. "I can do that." She'd try anyway.

MacAuley nodded. "Metro headquarters on King."

Roxy waited till the detectives drove away and broke out into a jog toward the Jeep. They didn't need know she was in a hurry to get to them. Or better yet, to get to Sarina.

She started Sarina's car and hit number two on her speed dial. What? Rafe meant a lot to her, but he couldn't replace her best friend as number one.

"Hey, gorgeous. I was just thinking about you." Rafe's voice was laced with sexy and promise. Too bad she was going to have to take a raincheck on that.

"I'm heading to Metro headquarters."

"Are you getting arrested again?"

"I didn't get arrested the first time." Roxy sighed. Everyone seemed to have a selective memory about what happened a few months ago. "It's Sarina."

"I have to do a few things here and I'll meet you there."

Forty-five minutes later, Roxy walked into the police station and asked for MacAuley at the front desk. The man in cop-tan picked up the phone and talked into the handset. He pointed at the door behind the desk as he hung up. "Detective MacAuley will be here in a moment to bring you back. Wait there."

She did as she was told. Standing by the back door, she got a huge dose of déjà vu. She'd been here before. But last time she was the suspect. This side of the equation was so much better. Which was why she needed to get Sarina on this side. So she needed some questions answered.

"Roxy." MacAuley held open the door. Just the man she needed to answer her questions.

"What are the charges."

"None yet. They're working on it."

"You can't honestly think she'd do this." She followed MacAuley through the slew of desks with cops and noise.

"It doesn't matter what I think. Her boyfriend is dead." MacAuley pointed at a chair along the wall. "Wait here."

"Fine." She sat on the chair and squiggled her body back and forth to show how she wouldn't move.

MacAuley nodded and walked into a room down the hall from where Roxy sat. Geary followed him in, carrying a file folder.

Sarina must be in that room. Roxy's foot tapped. She'd made a squiggle-promise to stay here. But that was before she realized Sarina would be so close. She inched back and forth. She couldn't get comfortable.

Probably because she didn't want to be here. She wanted to be in that room. But that wasn't going to happen.

It didn't mean she couldn't check out the door. She'd still be out of the way. Roxy stood up and tugged at her pants. *Just getting comfy.* She looked around, but none of the cops in the room seemed to notice or care that she was on the move.

She walked over to the door. The doorknob called to her. It wanted to be turned. Which would tell the two cops in the building who didn't want her involved that she wasn't sitting where she was supposed to.

There was no window to look into. Nothing. She pressed her ear to the metal. Closing her eyes, she pushed herself closer. Not one sound. Damn. That always worked on TV.

The door next to the one she was leaning against opened. Crap. She moved across from the door and leaned on the wall. She picked at her nails and looked up at the cop that walked out the door. He looked like he was going to say something, but "Single Ladies" played from his pocket.

Saved by Beyoncé. He answered the call. "Yeah... I'm on my way..." He walked down the hall, leaving the door he'd come through open.

Roxy waited for the guy to turn a corner and then she peeked around the door of the open room. Orange chairs set up like stadium seating faced a two-way mirror. A desk behind the chairs stood empty. No one was there.

Convenient.

"You said you were with Roxy at eight P.M." Detective Geary's tone was all business as he sat across from Sarina on the other side of the glass. And since he was questioning the timing of that night, he knew she hadn't been with Roxy. *Shit*.

Sarina picked at something on the table in front of her. "I said I was with Roxy that night. You didn't mention a specific time."

"Let's go over this again." Geary's eye ticked as he stared at Sarina. The guy needed some yoga in his life —or some good weed. "What were you doing the evening of June twenty-eighth? No, let me rephrase. Tell me where you were from seven P.M. to nine P.M. on June twenty-eighth."

"Starting at seven?" Sarine lifted her head and looked at MacAuley, who sat next to Geary. He was the kinder of the two. Less scary. "I was waiting for Cliff at my apartment."

"Why?"

"We were going to the Roswell UFO Festival. I was originally supposed to pick him up, but he said he was still packing and he'd call when he was ready. But he never called. I texted him a few times and just gave up. I called Roxy and she invited me over to watch a movie."

"Was it weird for Cliff to just blow you off like that?"

"Not really. He wasn't exactly a good boyfriend."

"So, you went to Roxy's and did what?" MacAuley's tone was much more pleasant.

"Ate ice cream and watched a movie." There might have been crying and man-bashing—but who's counting.

"You didn't go to see Cliff at all?"

"Nope." She gulped, like she was trying to hide something. Didn't Sarina know these two were like bloodhounds? If they thought she was lying, they were going to ask and ask until she'd say anything to shut them up. Or maybe that was just Roxy.

"So maybe you can tell me." Geary pulled something out of the folder in front of him. "Why was your car parked in front of his apartment at 7:45?"

Sarina's face dropped. She stared at the picture with wide eyes. "I just drove over there to see if he was home."

Crap.

"I thought you said you didn't go over there?"

"I didn't see him."

"Was he home?"

"I have no idea. I didn't even go to the door. I sat in my car for a few minutes and watched his place."

"Watched it for what?"

Sarina sighed and a tear slid down her cheek. "I figured since he was late for our trip, he was probably with someone else. I wanted to see if I could see anyone there."

"Was there?"

"Not that I could tell."

Geary gave a look that said he was channeling bad cop. "What does that mean? What could you tell?"

"No one came by the windows and the lights were off."

"Did you see anyone walking around? Anything suspicious?" MacAuley still seemed to be on her side. He was fully in good-cop mode.

"No." Sarina looked to the side. "I don't remember anything weird, but I was only there for a few minutes."

"Did you get out of the car?"

Sarina didn't look up from the table. *No. No. No.* She told Roxy she hadn't left the car. "I just went to the windows."

"And what did you see?" MacAuley was so calm, Roxy almost felt at ease. But she knew it was all an act. The man was a cop trying to get the bad guy—or gal, as it were. And their main suspect was right in front of them.

"Nothing." Sarina sniffled. "I swear. I put my hands next to my eyes and tried to see inside, but there wasn't anyone there. So I went back to my car and went to Roxy's. I figured he forgot about me, maybe fell asleep."

"Really? You didn't think he was with someone else?"

"I wasn't sure, but there was no way to tell. So I left." Sarina was trying to play it cool, but she was so not cool. Especially since Cliff had made it his life's mission to sleep with anything that moved. Hell, he probably didn't even require movement.

"You were stalking his house." Geary sifted through the pictures in front of him.

"I wasn't stalking. I was checking. I was worried since we had plans."

"So, here's what I think happened." Geary stared at one picture. He didn't indicate why, just stared. "I think you were mad that Cliff stood you up and went to his apartment. He was there. You were so angry you accidentally killed him. You didn't mean to. But all the emotions of being forgotten were just too much to handle."

"I didn't." A sob crested from Sarina's chest as she leaned toward Geary. "I swear. It's not like that at all."

"Look at this picture. Look at your face." Geary dropped the picture in front of Sarina. "Look at the anger in your eyes. Look how you're gripping the steering wheel."

"I didn't..." Sarina hiccupped and turned away.

"Geary, why don't you get her a bottle of water." MacAuley picked up the picture and stared at it.

"Fine." Geary stood up and left the room.

Roxy could hear him push a mountain of air through his lungs in the hallway before he turned and stood in the door of the room where Roxy had her face plastered to the two-way mirror.

"You shouldn't be in here." Geary didn't waste time with pleasantries, like *hello* or *oh, it's you*.

"Probably not, but I had to see. She shouldn't have to go through this alone." Roxy turned her attention back to MacAuley and Sarina. Her shoulders sagged against the table as she cried. MacAuley had moved his chair next to her and laid an arm around her.

Geary stood next to her and watched.

"Aren't you supposed to be getting water?" Roxy pointed out.

"That's just something we say to get the witness alone."

"You never left me alone."

"I was afraid you might try something. MacAuley didn't need to go out on any limbs for you." Like MacAuley would have done anything illegal for Roxy. They'd just met at the time. He wasn't the type. And Roxy wasn't the type to ask him to. That would be a shitty thing to do.

Which means he thought Roxy was that shitty of a person. "Why do you hate me?" Roxy didn't look at the detective. Just kept watching MacAuley comfort Sarina.

"I don't." His voice was aimed at the glass.

She didn't want to look, but she needed to see if he was showing any tells that said he wasn't speaking the truth. Something told her he wasn't. "You don't? I've been involved in two murder investigations, and you've been mean both times."

Detective Geary turned to her. The look wasn't hatred, more like *hide the knives from the crazy lady*. "Do you hear yourself? Two murders is not normal."

"I know it's not normal, but it's not my fault. These things just happen."

"These things don't just happen." Detective Geary sighed. Of course he did. His annoyance with her dictated there'd be at least one. "I don't hate you. But I see how my partner looks at you."

"Looks at me?" Roxy probably shouldn't interrupt the man she was trying to not be hated by, but he was talking crazy.

"Are you ready to talk?" MacAuley handed Sarina a tissue and leaned back away from her.

Sarina nodded.

"We should focus." Detective Geary turned from Roxy and folded his arms. He didn't kick her out. Seemed like a win. Although she really wanted to finish their conversation. What did he mean by the way his partner looked at her?

The look on Geary's face said he was done talking and she wasn't about to ask him.

Like the number of licks to the center of a Tootsie-Pop, the world might never know.

CHAPTER 9
YOU HAVE THE RIGHT TO REMAIN SILENT. ANYTHING YOU SAY CAN AND WILL BE USED AGAINST YOU IN A COURT OF LAW. ~ MIRANDA WARNING

MACAULEY SAT BACK and looked at Sarina, "Can I ask you something?"

"Sure." Sarina nodded.

Roxy's answer would have had more attitude. And she couldn't help but wonder if Sarina had said no, would that mean the interrogation was over. So many responses, and Sarina had just let them slide.

"We have someone else coming in today claiming to be in a relationship with him. Did you know he was seeing someone else?"

That son of a... Roxy was going to kill him. *Oh wait.*

Sarina sighed. "I know he'd cheated in the past, but I thought things were different now. He'd been faithful lately."

"Are you sure?"

"With Cliff, I could never be sure of anything. I wouldn't bet my life on it, but we'd been doing things together. It was different. A few months ago, I walked away and he'd begged me to come back. He said he'd change. And he had."

"Guys like that don't change," MacAuley said.

Amen. Roxy had tried to tell Sarina that a million times. Maybe not with that nice of phrasing, but it all meant the same thing. Cliff was a dick.

"I know. I keep hoping though." A tear slid down Sarina's cheek. "Kept."

MacAuley looked Sarina up and down as she dabbed her eyes. "We're looking into a few women who claim they had a relationship with Cliff."

Women?

"Plural?" That got Sarina's attention as her head snapped around. A long sigh escaped her and she hunched in on herself. Cliff seemed to have that effect on her. "I don't know why I'm surprised anymore."

"You really didn't know. You didn't know anything about them."

"No." Sarina coughed as her tears dried, and a resigned anger seemed to have taken their place.

"Would you like something to drink?" MacAuley looked at the two-way glass before standing up. Sarina's cough faded as she nodded.

"I'll see where that water is and be right back." MacAuley opened the door and stepped out. Closing it, he stepped around the wall into the viewing room. "So, what do you think..." His voice dropped off when his eyes landed on Roxy. He was either surprised Roxy was standing there or it was shocking that Roxy and Geary were sharing a room and not lobbing insults. Not that Roxy lobbed insults at Geary that often. He was scary.

"I think you're barking up the wrong girlfriend." Roxy felt that was a given, but the interrogation twins needed the reminder.

"What are you doing in here?" MacAuley looked at Geary. Like he had the answer.

"Don't look at me. You invited her here." Geary raised his hands, and Roxy nearly got poked in the eye by the file he was holding.

"I think she invited herself." MacAuley sighed, and said to Roxy, "I thought I told you to wait on the bench."

"You told me to wait. Did you specify where?" He totally did. She'd even squished her butt in the seat. But she batted her eyelashes and tried to go for the whole innocent, *who me* look.

"You know I did." MacAuley shook his head and turned to Geary. "What do you think?"

"She's really convincing. But she could be lying."

Sarina lie?

Geary glared at Roxy. She might have said that out loud. But really, Sarina was too sweet to make up stories. Or kill someone. "You can't think she would lie. I mean, look at her."

"Looks can be deceiving." Geary tapped the folder in his hands. "Anyway, have you seen the company she keeps?"

Wait. "I'm the company she keeps."

Geary's lip quirked. It looked like it might be the

makings of a smile. If Roxy believed he actually smiled. Jerk.

MacAuley didn't even pretend. A laugh bellowed from his throat. They were both jerks.

Roxy huffed. "Are you both done with her?"

"Not yet." Geary's lips edged into a smile. He was good looking when he smiled. Dark skin. Full pink lips. And he had perfectly straight teeth. Who knew? He should smile more often. Even if it was at her expense.

"Can I see Sarina?"

"When we're done."

"She's answered all your questions. It's your fault you don't believe her." Roxy was getting mad just thinking about it. "I mean, asking again and again isn't going to get a different answer."

"You can talk to her when we're done." Geary's face lost its smile. Pity.

"Go sit on the bench and we'll call you."

"Okay." Roxy looked into the room where Sarina was hanging her head. Sarina's forehead rested on her arm. Her shoulders might have been shaking. She might have been crying. Dammit.

There was no way Roxy was going to sit on a bench when Sarina was in trouble.

"Out," MacAuley told her. Geary seemed to have disappeared, which was good since MacAuley was reprimanding her like a toddler.

"Can't I just wait here?" Roxy's voice hitched. Sarina's shoulders were definitely shaking now.

"You can either go to the bench in the hall or I'll have a cop escort you out of the building."

Tears burned the back of Roxy's eyes. "It's Sarina." Her best friend. Her sister. The person she wanted to grow old with—well, in addition to Rafe. Maybe they'd share a two-flat like Lucille Ball and Ethel Mertz. Sarina was her best friend since grade school, but there was so much more to it than that. She was family.

"I know how much this means to you. But this is our job." MacAuley's eyes softened. He was such a nice guy.

All that BS Geary spewed earlier flittered through her mind. But he was way off. She'd seen how MacAuley leaned into Sarina and how sweet he'd been to her. He was just a good guy to everyone. MacAuley rested his hand on the back of her arm. "Go sit out in the hall and we'll send her out to you as soon as possible."

Geary shook his head as he walked out of the room. For goodness' sake. MacAuley touched her arm, not her... Never mind.

Way off.

She let him lead her out into the hall. "How long?"

"It shouldn't be longer than ten minutes or so."

The ten minutes she could live with. Maybe. It was the "or so" that was going to take some patience. She walked back toward the bench as he shut the door to the viewing room with a click. Locked it.

Fine. She could do what she was told. She always could. She just normally chose to not do it. But this time she was going to wait for Sarina.

She could do patience.

CHAPTER 10

PATIENCE IS NOT SIMPLY THE ABILITY TO WAIT—IT'S HOW WE BEHAVE WHILE WE'RE WAITING. ~ JOYCE MEYER

SHE DID NOT DO PATIENCE.

Her knee bounced. Her butt wiggled. But her eyes wouldn't leave the closed door down the hall. It wasn't opening. What more could they possibly have to ask her? They'd covered that night over and over again.

Unless they were trying to trip her up. And Roxy wasn't there to catch them. Damn cops trying to trick Sarina into admitting to killing Cliff. And given Sarina's desire to do just that, she might say something that made her look guilty.

Roxy stood up and stared down the hall. She'd sworn she'd stay. Like a dog. They'd probably send her to obedience school if she barged in the room. Or they'd arrest her for obstruction. She'd seen *Law and Order*. She knew how it worked.

She stared. She glared. The door still didn't open. Roxy tried not to think about all the ways in which they could skew Sarina's words. And what if Sarina told them about her dream of Cliff's demise?

Crap. She had to stop, or she'd barge in the door and pull Sarina out and do a *Thelma and Louise*. Roxy didn't want to drive off the side of a cliff today. She wrapped her hand around her hair and lifted. She should have put her hair up. But who would've thought she'd end up in the Vegas precinct sautéing.

The hall was just unpleasant. The smell of sweat permeated the air. Although that might have just been her. She could feel the sweat bead at the nape of her neck. She didn't like waiting. Especially when she couldn't hear what they were asking and what Sarina was saying.

It had to have been ten minutes. She pulled her phone from her pocket. Three minutes. Three? The longest three minutes of her life. And that counted the time she was stuck in that interrogation room herself.

She leaned her head back and just breathed while she watched cops walking back and forth. The room was full of bustle and the hum of noise. But nothing could take her mind off of that darn room down the hall where they were keeping her BFF hostage.

An hour later—or maybe it was only six minutes. She checked her watch. Okay, eight minutes— the door popped open and Sarina came out the door. Laughing. She was actually laughing while Roxy freaked out.

Sarina walked down the hall, MacAuley at her side. He wasn't calling her a murderer or slapping on the cuffs. So, progress.

Roxy stood up as she approached. She ran up to her best friend and pulled her close. So close. Roxy didn't want to let go.

"You're squeezing me," Sarina hissed.

Okay, maybe Roxy was holding on a bit tight. She pulled back. "Are you okay? They didn't hurt you, did they?"

"I'm fine."

"You were watching the whole time. When do you think we hurt her?" MacAuley shook his head.

"You made me leave and sit here."

"For like five minutes." Geary came up behind MacAuley.

"A lot can happen in five minutes. Mindy Swanigan got knocked up after a game of five minutes in heaven. I mean, really, if you're going to be stuck paying for something for eighteen years, it should last longer than five minutes."

"Is there a point here?" Geary didn't even stick around for the answer. He walked away toward a desk against the far wall.

"A lot can happen in five minutes." Not that Roxy thought MacAuley would hurt Sarina. Hell, neither would Geary. He'd just glare her into submission.

"Excuse me." An older woman hobbled into the room. Wide hips in pink spandex. Fluttery pink sleeveless top. Blond hair held up with a green banana clip. "I'm looking for a Detective MacAuley."

"I'm Detective MacAuley."

"I'm Celeste Foster-Robbins." Cliff's mother. It had to be. She held out her hand, wobbling as she shifted from one foot to the other. She almost looked like him. Except he was scrawny and a womanizer.

The detective shook her hand and led her to the bench. "Ms. Foster-Robbins. I'm so sorry for your loss."

"Thank you." She sat on the bench with a sigh.

"Let me get my partner and we'll go into a room for privacy."

"Sure." Celeste's eyes were rimmed in red. The poor woman must have been crying all night. Which was understandable, since she'd lost her son.

"Ms. Foster-Robbins." Sarina looked at Celeste like she was the holy grail of parents.

"Did you know my son?"

"Yes. I'm Sarina. We were dating."

"I don't know you." Cliff's mom's eyes narrowed in skepticism or anger or both.

"I'm so sorry. We were supposed to come by for Mother's Day a few months ago, but Cliff had to work."

"I don't know who you are or what you're talking about. Cliff and his fiancée came by on Mother's Day."

Fiancée?

The word hung in the air. *Fiancée.*

"His what?" Sarina's skin was almost as pale as Roxy's. She heard the word. She knew what the word meant.

"My son and his fiancée bought me a beautiful crystal candy dish."

Candy dish? The candy dish Sarina had bought? The one Roxy had helped her pick out after they'd spent over two hours walking around The District at Green Valley. Two hours of mall walking and Sarina hemming and hawing about what to buy.

Roxy wanted to choke him out. She'd always

figured the guy was a man-whore. But a fiancée? A fiancée who commandeered the Mother's Day gift Sarina purchased. Roxy waited for Sarina to say something. Anything.

When Sarina didn't yell or cry, Roxy turned her way. Her eyes were wide as she stared at the door. Roxy couldn't help but look.

Roxy wished she hadn't.

A girl who could be Sarina's tacky twin walked in. Sun-kissed skin, blond hair and big tits. She carried two bottles of water. "Momma, you forgot your water."

"Thank you, Kandi. You are a dear. The cops said to wait here."

Kandi looked Sarina up and down. "Who are you?"

"She's no one." Celeste— or Momma— said.

Kandi was calling her Momma. Ugh.

"She's Cliff's girlfriend." Roxy glared at the dime-store Sarina. "Who are you?"

"I'm his fiancée." Kandi's bleach-blond hair was pulled away from her face by a red banana-clip. Did she borrow that from Momma? "You're not his girlfriend. Just because a man slept with you don't make it serious."

Well at least Kandi knew her fiancée was a cheating man-whore. That didn't explain why she was planning on marrying him. But if Roxy could figure that out, she'd be rich. She'd start a women's support group to keep women from falling for useless men.

"He said he loved me." Tears pooled in Sarina's eyes.

"He didn't love you." Kandi held up her left hand. "You ain't got the ring on your finger."

That had the desired effect. What blood was left drained from Sarina's face. Stricken would have been a step up.

Oh hell no. Bottle-bitch was not about to step on Sarina or her feelings.

Roxy leaned in to look at the mini-diamond on Kandi's finger. "Does a ring mean anything if the guy is sleeping with other women?"

"What about the whore sleeping with another woman's fiancée?" Kandi stepped into Roxy's space. Of course she did.

"What about the guy who has a fiancée, a girlfriend, and was sleeping with a few other women?"

"You're lying. You're just jealous." Kandi's spit the words in Roxy's face. "My Cliff wasn't like that."

"But you admit he was sleeping with Sarina. You called her a whore."

"I don't admit nothing. She's probably just some DJ-draper, hanging all over him."

"I don't drape." Sarina managed to find her voice. And the voice was angry. Go girl.

"Well, my man wouldn't be into that."

"He wasn't into blond hair and big tits?" Roxy nodded to Sarina.

"Is there a problem?" MacAuley appeared out of nowhere. He should wear a bell, or at least announce his movements.

"No problem." Roxy didn't need him to know what

was going on. He'd find a way to use it against Roxy, or worse, against Sarina.

"This person is making Momma cry." Kandi's nasty glare softened as she moved to Cliff's mom and grabbed her hand. Celeste didn't look like she was going to cry, she looked like she was eating up the drama. Like she was pretending she was a Kardashian. "Maybe we should come back tomorrow."

"We're done with you both." MacAuley looked from Roxy to Sarina. "You can leave."

"Happily." Roxy grabbed Sarina's arm and pulled, but she was immovable. Those tears were still there. Fresh. Like the pain in Sarina's eyes.

Sarina said to Celeste, "I loved your son. He was my everything."

Celeste nodded but didn't say anything. Probably best. Nothing she could say at this point could make any of this better.

Sarina nodded to MacAuley as she walked past and out the door. Roxy followed. Pride burrowed deep into her bones. Sarina had laid it all out there. She didn't hide. She was a freaking warrior.

"You are awesome." Roxy ran up to Sarina and wrapped her arm around her BFF's shoulder.

"How am I awesome? I just found out my boyfriend is engaged and his mom doesn't even know who I am. He never mentioned me because his fiancée would get upset."

Probably not. The creep. "That's on him. He was a shitty person, but you're not. You told his mom exactly how you felt. You got some balls there, West."

"Too bad I didn't have them earlier. I could've left him long ago."

"You have them now. That's all that matters."

"Are you okay?" Rafe walked in the front door of the precinct. He wrapped his arms around Roxy.

"Which one of us are you asking?" Roxy held on tight. He just smelled so darn good.

Rafe pulled back and looked into Roxy's eyes. "Well, I was asking her, but do I need to ask you?"

"No." Roxy melted against his chest. "I'm okay." Now. She left the warmth of his arms.

"I'm okay." Sarina nodded to the door. "I just want to go home."

"Hold on." A voice called from behind them. MacAuley. "Sarina West. You're under arrest."

Wait. What?

"What are the charges?"

"Second-degree murder." MacAuley pulled out cuffs and slowly snapped them around her wrist. Her arms were pulled behind her back. It looked so uncomfortable. And she looked so scared.

"Is that necessary?" Roxy asked.

Rafe ignored her and addressed MacAuley. "You just let her go."

"We received fingerprint analysis back from the weapon," MacAuley whispered to Rafe. "The only prints on the turntable are Sarina's."

"He was teaching me how to mix," Sarina cried.

"She wouldn't do this." Roxy was going out on a limb with that one. But it was Sarina.

MacAuley checked the cuffs as he guided Sarina

toward the cop standing off to the side. "Take her inside, Officer Bates."

Sarina's eyes were red rimmed and leaking again.

"Wait." Roxy ran over to her, wrapping her in an unreciprocated hug. "We'll find out who did this. I swear."

Rafe walked over. "Watch what you say. From here on out, only talk when a lawyer is present. You got it?"

It was probably hard to see Sarina's nod since Roxy had her in a vise grip. "My phone is at the office with my purse," Sarina muttered. "Grab it before someone steals it."

"I will, and I'll get you out as soon as I can."

Sarina sobbed as the officer named Bates pulled her away and through the back door. Yeah, she was a hardened criminal.

"She couldn't have done this." Roxy was begging MacAuley to understand, but how could he not.

The detective actually looked upset. "All I know is the evidence says otherwise. Her prints are on the murder weapon. I'm sorry, but I have to get back." He turned and disappeared through the door they'd just taken Sarina.

"She didn't do anything wrong," Roxy managed, trying not to hyperventilate.

"I know that and you know that, but that's not what the police think. She has motive and opportunity." Rafe wrapped Roxy in a hug.

"But it's not like her," she said into his shirt.

"I know." His lips ghosted along her forehead. Warm lips. Soft and sweet.

And somewhat hot. Not that she had time for any of that. "We have to clear her name."

"I know," Rafe said. He kept her close. "We will. So, where are we starting?"

"Hell if I know." She had no idea where to start.

"How did you get here?" Rafe guided her outside the building and into the parking lot.

"Sarina's car." Roxy pointed to the pink Jeep in the corner. "I'll drive it back to M&J for Sarina, if she needs it when they let her out."

Who would be able to shine some light on this? Maybe if she knew who Sarina had called. *Sarina's phone.* "Let's go to the office. I need to pick up Sarina's purse."

CHAPTER 11
REALITY CONTINUES TO RUIN MY LIFE. ~ BILL WATTERSON, THE COMPLETE CALVIN AND HOBBES

ROXY PULLED Sarina's car into the parking lot and parked next to Rafe's idling truck. Cars lined the lot in the strip mall, and an orange Charger sat in front of the door Roxy needed to enter.

Shit. Karan was here. Which meant she'd want to know why Roxy wasn't twiddling her thumbs in front of Gromme's house. She'd also want to see the pictures Roxy had gotten this morning.

Roxy wasn't exactly sure she'd gotten anything usable and she hadn't had time to find out. Who Gromme was giving conjugal visits to wasn't high on Roxy's priority list when Sarina couldn't even get a conjugal visit. So she needed to get in the door without anyone seeing her.

"Give me a minute." She held up a finger to Rafe and ran up to the office.

Roxy couldn't see in through the glass doors. Not with Vegas sun glaring against the window. With no idea what lay behind, she opened the front door.

The phones were quiet. No one sat in Sarina's chair. One of the PIs or process servers must be taking the calls from their desk. It's not like they could replace Sarina—the perk of once sleeping with an owner. Sarina was given a job for life so she wouldn't press sexual harassment charges against the company. Said owner wasn't so lucky. He was forced to move to Utah by his very angry wife. On a pig farm. Guy was suffering for his mistakes.

Hopefully that juice was worth the squeeze. A pig farm felt like one hell of a squeeze. And not worth it. And Roxy loved Sarina more than life itself.

Roxy slipped behind Sarina's desk and opened the top drawer. Found Sarina's purse and phone.

"Roxy?" John Sherwood stood in the doorway Roxy had just come through. The sun danced on his black balding scalp before it was sucked up by the closing door, leaving him in the darkened entrance. The owner who hadn't gotten caught dipping his nib in the office ink.

"Hi, John. Just stopped to grab Sarina's things." She slung the purse strap over her shoulder.

"Have they sent her home? Tell her to take all the time she needs." Obviously he didn't know Sarina was an overnight guest of the Las Vegas Metro. That rumor hadn't made its way here yet.

"I'm sure she'll appreciate it" —since she was not allowed to leave her current digs. "I just thought I'd bring these things to her."

"Roxy?"

Crap. The voice that launched a thousand cats into

high pitched caterwauling. "Shouldn't you be..." Karan noticed John and smiled. "... working?"

"I am working. You gave me the afternoon off to deal with the Sarina issue." Was that a lie. Yes. Did Roxy care? No.

"That's what I like to see." John's skin glowed as he smiled. "Teamwork makes the dream work."

John liked clichés.

Karan's teeth bared in an attempt at a smile. She looked more like she was going to eat her young—or Roxy. And not in a good way. "That's right. I forgot."

John smiled some more. "How's the Gromme case coming? Angela's been calling." Angela— the wife— was an old friend of John's.

"I'm working on it." Karan nodded. If getting her nails done with little diamonds was working on it...

"Shouldn't you be watching him?" John was turned away and must have missed the laughter bubbling through Roxy's chest.

Karan's eyes narrowed. She didn't miss it and Roxy was going to pay dearly for that giggle.

Worth it.

"I was waiting for my little shadow to get back." Karan walked over and put her arm around Roxy. Karan's impossibly sharp talons dug into Roxy's shoulder and squeezed the air from her lungs.

Ouch.

"I'm back, but I have to go to Sarina." Roxy ducked and weaved. Air filling her lungs. "Great to see you."

Before anyone could say anything else, Roxy shot out the front door. She ran for the truck and hopped in.

Karan would be outside soon, and she'd be out for revenge.

"We should go." Roxy clicked her seatbelt into place.

Rafe didn't throw the truck into reverse and peel out of the lot. He was still staring at his phone. "Where are we going?"

The front door of the office whipped open, and dark brown Medusa hair swirled around a pinched face. *Crap.* "Can we go anywhere but here?"

Rafe looked up and saw Satan's mistress stomping closer. "What did you do to piss her off this time?" He laughed. Which was fine, because he also shifted the car into gear.

"I was breathing."

"She took offense at your breathing?" Rafe backed up and drove out of the lot. Karan stopped mid-lot and pulled out her phone.

"Pretty much."

Karan might not have taken offense at it, but she sure as heck wanted to squeeze the breath from Roxy's body. Roxy's phone chimed.

You have to come back sometime. I'll wait.

Karan was one scary chick. Somehow, that felt like a threat.

"Did you get Sarina's things?"

Sarina. "Yeah." Getting her mind back on her best friend, Roxy sat in the passenger seat of Rafe's truck, fuming—over Karan or over this whole situation, she wasn't sure. Well, maybe both. "He had a fiancée."

"Who had a fiancée?"

"Sarina's Cliff." Although he wasn't really Sarina's.

"A fiancée?" Rafe had the right amount of indignation. He was such a good guy, and not just because he didn't have a fiancée. That was a pretty low bar.

"Yeah, she's at the precinct."

"Asshole." Such a good guy.

"Right."

"So, what are we looking for?"

"Someone. Anyone who might know what's going on." She scrolled through the missed calls. Nothing. She flipped to the placed calls.

"We could talk to the fiancée."

"I doubt she'll talk to me. I figured we'd start somewhere else. If possible." Roxy would love to talk to the fiancé, but given her attitude, there was a good chance Roxy would get arrested. She scrolled down. The girl placed a lot of calls. "Davis."

"Who's Davis?"

"Cliff's lying-douchebag of a best friend." She clicked call and it immediately went to voice mail. He was probably screening his calls. She put the phone down and took a deep breath. "I need to find out if anyone had anything against Cliff." Besides her and Sarina, anyway.

"If he's a liar, do you think he'll tell the truth?"

"Who knows, but it's the only lead I've got right now." Only lead that might actually talk to her. She texted his number to her own phone and clicked to call. Immediately to voice mail. "Dammit."

"What?"

"He's screening his calls. He won't answer."

"Let's go see him then."

"Sarina doesn't have his address." She entered the number to the search engine. Nothing. Unlisted. "I could run it through LexisNexis, but I don't want to go back to the office."

Rafe rolled up to a red light, his hand draped over the steering wheel. "Karan doesn't bite."

"That you know of."

"Give me a minute." Rafe placed a call.

A voice came over the speakers in the truck. "Ruiz."

"Hey, Sal!" Sal was Rafe's supervisor at Pura Vida. "Can you run someone for me? I have a phone number and first name."

"One sec." Shuffling was heard over the line. "Ready."

"First name Davis." He took Sarina's phone, gave the number to Sal, and waited. More shuffling. Some clicking.

"Here we go. Davis Simon. North Las Vegas."

"Can you send me the address?"

"Sure thing."

Roxy's stomach growled. They'd been heading all over town all morning. She checked her phone. Two PM. They'd been going most of the afternoon too. She forgot lunch. She never forgot lunch.

Rafe clicked end. "How about we go get something to eat?" He must have heard her stomach ask for food.

"Let's do it." She attempted a smile. They had the address, and they could check on the lead after they ate. It was best if she wasn't hangry when seeing one of Cliff's awful friends.

CHAPTER 12
IT'S 420 SOMEWHERE. ~ UNKNOWN

AROUND NINE THE NEXT MORNING, Roxy stared out the truck window as Rafe drove up to a U-shaped run-down apartment building on the border of North Las Vegas and parked in the lot. Stairs on the outside of each building led to the upper floors.

She'd wanted to visit Davis Simon yesterday, but after their late lunch Rafe pointed out they'd have a better chance of catching Davis at home in the morning.

"Can you go into the glove box and grab my gun?"

Roxy opened the compartment and pulled out a Glock. "Shouldn't this be locked up in a safe?"

"I have the safety on, and the magazine is in the center console." Rafe took the gun, opened the center console and pulled out a magazine, checked that, and slid it into the gun.

She could admit, it was hot.

"4600." Rafe pointed to the building to the right.

He stepped out of the truck and slid the gun into a holster at his back. "Unit thirteen."

They walked to the end of the building. Ten. Roxy sighed. "Thirteen must be upstairs."

Climbing the metal staircase decorated with gang symbols and what appeared to be a used crack spoon, Roxy thanked her lucky stars Rafe was with her. This was no place for a woman alone. Hell, this was no place for anyone alone.

"Stay close." Rafe must have read her mind. Or it could be that she was so close, if he stopped fast she might be permanently lodged where the sun don't shine.

Rafe knocked when they reached a gray door with 13 in black lettering. The door swung open. Davis Simon.

Now Roxy remembered him. Light brown skin. Long dreads. He looked like the type of guy who'd be right at home in a Cheech and Chong tee. As it was, he was wearing a tank top with My Little Pony on the front.

He smelled like a cannabis dispensary. There was smoke practically billowing from the apartment. "Hey." His bloodshot eyes landed on Roxy. "Whoa, I know you."

"I'm Roxy."

"Yeah. You're one of Cliff's tasty nuggs."

"Thanks?" Roxy wasn't sure if a tasty nugg was good, but tasty things were good. She was going with compliment.

"Who's the dude?" Davis nodded to Rafe.

"The dude is Rafe. Do you have a minute for some questions?" Rafe rolled his eyes as Davis winked at Roxy.

"I don't talk to cops. Got no beef with 'em or nothin'. Just not my scene. You know?" Davis said... to Roxy's chest. "I'm a lover, not a fighter."

If Roxy was supposed to be swooning at this, she was failing miserably. There was no swoon. The way he said "lover" was as welcome as the crack spoon.

"We're not the police." Roxy bent her knees and lowered her head until Puff the Magic Gaggin' was looking at her eyes, not her nips. "We were hoping to come in and talk for a minute."

"Talk, huh?" Davis licked his lips and rubbed his belly like he was making a wish. Since his eyes were back on the girls, she could only imagine what the wish consisted of. Probably not talking. "I'll talk to you, but I ain't talking to the cop."

"He's not a cop."

"He looks like one."

To be fair, Rafe did look like a cop. Probably the years he spent on the force before he joined the private sector.

"Fine. Talk to Roxy, but I go with her." Rafe nodded toward the inside of the apartment.

"I got like ten minutes, dude."

"You have somewhere to be?" Roxy couldn't imagine he was busy given his current state.

"Conference call." Davis stepped back and let them enter his smoky lair.

"Aren't you high?" Roxy might have said that, but

she wasn't sure. She could practically feel the pot in the air killing brain cells.

Davis crossed the room and sat on a leather couch. "I do my best coding when I'm lit."

The place was nice, considering the neighborhood. Black leather furniture and small glass tables. Black shelving stood against the side wall, covered in decorative bongs and paraphernalia. A black table on the other side of the room held an elaborate computer system and multiple monitors. What appeared to be computer code was on one of the screens.

"So, you're a computer programmer."

"Yep." Davis leaned back and his eyes closed. His chest rose and fell with rhythmic grace.

"Hey, buddy. Wake up." Rafe sat next to the guy and slapped his knee.

Davis's eyes popped open. He looked from Rafe to Roxy. "Hey, I know you."

As Roxy's mother would say, bless his heart. This was turning out to be a dead end.

Speaking of dead. "I'm looking into Cliff Foster's death." Roxy sat on the table in front of the couch.

"Okay."

"I'm trying to find out who would want him dead."

"Everybody loved Cliff." Davis leaned forward and picked up a bong. "He always had the best stash."

Rafe took the bong away from him and put it on another table, out of reach. "Could someone have been after his stash?"

"Nah, that shit's locked up tighter than a virgin's... ouch."

Rafe's fingers were wrapped around Davis's knee. His knuckles were white—the only indication he was getting pissed. His face was impassive.

"Dude. Stop touching my knee. I don't go that way."

Roxy tried to sound patient. "Davis. Could anyone not like Cliff or his stash, and want him dead?" Besides her and Sarina, naturally.

"Hell, it could have been any of his women. That dude attracted the crazies. You know what I'm sayin'? He had this one girl, long blond hair, hot as shit, but looney as a tune. Possessive. And into, like, aliens and shit. She probably did it."

"What was her name?" Please don't be Sarina. Please don't be Sarina.

The wheels in Davis's head were obviously spinning overtime as his face scrunched in concentration. "Sara. Uh... Sarri. Sarina."

Son of a...

"She even called looking for his mom." Davis shook his head.

"So, if she was looking for his mom, she probably didn't kill him." Why was she the only one seeing this logic?

"Or she could be some evil mastermind. Like Darth Vader and shit."

If this wasn't so darn important she'd laugh. Sarina an evil mastermind was ridiculous. "When she called, why did you say you and Cliff weren't talking?" Roxy wanted to say he might be an evil mastermind, but that obviously wasn't a thing.

"I didn't want any of his women showing up at the funeral. Chick fights aren't as hot as they say. They never rip off each other's clothes."

"What a tragedy." Rafe sighed. "How many women did he have?"

Davis pursed his lips and sighed. "Like, three, maybe. His fiancée, the girlfriend, and some new chick."

"Does the new chick have a name?" Roxy asked, and see? She sounded calm. Ish.

"I couldn't tell you. There were so many."

Rafe shook his head. "What about friends?"

"He had lots of friends. Man, he had the best stash."

"You mentioned that. But would any of his friends get mad because he withheld his stash? Maybe killed him?" Roxy hated wading through this guy's ramblings.

"Why would any of us want him dead? He got us into the best parties. Well, except Pauly P."

"The guy from *Jersey Shore*?" Roxy hadn't talked *Jersey Shore* in ages. She and Sarina used to love that show.

"No, he wishes. Paul Krasuski."

"Wouldn't that be Pauly K?" Where the heck did the P come from?

"P stands for pus..." Davis cringed when Rafe's knuckles went white again. "...something else."

"Why is he— Never mind." She didn't want to know. "What did Pauly have against Cliff?"

"Cliff stole his gigs. Pauly was growing his fan base,

even got a DJ gig over at the Luxor. He was rising to fame and Cliff came along and stole the gig."

"How did he manage that?" Roxy was not only curious as to how one stole another person's gigs, but how Cliff managed with his awkward transitions.

"His last girlfriend. Delany or Destiny or something."

"So, not the fiancé, and not the new one. It was the girlfriend?" Roxy was having trouble keeping track.

"Nah. This was the one before the new one."

Another girlfriend. Ugh. "What happened to her?"

"I think he broke up with her. That Sarina chick was getting jealous and threatening to leave. So he had to thin the herd, if you know what I'm sayin'."

She so wished she didn't know what he was saying, but she had a feeling she understood.

"Hey, I gotta get to work. Code's not gonna write itself." Davis got up and retrieved a cordless headset from the computer desk. "But that would be awesome."

"Thanks." Roxy followed Rafe out the door. As she closed the door, Davis's voice changed.

"Good afternoon, sir. I am analyzing the control flow for that code. I think the previous programmer..." He actually sounded like a fully functioning human. Who knew?

"Do you have time to check out another lead?" Roxy asked Rafe as they stepped over the spoon and other local flavor on the way down the stairs.

"I don't want you going alone."

Rafe had a point. She didn't want to go alone, either. "Can you get us another address?"

He nodded and called Sal once they were back in the truck. Then he removed the Glock from the holster, ejected the magazine, and handed Roxy the empty gun. She put it back in the glove compartment while he dropped the magazine into the console. Before the ignition sparked, Rafe had the address for one Pauly Krasuski in Summerlin.

CHAPTER 13
DJS ARE THE NEW ROCK STARS. ~ DJ GODFATHER, LIVE MASHUP MIX 1

SUMMERLIN WAS an area in Las Vegas with a suburban feel. Kids flooded the streets on bikes and skateboards and scooters. Parents pushed strollers and nodded to each other in their secret-affluent-ways.

Roxy had grown up in an affluent part of Las Vegas; her father had been a casino director back in his heyday. But she hadn't fit in. To be fair, neither had her father. That was probably why he'd given up all the money a few years ago to live off the land with his toddler girlfriend. Okay. She wasn't a toddler, but she'd gone to high school with Roxy—at the same time.

Her mother always fit in. She was a transplant from the deep-south cotillion crowd. After she'd divorced, she'd found the first doctor she could and married her. Yeah, she'd come out of the closet, but she'd managed to make that trendy, too.

Rafe pulled the truck up to a single-story tan house with red terracotta roofing. A meticulously kept rock-lawn covered the front yard. The only green was a tree in the center. The garage door was open, a white van sitting inside.

Roxy and Rafe both got out and walked up the driveway. As far as she could see, there were no markings on the outside of the van. A few scuffs along the door. It looked like the vans your mother warned you about when you were a kid. The ones that held weird men offering lollypops and puppies.

The door from the garage to the house opened and a big burly guy walked through it. Stringy dark-blond hair, no neck, and he had to be way over six feet tall. He towered over Rafe. His muscles bunched as he carried a box. A face as big as Roxy's was tattooed on his bicep. The guy was a skyscraper disguised as a human.

His eyes found Rafe and narrowed. "Who the hell are you?"

"Mr. Krasuski?"

"Who's asking?" Pauly's arm flexed and the tattoo winked at Roxy. Winked. Like it dared her to meet him in a dark alley.

Not without Batman, my friend.

"I'm Rafe Amato." Rafe held out his hand, but Pauly just glared at it over the box.

Maybe a woman's touch would help. "I'm Roxy Horne. We're here because of Cliff Foster." All she could think was how easy it would be for this man-skyscraper to toss her in the back of the pedo-van. What might happen after that was just too disturbing to think about.

"You work for that bastard Cliff?" A vein under his

eye pulsed. Okay, a woman's touch wasn't enough, and where was an anger management class when you needed one?

"No, Cliff's dead." Rafe didn't flinch at the newfound hostility Pauly was displaying.

Pauly tossed the box into the back of the van. Like he was tossing a toothpick. "What do you mean he's dead?"

Were there different definitions of dead?

He must have decided no, because he kept talking. "The drugs finally got to him, huh?"

"Drugs?" Roxy rejoined the conversation. "I didn't know he did drugs."

"No, he didn't do drugs. He sold them."

"Are you sure?"

"Well, it was just a rumor, but he was a bad dude."

Interesting. She didn't believe she could think any lower of Cliff. But selling drugs? Although, this could just be a way to throw them off the track. "Did you have a beef with Cliff?"

"I didn't do it."

"We don't think you did." She was so lying. When you looked up crazy psycho-killer in the dictionary, his picture was probably right there next to this van. "I'm trying to find out who would."

"Take your pick. The guy was a total douchebag. Slept around. Had no respect for women or spinning." He wasn't exactly giving them anything they didn't already know. Or clearing his name.

"Have you seen him lately?" Roxy moved toward

Pauly and leaned against the van. Casual. Trying to keep him calm, keep him talking.

"We mighta had a few words at the Pura Vida club last week." Pauly shook his head.

If Rafe hadn't already figured it out, Roxy would need to get him to find that security footage.

Pauly sighed. "That guy just didn't know when to quit."

"What was it about?"

"Luxor. He stole that gig from me."

Now they were getting somewhere. Eliminate the competition and he'd have all the gigs. "When was the gig?"

"It's next week."

Motive didn't get any better than this. Sarina would be out before dinner. "So, you'll be taking his place?" *Cha-Ching.*

"I haven't heard anything, but I doubt it. I've got a regular gig in LA. I would've taken time off to play the Luxor. I mean, who doesn't want to get booked there on the regular? It could open doors. But now there's not enough time for me to find a replacement. And I can't do that to the guys in L.A. They've stuck by me."

There went his main motive. "But you wanted him dead." On the other hand, if wanting him dead was motive, they'd all be prime suspects.

"No. Not dead." Pauly stopped talking when the door to house flew open.

A little girl in light-brown pigtails ran out of the house. Her footy pajamas were covered in rainbows and unicorns. She ran into his arms. "Daddy, can I have a drink before breakfast?"

All the anger and posturing slipped from his face. If she was into wanting kids, her ovaries would have exploded at the love on his face. But since kids were the furthest thing from her mind, they merely gasped.

What? She was human.

"Yeah, baby." The smile he gave the little pig-tailed cherub was blinding. "I'll be right in."

He put the little girl on the ground, and she ran inside the house. "Sorry, my wife is at work. I'm trying to get ready for this wedding I'm doing tomorrow night and keep the house in order." Pauly slammed the truck door closed and locked it up. "I didn't want Cliff dead. I wanted him to chill out. There was room enough for all of us. We could've worked together so that we all had a piece of the pie. But he wasn't a sharer."

"True." He didn't like to share his things, but he expected everyone else to share him. Speaking of... "What about his girlfriends? Did you know any of them?"

"No. I'd be surprised if he did. He slept with whatever was closest."

"So you never met any of them?"

"There was one. Umm... Kandi or Sandy. They were fighting at Pura Vida Wednesday night."

Kandi. The fiancée. The woman they'd met a few hours before. Maybe the bride-to-be wasn't as happy with her betrothed as she pretended to be. It was something. And right now they needed something.

"Was there anything else?" Pauly crooked his

thumb at the door to the house. "I need to get my daughter some milk."

"Nope." Dammit. She needed something because Pauly might have a dumbass name, but he was way too sweet to be a killer.

CHAPTER 14

ONE OF THE MANY LESSONS THAT ONE LEARNS IN PRISON IS, THAT THINGS ARE WHAT THEY ARE AND WILL BE WHAT THEY WILL BE. ~ OSCAR WILDE

"HE'S way too nice to be a killer. Did you see him with his daughter?" Roxy couldn't believe they'd been having this discussion the whole trip across town on the way to the precinct. Pauly might have been a tatted-up skyscraper, but he was so sweet to his kid.

"I was there. I saw them. But remember last time we thought the suburbs couldn't house a murderer?" He had a point. A white picket fence didn't mean they wouldn't stab you with the pointy end of the picket. "I want to see the video footage of that fight before we make a final verdict."

"Fine. He's still on the list." Roxy just wanted to narrow it down a bit, but Rafe was apparently against that. "Can we at least agree to remove Davis?"

"Fine. He's off for now." Rafe opened the front door of the precinct. Yesterday, Kandi had said she and Cliff's mom wanted to come back tomorrow. So here Roxy and Rafe were, walking toward the check-in desk. The room was crowded with people, except behind the front desk. There was only one cop handling all the people.

Rafe walked up and smiled. "Rafe Amato for Detective MacAuley."

"One minute. Let me see if he's in." The policewoman behind the desk picked up the phone, and paused to nod to the man next to Rafe. "Sir, Officer Ramirez is not available. Can I take a message for her?"

The guy next to Rafe huffed and puffed. It could be because he was overweight, but it seemed more than likely he was pissed the officer wasn't on-site. Roxy could relate. If MacAuley wasn't here, she was going to be pretty pissed as well. She might even huff and puff.

And yeah, MacAuley deserved a day off. Just not today.

"Sir." The cop behind the counter motioned to Rafe. "The detective will be out in a minute."

"Why do they get help first?" Huff-and-Puff whined.

"The officer they need is available." The woman behind the counter was obviously holding back her own huff and puff. "I can get you another officer if that would help."

"I need Ramirez."

"I can leave her a message and she'll get back to you as soon as possible." The poor officer was trying, but the guy just didn't want to get it.

MacAuley opened the metal door. Thank goodness. Roxy had no interest in finding out how the saga between Huff-and-Puff and Ramirez ended.

"Twice in one week." MacAuley motioned for them to come through.

"We're stalking you." Roxy smiled.

"This is Vegas. There are better people to stalk." MacAuley laughed as he led them to his desk on the far side of the room. Cops sat at their desks or stood around talking guns or handcuffs or donuts. Whatever cops talked about when they thought no one was watching.

"True, but we need to talk to Kandi." Roxy sat on the chair next to his desk. "And you have her, so here we are." Rafe leaned against the desk and picked up a golden paperweight.

"Kandi the fiancée. What do you need with her?"

"Information." Duh.

"I thought I told you to let me handle this."

"To be fair, you say that all the time."

"And you don't listen." MacAuley sighed as he dropped into his desk chair. "That tracks."

"Can we talk to her when you're done?"

"She's already left."

Seriously? It was barely ten in the morning. "When I'm here, I'm usually stuck in that hell for hours."

"She was more agreeable."

"I'm agreeable." She curled her lips in a pout. It wasn't the best way to show how agreeable she was, but she figured she might get some sympathy or something.

Rafe laughed. MacAuley rolled his eyes. Or not.

She'd be offended, but why bother. It was hard to argue how agreeable you were when you were pouting. And arguing.

New tactic. "Can we talk to Sarina?"

"She was moved to the Clark County Detention Center."

The detention center? Roxy's heart twisted. Sarina didn't belong there. She belonged in a kitten café, not doing hard time. "Already?" The one time she wanted the wheels of justice to spin slowly. "What about bond?"

"The judge won't set it till tomorrow."

"She can't be in that place all night. It's Sarina. She's not jail material." Roxy's heart pulsed in her ears. Sarina was a Hallmark movie, not someone from HBO.

"And what is jail material?"

She had no idea. "Not Sarina. You can't think she did this."

MacAuley sighed. "It doesn't matter what I think, it's what I can prove."

"Well then, prove she didn't do it."

"I'm working on it. He had a long list of people who didn't like him. It's going to take time to get through them all."

"We could help?" Yeah, she was practically begging. But she needed all hands on deck. That meant her hands and Rafe's needed to be in the mix.

"No." MacAuley didn't even pretend to think about it.

"Come on." Yeah, begging again.

"Let's try something different." MacAuley stood up, like he was done with the conversation. "Stay away from this."

"Mac, we need you," a cop called from the other side of the room.

"Be right there." MacAuley turned to Roxy. "I'll see you out."

Dismissed. She stood up from the chair. "Can I go see her?"

"Tomorrow." MacAuley actually looked upset. "Don't worry. I'll check on her before I go home."

"Thanks." She walked back the way they'd come, followed by Rafe and MacAuley.

Rafe stepped in front and opened the door. He broke his silent streak and turned to MacAuley. "Do me a favor, call me or Roxy if Sarina needs us."

"Of course." MacAuley held the door until they walked through.

Roxy turned to say thank you, but metal slammed in her face. Apparently MacAuley was in a hurry. The front desk area was quiet. The crowds gone. She stood outside the door, not knowing what to do.

Rafe slid a hand along Roxy's cheek. Her eyes closed as his thumb drew little circles on her chin. So relaxing. "We should go home. You look tired."

Her eyes popped open. "No. I can't sleep knowing Sarina is in that jail. She's as hardened as a tulip. They'll tear her apart." Roxy pushed down the ball of dread threatening to come up with her breakfast.

"She'll be okay. We'll help her. Tomorrow." He ghosted a kiss on her forehead. "I promise. But there's nothing we can do today."

"Okay." She walked toward the door, Rafe's arm draped over her shoulder. It felt so good to have him by her side. A balm for the worry that was strapped to her shoulders.

She cuddled closer to him, soaking up all the balm. His arm pulled her into his side. More balm. Too bad it wouldn't matter. There wasn't enough balm in the world to make the worry go away. No way she was going to sleep until Sarina was back at home.

CHAPTER 15

WHEN YOU'RE IN JAIL, A GOOD FRIEND WILL BE TRYING TO BAIL YOU OUT. A BEST FRIEND WILL BE IN THE CELL NEXT TO YOU SAYING, "DAMN, THAT WAS FUN." ~ GROUCHO MARX

THE NEXT MORNING, Roxy's eyes were grainy. Her hair was in a knot and she was pretty sure her shirt was on inside-out—but she was too damn tired to check. And after the interrogation and multiple pat-downs, she might not care for a while.

She sat on the metal stool in the visitation booth at the Clark County Detention Center. The air was sour with the smell of molding dreams.

And Sarina was in here. In this deathtrap and happiness-vacuum. She must be miserable.

Where was she? Roxy wanted to stand up, but she'd been told to sit. She didn't want to piss off the guard standing at attention next to the metal door. She didn't want to do anything that might hinder Sarina from coming through that entrance.

Any minute. Roxy stared at the scuffed metal and willed it to open. She'd finally get to talk to her. Sarina would tell Roxy that she was okay. After all, it had been one night and MacAuley said he'd come to check on her. If there was a problem, he would have told her.

Sarina would be out any minute and she'd smile. And then Roxy could finally breathe.

The metal door clanged open. Sarina shuffled inside, the dark blue jumpsuit hanging off her tiny shoulders. She would never not be hot, but right now she was more mess. She looked smaller, somehow. Frail.

There was no smile on her lips. Her hair was scraggled down her back and her eyes rimmed with worry. Wait. Not just worry. Roxy picked up the corded phone on her side of the glass as Sarina did the same on her side. Roxy wanted to start with hi, but who had time for that when her friend had a shiner. "Did someone punch you?"

"It's nothing."

The heck? "It's not nothing." Roxy willed the glass between them to disappear. She wanted to hug her and brush her best friend's hair into a cute pony. They'd talk boys and lip gloss and who the hell did this to her, so Roxy could kick the bitch in the twat. How dare anyone lay a hand on her best friend. Roxy was ready to throw down.

"I just need to get out of here."

"When do you meet with the judge?"

"I already did."

"Then why aren't you out?" Dread or something like it balled in Roxy's throat. Sarina couldn't stay here another night.

"My parents are on the way with the money. They

were performing in LA." Sarina's parents. Her father was a brick house of a man who threw Sarina's slip of a mother in the air every night on stage as they spun on roller skates. God bless them for making spousal hurling into a lucrative career.

None of that mattered right now, though. Getting Sarina out of here was the priority.

"I can post bail." Roxy could scrape together a few bucks to get Sarina out. She had to.

"Do you have an extra twenty-five thousand lying around?"

Or not. "Dollars?" She barely had twenty-five *dollars* lying around, let alone adding the thousand.

"I'm wanted for murder. And it was gruesome." A tear slid down Sarina's cheek. "I didn't do it."

"I know, sweetie." Roxy flattened her hand on the glass.

Sarina mimicked the movement. All that separated their palms was a half inch. And what a pain that half inch was. "Why won't they believe me?"

"The turntable had your prints on it."

"He was showing me how to mix music. He stood behind me and helped me do the mashups. It was so romantic, like *Ghost*. It was the same day I made the salad for our alien trip. Everything was so perfect that day."

"I thought you made that salad at your house." Roxy didn't like where this was going or the look on Sarina's face as Roxy asked, "You brought the salad to my house the next night."

"I grabbed it from Cliff's house before I came over."

"You went inside?" The lump in Roxy's throat was revolting. Any second she was going to be holding it in her hand. Or it would be plastered on the damn glass.

"I did. He wasn't home."

"Did you break in?" *Oh my goodness.* How exactly should one respond when they found out their BFF was performing B&Es—not sanctioned by Roxy?

"No. I have a key."

"You have a key to his place?" Why would he give her a key and not introduce her to his mother? Seemed bass-ackward.

"He didn't know I had it."

Could this get any worse? "So, let me get this straight. You stole a key to his house. And then used it to get into said house on the night he was killed. Is that about right?"

"It's not like that." Sarina curled her finger in the phone cord. "I had a key made when I started helping him pay his rent."

"You helped him pay his rent?" Roxy tried really hard not to sound judgmental, but she had a feeling her voice hadn't gotten the memo. He didn't deserve for her to pay for his coffee. "Do the police know all of this?"

"Yes."

She was so screwed. The police had everything they needed to keep Sarina in this place for years. Which was probably why the bail was so darn high.

"I didn't do it." The desperation in Sarina's eyes was enough to make Roxy's prickle with tears.

"Do you know who did?"

"I don't know who would hate him that much."

Tears were streaming down her face in full force. "Or hate me."

"No one hates you, Sarina. This is just some big misunderstanding." Roxy hated to ask the next question. Her friend had been through so much with the whole surprise fiancée. And now this. "Was Cliff seeing someone new?"

"I didn't know he was seeing anyone, let alone someone new."

"Think. Did he mention a new friend or coworker?" Did DJs even have coworkers?

Sarina stared at her hands before shaking her head. "No. I'm sorry."

"It's okay." Roxy looked at the clock on the wall. They had three minutes. She hated to leave, but the guard didn't look like he was going to let them have a sleepover. "I'll call your mom and we'll be back. Hopefully tonight."

"You can't come back. Your aunt's fiftieth is tonight."

"That's on Saturday."

Sarina shook her head. "Today is Saturday."

Crap. "I'll come back, and we'll head over together." Kill two birds one stone.

"I can't go, Roxy."

"Why?"

Sarina truly did look worried. "I just want to spend some time with my parents and talk to their lawyers." Yes. Lawyer with an s. Tossing one's spouse was profitable.

"You have to go." Yes, Roxy was whining, but her

family was best experienced with a buffer. "I can't go alone."

"You're an adult."

Debatable.

"And I'm in jail." Sarina had a point. "Take Rafe."

"I don't think our relationship is at that point yet. He can't meet my whole family. He still doesn't know I pad my bra when I wear that black dress."

"One minute." The guard almost looked like he wanted to laugh. But he probably got in trouble for showing human emotion. That would explain Detective Geary.

"I'm sorry, but I have to spend time with my family." Sarina almost looked like she wanted to cry.

Join the club. Not that Roxy would say that out loud. Sarina had enough to deal with. "Don't be sorry. You take all the time you need with your family. I'll text you later." Roxy was a terrible person. She was whining about a family party when Sarina was in jail with a black eye.

"Time." The guard wasn't smiling this time. They needed to do a better job of entertaining the statues.

"What about the eye. What happened?" Roxy asked the question, but Sarina didn't look interested in answering.

"I have to go." Yep, not answering. Sarina hung up the handset and walked out the metal door— disappearing, leaving Roxy alone.

Roxy stood up and left visitation, reaching in her jeans pocket for her phone. It wasn't there. No phones allowed. Damn rules. She walked out of the building and straight to Rafe's truck. She threw open the passenger door.

"Is she okay?" Rafe's stare was intense. He must have seen the look on her face. And that look must have been worse than she thought.

"I'm not sure." Roxy found her phone and dialed Sarina's parents. "Mrs. West, it's Roxy."

"Roxy, is everything okay?" That was the question of the day right there.

Too bad Roxy couldn't answer that. "I'm not sure. I wanted to find out how far away you are."

"We'll be there in twenty minutes."

Twenty minutes. Deep down Roxy was hoping they'd say they were already there. "I'll be in the lot when you get here."

Roxy ended the call and sighed.

"What's the ETA?" Rafe dropped his cell phone into the center console.

Estimated time of arrival. "Twenty minutes."

"That's good."

"It's not fast enough. She had a black eye." Saying the words made Roxy want to hurl. What happened in that damn place?

"Wait. What? How?"

"She wouldn't tell me." Roxy eyed her phone. MacAuley should have told Roxy there was a problem. After hitting his number, she waited for him to answer. And waited. His outgoing message clicked on, telling her to leave a message.

She had a message all right.

"Why didn't you call and tell me Sarina had been

hurt? What the hell happened? You had one job, MacAuley. One job..." The phone disappeared from her hand.

"Hey MacAuley, call when you can." Rafe ended the call and handed the phone back to Roxy.

"I had everything under control."

"Yeah, piss off the cop who can help us in this situation."

"Since when are you on his side?"

Rafe slid his hands along the steering wheel. His eyes were guarded. "When he started to hold Sarina's life in his hands."

Good point. Dammit.

CHAPTER 16
YOU CAN TAKE THE GIRL OUT OF THE TRAILER PARK, BUT YOU CAN'T TAKE THE TRAILER PARK OUT OF THE GIRL. ~ UNKNOWN

TWO HOURS LATER, Sarina was safely at home with her parents. She still wasn't talking about the eye, but her mom said she'd reach out if she found anything out. Rafe and Roxy were sitting in front of the fiancée's house.

Roxy should be thinking about the impending interrogation, but all she could think about was her Aunt Tutie. Last Christmas, Aunt Tutie pinched Roxy's cheeks seventeen times, all while saying how old Roxy was looking. She also regaled everyone with the story of Roxy's stained tights and leotard at her first dance recital, all thanks to her first period. It was a day of firsts that never needed to be relived.

Roxy had quit ballet, and she sure would have given up future periods if it didn't beat the alternative.

"How are we playing this?" Rafe asked.

"Uh-huh." Roxy had no desire to deal with family on a day like today—a day that ended in Y after she escorted her friend out of jail. But she couldn't invite

Rafe. Introducing him to family was relationship suicide. Introducing him to *her* family, anyway. She needed a good excuse not to go.

"Are you okay?"

"Uh-huh."

Sarina was a professional buffer. She knew when to run and when to stick it out. She knew Roxy's family better than Roxy. Mostly because Roxy was too busy dealing with her own crazy to deal with her family's.

Not that Roxy blamed Sarina for bailing on the whole Horne family festivities. Sarina had her own issues. And those issues were bigger than the family problems that Roxy had. That's it. Maybe if she kept them asking questions, she could "accidentally" miss the party. Her mom couldn't possibly be upset if Roxy missed the party trying to keep Sarina out of jail. Right?

"Roxy? Maybe we should just head home."

Wait what? "Home?"

"You seem distracted. We can come back."

"No." She couldn't head home. Home meant heading to the party.

"I'm just trying to figure out what to say. Let's go in." She smiled at Rafe, who looked a bit worried. No need. She was worried enough for the both of them.

Rafe gave her a look like she'd just flown over the cuckoo's nest. "How do you want to play this?"

"We'll play good cop, bad cop."

"Which one are you?" Rafe picked up the fob from the cup holder and opened the driver's door.

She opened her own and slid out. "I'm obviously the good cop."

"Obviously." Rafe hit the locks as they walked up to the front door.

Run down didn't really do the place justice. The concrete path was cracking and sinking. The awning over the front door was a modern marvel. The supports on both sides had rusted away from the house and hung down like defective windchimes, and yet the awning was still overhead. Well, overhead as long as you ducked down or were a short twelve-year-old.

The aluminum front storm door rattled as Roxy tapped on the frame. The cheap knockoff Sarina from the precinct appeared when the inside door opened. "Who are you?"

Hello to you, too. "Hi, I'm Roxy Horne and this is my... associate, Rafe. We need to ask a few questions."

Kandi's bleach-blond hair was still in that red banana-clip. A yellow T-shirt clung to her chest, leaving little to the imagination. Her nipples were large and pointy, in case anyone was wondering. Roxy wasn't wondering, she'd never wondered, yet here she was.

"What kind of questions?" Kandi's not-blond eyebrow arched as she spun the tip of her ponytail around a red nail. A smile curved her lips.

This was better. She wasn't glaring at Roxy. Heck, she wasn't even looking at Roxy.

Kandi's eyelashes batted. "And you are?" Her voice was throaty. Maybe she was coming down with a cold.

"Rafe Amato."

"Rafe." The way Kandi said his name was all breathy sexual innuendo. Not a cold.

He smiled. "Nice to meet you."

Kandi's eyes grew wide. She swooned. Actually swooned.

Not that Roxy blamed her. Rafe was naturally hot, but add that smile, and damn…

"I'm so sorry for your loss." Rafe edged his way past Roxy so he was in front of the swooning almost-widow.

"Thank you. It's been so hard."

"I'm sure." Rafe opened the storm door. "I know this is a terrible time, but we could use your help."

"Sure." Kandi stepped back, motioning Rafe in the house. Roxy followed—even though she was positive Kandi didn't mean that motion for her.

Kandi led them into a cozy living room with kitschy pictures on the wall. Paris. The Tower of London. All fuzzy-velvet-style art. In the center of the room sat a light brown rug with a mystery stain almost covered by a round green coffee table that looked like it barely survived the 70s.

"What can I help you with?" Kandi sat on a faded brown leather couch held together on the sides with duct tape. Rafe sat across from her on a matching chair, while Roxy stood off to the side, leaning against the wood-paneled wall. Given the googly-eyed stare Kandi was giving Rafe, he was going to play nice cop.

Rafe leaned in. "When was the last time you saw Cliff?"

"I saw him last Thursday. He was supposed to work some party in Reno, so I wanted to see him before he left."

Reno? Liar. He was supposed to be heading to Rachel, Nevada, to chase aliens with Sarina. Roxy couldn't muster the words to say that out loud. It sounded ridiculous in her head.

"So you didn't see him on Friday?"

"No." Her eyes shifted right to left. Very... shifty. Although her eyelashes were fluttering, so maybe it was just her way of flirting.

Either way, this was taking too long. "You didn't see him with the sex worker?"

Kandi's eyes rolled toward Roxy. "Why would I see him? Do you think he'd bring her home to hang out with me?" Sarcastic much?

She kind of looked like the three-way type. So, no, it wasn't out of the realm of possibility.

"Anyway. He just took a woman home, doesn't mean anything." Kandi's empty stare might mean she was lost in her thoughts. Or maybe even she didn't believe the words coming from her mouth.

Cliff wasn't exactly a drive-a-sex-worker-home-out-of-kindness kind of guy. He was more like a bury-a-sex-worker-in-the-desert kind of guy.

"He was changing. He'd been trying really hard." Kandi swiped away a tear with the back of her hand. "He might have known that girl he drove home, but he wouldn't cheat. He promised. That's why we were getting married, so he wouldn't be tempted."

Was that how that worked? Roxy must not have gotten that memo. Cliff definitely hadn't gotten that memo.

A tissue appeared in Rafe's hand, and he offered it to her. Kandi looked up at Rafe and her lips curved in a watery smile as another tear slid down her cheek. "Thank you."

"No problem. I know this is hard." He moved to sit across from Kandi on the green table. Somehow, even that seventies-reject looked good when Rafe was on top of it.

"You have no idea." She shook her head.

"I get it. My wife cheated on me."

Kandi glared at Roxy.

"Not me." Roxy threw her hands up to defend herself. From what? She had no idea.

Kandi didn't stop glaring until Rafe spoke again. "It was so hard to know she was disrespecting me. That she didn't love me the way I loved her."

Kandi sniffed. "But he loved me."

"Yeah, you were lucky. But you deserved so much better." Rafe rested his hand on hers. "You deserve a guy who will worship the ground you walk on and treat you like a princess."

Princess? *Gag*.

Kandi was lapping it all up. Her tears were drying as she nodded in agreement. "He wasn't always bad. We had our problems, but he promised no more screwing around."

"What about Sarina?" Roxy might have said that out loud. The glare Kandi threw said, yep she had.

"That bitch in jail? She's the one who killed him."

Roxy's temples pulsed. Her fists clenched. She was inches away from landing her own ass in jail. And it would be so worth it.

"Kandi, do you mind answering a few more questions?" Rafe's tone was calming. Probably for Roxy's benefit. "I really need a bit more information."

Yep. Definitely for Roxy's benefit. He was looking right at her as he said it. She unclenched her fists and her teeth. She unpuckered the cheeks that had been inches away from landing in jail.

Kandi took a deep breath. Probably for Rafe's benefit. "I'll answer your questions, but not hers."

"Fair enough." He smiled. "Is it true you and Cliff were fighting last Wednesday at Pura Vida?"

Fresh tears streamed down her face as she nodded.

"What were you fighting about?"

"He cancelled the cake tasting, because he wanted to push back the wedding."

"Why?" Roxy couldn't stop the question from popping out of her mouth.

Kandi glared at Roxy like she could read her mind.

It wasn't like Roxy asked anything bad. It was the natural progression in the conversation. If she'd said something about how Cliff probably knew what a manwhore he truly was and didn't want to get married because then he'd have to stop paying all the sex workers in the Vegas valley, that would be bad. Also untrue. Marriage wouldn't have stopped him.

"Why would he want to push back the wedding?" Rafe brought Kandi's attention back to the conversation.

"He was a romantic." Kandi's lips turned up into a small smile. Almost wistful. "We had plans for our day. A big dance floor in the center of the yard. Catering from Spago with a huge chocolate fountain for dessert. A bounce house off to the side."

Roxy was right there with her until the bounce house. That just sounded like an opportunity for drunk guests to end up in the emergency room.

Rafe nodded. "Sounds like the perfect wedding."

"It was going to be. I didn't need all that, but Cliff wanted to give me the world. He wanted all my dreams to come true. That was the type of man he was. That's why I loved him." Kandi wiped away another onslaught of tears.

Whether Cliff loved Kandi—or Sarina—or anyone other than himself was still in question. Did he truly want to give her a dream wedding, or were these all excuses? Only Cliff knew. But there was no question that this woman was smitten with him. Listening to Kandi was like listening to Sarina. How had that trash-compactor of a man attracted these loyal, loving women?

"Then why did he want to postpone?" Rafe asked.

"He ran into some cash problems."

"Didn't he just land a regular gig at the Luxor? That must have paid well." Since Rafe ran the security at Pura Vida, he had a little insight into the inner workings of the entertainment scene.

"I wish. He landed the gig by taking a huge pay cut. Heck, he wasn't even getting paid. He signed a contract that he'd get all the proceeds from his CD and T-shirt sales."

Rafe's eyes widened, but he reined everything back

in and narrowed his eyes in sympathy. "That sucks. Why did he take the gig?"

"He said it was exposure. But I think that crappy manager of his negotiated a bad deal and Cliff didn't want to admit it."

"You don't like his manager?"

"No one likes Fissure."

"Fisher? Like the YouTube DJ guy? Is that his last name?" Roxy asked another question. Sue her. But this might be a lead.

"No. Fissure." Kandi rolled her eyes. Again. "F-I-S-S-U-R-E"

"Oh, like a crack in the earth."

"I don't know." Kandi either gave up glaring or didn't realize that question came from Roxy. "It's like a stage name or something. Fissure. Dumb name, right?"

Not only a dumb name, but why on earth would a person trust their entire career to a man named after a crack caused by some kind of damage?

Kandi continued. "Cliff always trusted him, but I think the Luxor deal made him see the light. He talked about leaving him."

"About leaving Fissure?" Rafe asked.

"Yeah, he was tired of the low-rent deals. He was trying to be the next Marshmello, not some two-bit wedding singer." Kandi tore at the tissue in her hand. "And he was good enough. He could've been big here in Vegas—playing for the big hotels. Or LA. Ibiza. He could've played them all. And all I wanted was to be his wife. Travel the world. But he didn't have the money for what we wanted."

Knowing Cliff, if he thought he'd be travelling the world, the last thing he'd want was to be tied down to one woman. But at this point, that didn't really matter.

"Did you know Sarina?" Rafe asked the question that would have gotten angry-eyes if Roxy had asked it.

"Not personally. She just followed my Cliff around like a lost puppy dog. He tried to get rid of her, but she just wouldn't take a hint."

A hint? Like when he made plans to take her out of town? Or when he'd spend the night at her place and talk about how much he loved her? What hint was Sarina supposed to take?

He was such a tool.

"What about a new girl? Was he seeing anyone new?" Rafe kept asking question after question while Roxy listened. She'd be annoyed, except Kandi tended to answer more willingly when he asked.

"He wasn't seeing anyone but me. Not on purpose." Delusional. Why did this man make intelligent women *Krazy* with a capital K. "That's why that Sarina chick lost her shit. She kept throwing herself at him and he kept pushing her away. But she was different."

Delusional.

"Different how?"

Kandi played with the tissue in her hand. "The way he talked about her, I always thought she was just a nerd. You know, not the killing type. But that's what they say, right? It's always the quiet ones. Gotta watch them the closest."

"If you didn't think it was Sarina, who did you think it was?"

"At first, I thought it was Pauly. He threatened him so many times."

"You don't think it's Pauly anymore?" Rafe asked the question Roxy wanted to ask. She didn't think it was Pauly, but as long as it wasn't Sarina, she didn't care who it was.

"Nah, it makes sense. She was a stalker."

"A stalker? Are you kidding me?" Roxy's hands curled into fists. This bitch's attitude was getting on Roxy's last nerve. "What is your defect?"

"We should go." Rafe must have stood, because he was at Roxy's side. His hand under her elbow, guiding her toward the door. "Thank you so much for your time."

"Thank you for being so nice." Kandi's eyelashes fluttered. If her eyes weren't rimmed in red, it might've been endearing. "Stop by anytime you need anything."

Roxy turned to Kandi. Her hand flexed as she cocked her arm back, ready to slap that breathy "anything" from her blond-haired, big-boobed mouth.

"Thanks." Rafe smiled as he took Roxy's other arm and walked toward the door. "We'll reach out if we need anything."

"*You* can reach out anytime."

You can reach out anytime. The voice in Roxy's head practically sang the words. Okay. It totally sang the words. Her feet hit the steps and the hot outside air slapped her cheek. For some reason, she was still being pulled. She planted her feet and yanked back. "Why are you dragging me?"

Rafe let go of her arm and stepped into her. "I've visited one friend in county lockup today, I'm not looking to go there to see you. And that shit back there, you were inches from ending up in cuffs."

She'd argue, but she'd thought the exact same thing. "You are... right." The words fell out of her mouth before she thought about the ramifications. But the look on Rafe's face said that no three words in the English language could cause her more grief.

"Wait. What?"

"We should go." She headed toward the truck. Hoping he'd take the hint that they should never speak of this.

"Oh no." Rafe jogged over and stopped in front of her. His smirk would have been so adorable, if it wasn't at her expense. "What did you say?"

"We should go."

"Not that." His arms wrapped around her as her head dropped to his chest. His mouth rested on the top of her head.

She couldn't look at him if she was going to repeat it. She could already feel her cheeks growing hot. She hated admitting she was wrong. Which was ironic, since she was wrong so often.

"You are right." She could feel that his lips were turning up into a smile. And his smile made her smile. "Are you happy?"

"I have to admit, that didn't suck."

She laughed. The man was nothing if not honest.

And that was incredibly hot. Honesty was such a turn-on. It was time for her to be honest.

"So, I have a question." She drew away. She needed space to ask this one. "What are you doing tonight? Would you like to meet my family?"

He smiled again. All white teeth. His lips were downright edible. "I'd love to."

His smile was contagious. She felt it all the way to her toes. He'd love to. Well, once he met the family, hopefully those wouldn't be the three words he'd regret.

CHAPTER 17
SOME FAMILY TREES BEAR AN ENORMOUS CROP OF NUTS. ~ WAYNE HUIZENGA

AN HOUR LATER, Rafe might not have regretted accepting her invitation, but Roxy did. She was regretting so many things.

"For so long I thought Roxy was into the innies, not the outies." Aunt Tutie's broad shoulder bumped Rafe's. "If you get my drift."

Rafe's hand rested on Roxy's back. Somehow her heart slowed with just that touch. And since her aunt was telling her boyfriend she'd thought Roxy was gay, Roxy was amazed her heart was thumping at all.

"I'm not gay, Aunt Tutie." Except for that brief period in college, but it was college and Brittany was pretty hot. Anyone would have tested those waters.

"I see that now." Tutie shook her head. "But you always show up with that blond girl."

"Sarina."

"Where is she today?" Aunt Tutie had a gift. If there was a question Roxy did not want to answer, she'd find it.

"She's with her family."

"Does that mean she's out of jail?" Roxy's mother walked up, her mouth opening a can of worms.

"Your girlfriend was in jail?" Aunt Tutie whispered the word "jail" like she was afraid she'd summon Lord Voldemort. Her hand grabbed at her heart as sweat beaded in the mustache on her upper lip.

"Yes."

"I've never met anyone who was in jail. Is it like *Orange is the New Black*?" Aunt Tutie was whispering again. "Did she have to be someone's bitch?"

Given Sarina's shiner, it might be more like it than Roxy wanted to admit.

"Don't be silly, Tutie. That's drama created for TV." Roxy's mom nodded her perfectly coiffed bun toward the other side of the room. "Uncle Chet is looking for you."

Normally, Roxy would be annoyed at being left with her mother and her pressed white pant suit. But right now she wanted to wrinkle her perfection and plant a kiss on her cheek as Aunt Tutie walked away, waving her arms as she flagged down Uncle Chet.

"Thanks." Roxy took a long pull from her drink. It was a chance to pause before her mom started the third degree.

Her mother ignored the thanks, looking Rafe up and down. "It's nice to see you again."

"You too, Mrs. Evans." He looked like a teenager in the principal's office—all nervous shuffling feet.

"As we discussed, please call me Olivia." Her

mother had met Rafe when Roxy had been shot during her own run-in with the law. Apparently, they'd talked. Rafe thought she was perfectly pleasant. He might have been distraught that Roxy was shot. That was the only explanation for finding Olivia Evans pleasant.

"Mom, where's Danielle?" The more amiable half of the Evans couple.

"She had patients, so she couldn't get away."

"That's too bad."

"Not really. If I could have skipped the party, I would have." Roxy's mom took a generous pull from her martini glass. "Sometimes I'm jealous of her career. She has the best excuses."

"You know, Mom, you could've skipped the party with a migraine, or your period."

"Don't be crass. Ailments are not justifiable excuses for missing a function." Her mom stopped drinking and glared. "You don't use those excuses on me?"

More often than not. "Not at all." Roxy took a drink, hoping the lie wasn't written on her face.

"I don't believe you." Her mom had lie-dar. At least when it came to Roxy.

"Why would I lie? I love seeing you."

Her mom laughed—an honest-to-God laugh, where her chest shook. "Now I know you're lying."

"Well, I like to see Danielle."

Her mom's smile widened. "She's pretty great." Then the smile cracked and her mom glared. "But that doesn't mean you can lie when Danielle's not around."

"I'm here, aren't I?" That Roxy didn't know

Danielle wouldn't be here, didn't need to be brought up.

"Hmmm." Her mom took another sip of her drink. And sip meant gulp in this situation. Her mother didn't gulp. It wasn't ladylike. And her mom was a lady. Which meant...

"Is everything okay?" Roxy asked.

"Why wouldn't it be?" Her mom's face became a mask of cold. "Is everything okay with you?"

"Not really. My best friend was in jail." Roxy never did learn how to fake it as well as her mother.

"Was? I guess that means her parents bailed her out."

"Yep. It's what good parents do."

"It's yes, not yep. And I wouldn't bail you out if you were in jail. Yet, I'm a good parent."

"Please, you would so bail me out. You wouldn't want the ladies in the Blue Bonnets to hear about your jailbird daughter." The Blue Bonnets. An uptight group of women at the golf club who claimed to be charitable. The operative word being "claimed". For every dollar they raised for cancer research, they'd spend a dollar-fifty on booze and crepe paper.

"They hear about everything. I was popular for over a month when you had that, that incident."

That incident. Her mother couldn't say the words. Apparently, it was traumatic when your only daughter was shot by a crazy person.

"A shooting equals popularity? Maybe I'll see if I can get shot again." Not gonna happen. That was not fun.

"Don't you dare." Her mom actually looked upset. "That was the hardest thing. I can't do that again."

And given the words, her mom was upset. The guilt clawed at Roxy's throat. "I was joking."

"A joke is supposed to be funny." Her mom's upset dried up like her tone. Along with Roxy's guilt.

"I agree." Rafe had a smirk on his face as he sided with the enemy. Traitor.

Her mom's lips curled into a smile. "See, even he knows you're not funny."

"It was one bad joke in a lifetime of wildly funny zingers."

"More like, we're still waiting for that wildly funny zinger in a sea of bad jokes." Her mom's lips quivered as she obviously held back a laugh. "Oh dear." Her eyes widened as she took another long pull from her glass.

Roxy knew that *oh dear* actually meant *oh shit* or some other version of swear word. Roxy followed her mother's gaze and totally understood. Swearing was a perfectly acceptable reaction to seeing her ex-husband's young wife.

"I'm so glad you're here." Stormy waddled up to Roxy, bright red dress swaying, and wrapped her arms around her. Waddled.

Roxy's former schoolmate-turned-stepmother was pregnant with Roxy's unnamed sibling. Her father was going to be a sixty-year-old new father. While his daughter was old enough to have her own kids. Not that she was going to have kids—but still. It was the principle of the thing.

Stormy let go when Roxy's father came over, and

stepped back so her husband could take his turn. His green pants and palm-tree-covered button-up short-sleeved shirt screamed old-Vegas Rat Pack. And after working most of his life in the casinos in Vegas, he was a walking Frank Sintra cliché.

"How's my favorite daughter."

"I'm your only daughter." Better use that line as much as possible. It might not be true much longer.

"You're still my favorite." He laughed, and she hated to admit she laughed a bit too. It was their joke. It was what they said...

Stormy wrapped them both in a hug. "You're both my favorite."

...until *she* came along.

Roxy wiggled out from the warm cocoon of her father's embrace to shake off the interloper. The interloper rested her hand on her stomach when she saw Rafe. "Rafe, it's so nice to see you again." Another set of people Rafe had met when Roxy was in the hospital.

The fact he stayed with her after that was a miracle. She'd gnaw off her own arm to get away from her family.

"Rafe." Her father held out a hand to shake and Rafe took it.

"Nice to see you, sir." Rafe's manners were so on point. It was adorable.

"Oh my goodness." Stormy bounced up and down. "I forgot to tell you. I saw Jenny Henderson last week. We were like best friends in high school. Remember her?"

Of course Roxy remembered her. The girl was in her homeroom.

Her mom downed the rest of her drink. "Didn't you get caught smoking with Jenny Henderson in the girl's locker room freshman year?" she asked Roxy.

"Yep."

Her mother's eyes narrowed, but she didn't mention how Roxy should say yes not yep. Apparently, having her ex's pregnant wife around was a buffer of sorts. Super. "Paul, your wife is best friends with the child that got your daughter suspended in high school."

"Well, everyone is a child at one time or another."

"Very true. She was just a child when your daughter was a child." Her mother's ire focused on her father.

"Olivia." Her dad's tone was scolding.

Her mom's eyes rolled so hard, it was a miracle they were still in her head. "I have to go."

"You don't have to leave." Roxy wasn't exactly upset her mom was leaving, but she didn't want her to leave mad.

"It's nothing like that. I'm bringing dinner to Danielle at the hospital." Her mom handed her glass to Roxy as she kissed her cheek. "Always a pleasure. It was nice seeing you again, Rafe."

"You as well, Olivia." He leaned in to kiss her mother's cheek.

And then she was gone.

"I didn't do anything wrong, did I?" Stormy's lips were drawn in a pouty frown.

Maybe being born—or at a minimum, dating outside her generation bracket?

"Not at all." Roxy's father gave Stormy a sweet kiss on the lips. Well, it would have been sweet if it wasn't Roxy's dad.

"So, I just wanted to tell you that Jenny Henderson finally finished rehab and she's getting married to a nurse over at Desert Rose Hospital."

"That's great." And it was great. Jenny'd had a hard time after high school. Addiction and crappy boyfriend after crappy boyfriend. She deserved a win.

"Speaking of friends. How's Sarina? Is she still in jail?" Her father frowned. "She's like a daughter to me."

"She's out. Her parents came back to town."

Her father nodded his head. "It's so hard when our kids are in trouble."

"Absolutely," Stormy agreed and rested her hand on Roxy's arm. "My heart goes out to her parents and the parents of the boy who died."

Boy? He was the same age as Stormy.

"Now that I'm a parent—"

Stormy was barely a parent. The kid was the size of a small squid.

"—I can totally understand how hard it must be to lose a child. I don't know what I'd do."

Roxy's eyes rolled. Shit. She was turning into her mother. But to be fair, her father's teen bride had that effect.

"She must be beside herself trying to figure out what happened."

Kind of like Roxy. She might not be Sarina's mother, but she was beside herself, all right. If she didn't figure this out, her best friend could end up in prison. And the best resource was probably Cliff's mother. This party was a necessary time-out, but tomorrow they had to move faster, before Sarina was afraid to drop the soap.

CHAPTER 18
A MOTHER'S LOVE FOR HER CHILD IS LIKE NOTHING ELSE IN THE WORLD. ~ AGATHA CHRISTIE, THE LAST SEANCE

THE NEXT DAY, Roxy and Rafe walked up to a small bright blue house in the College Park neighborhood of North Las Vegas. Rafe parked his truck along the curb, next to the low white brick wall surrounding the single-story house. Black bars covered the windows, and the front door had a matching metal security door.

A white metal gate hung open at the bottom of the driveway, allowing them access to the pocked concrete walk leading to front door.

Roxy's checked for a doorbell. Nothing. The metal bars of the security door prevented any knocking. Not a bad idea.

Rafe came up behind her. "Could you try to not start any trouble today?"

"I don't start trouble."

"True. It just manages to find you."

"I can't help it I'm easy to find." She checked along the doorjamb one more time. If only a knocker was easy to find. There had to be some way to get a hold of these people.

"Why aren't you knocking?"

"Where would you like me to knock?" Roxy gestured like she was presenting letters on *Wheel of Fortune.*

Rafe banged his knuckles against the edge of the security door, making it rattle. A voice called from inside, "Coming!"

Rafe smiled but managed to refrain from saying he told her so—just one more indication he valued his life.

The door opened and Celeste Foster-Robbins stood in the opening. She looked the same as the first time Roxy saw her at the precinct. Her eyes were still rimmed red. Just her outfit had changed. Her light blue floral muumuu hung down to her Crocs-covered feet.

"Hi, I'm Rafe Amato and this is my associate, Roxy Horne. We need to ask a few questions."

Celeste sniffed. "Are you with the police?"

"We're working in conjunction with their investigation."

"That crazy girl did it."

That Roxy was the crazy girl's BFF wasn't something she was going to tell this woman. They needed her help, and saying they were aligned with the enemy wasn't going to make that happen. Roxy pasted on a smile. "We're making sure the charges stick."

"Thank goodness." Celeste opened the door and ushered them in. "Them cops aren't doing their job. That girl is out on the street, you know."

"We're well aware, and we want to help you." Roxy nodded as she walked inside. White tile floors, with a couch that looked to have been bright blue at one point. Now it was a hazy shade of blue. The décor was mainly oak-adjacent furniture covered in figurines and knick-knacks. Doilies covered everything.

Roxy waited while Celeste closed the door and ambled to a recliner next to the couch.

"...I don't know..." A voice came from an open door behind the recliner. A teen boy with acne sat in a purple gamer's chair. Headphones covered his ears, and a microphone hung in front of his mouth.

"That's my Michael's son, Jared." Celeste dropped onto the recliner.

Roxy waved at Michael's kid Jared. Whoever Michael was. Rafe nodded.

Jared didn't seem to notice them. He raised a fist as the television flashed and red slid down the screen. His smile faded as he looked back at the screen. "Dammit." He threw his headset down on his lap as the screen went black. "I'm dead."

"That sucks." Roxy stepped into the doorway. The chair he sat on wasn't just purple. It was purple and black leather. By far the nicest piece of furniture in the place. "Nice chair."

"Thanks." A tear shimmered at the corner of his eyes. "I got it from my brother."

"That is a really cool gift. Is your brother older than you?"

"He was. I mean, he was my stepbrother, but Cliff was like my brother. He was always there for me."

The pain in the kid's eyes was evident. He might not be Cliff's brother by blood, but he was taking it as hard as a sibling.

"Shit. I'm so sorry." Jared wiped away a tear and took off his headset. The side of his hand was bruised.

"What happened to your hand?"

He stared at the fading bruise and tilted his hand. "Oh. Nothing. I fell. I've got to get back in the game. Greg's losing his shit without me."

"Wouldn't want to upset Greg." Roxy didn't buy the whole falling thing, but she didn't think now was the time to pry.

"True." Jared attempted a laugh as he repositioned the headset.

"Don't forget you have algebra homework," Celeste called from the living room.

Jared covered the microphone, yelling back, "After this game, Mom." He pulled the microphone closer to his mouth and said, "Keep your pants on. I'm jumping in."

Roxy stepped back into the living room. Celeste was smiling, shaking her head. The shaking was probably because Jared was practicing killing zombies instead of learning algebra. The smile might be because he called her Mom.

"Is he your son?" Roxy thought she knew the answer to that one, since Jared just said that Cliff wasn't his brother. But she had to start Celeste talking somehow.

"No, but I've been raising him since he was nine.

His momma died in a car accident a few years before I met his father."

"That's too bad." And it was too bad. Roxy wasn't thrilled with her mother, but she couldn't imagine a life without her.

"He had a rough start. He was in the car when his momma died."

Roxy eyes filled with tears. "That's terrible. But it's good he's still here."

"Yeah. He was in the passenger seat without a seatbelt. He flew through the windshield. Shattered his leg." Celeste ran a hand down her face. "They told Michael he'd never walk again."

Roxy hadn't seen the kid walking around, but he had kicked at the TV. "He seems to be moving around okay."

"Three years of physical therapy and a lot of prayers." Celeste smiled like a proud Mama. "That's where we met. In the hospital. I'm a physical therapist. I wasn't Jared's therapist, but I'd see my Michael outside crying every time they came in.

"I used to bring Cliff into work with me during summer breaks. Cliff helped Jared walk again. He encouraged him and became his biggest cheerleader. Cliff pushed him to stand up. He'd hold out a candy bar and tell him he could only have it if he walked over. That kid would do some amazing things for chocolate. Although, I don't think it had anything to do with chocolate. I think Jared just looked up to him and they became friends. Then Michael and I became more than friends." So much maternal-type pride there in her smile. "That kid has overcome a lot, but he's never given up. He's a good kid. Straight A's."

"He must be upset about Cliff."

"He is. We all are." She pulled a tissue from a box on an end table next to her recliner. She dabbed at her eyes. "I'm sorry. I can't seem to stop crying."

Roxy wanted to say so many things, but she didn't think anything she could say would help. Thoughts and prayers wouldn't bring her son back. Her condolences wouldn't make the ache go away. "There's no reason to be sorry. You suffered a great loss."

"I just wish I could stop crying. No. I want him to come through that door and tell me it's all a joke." She sniffed.

"Was Cliff a jokester?"

"He was." Celeste giggled. "He put shaving cream in Michael's work gloves. It was such a mess. But so funny."

"Did Michael find it funny?" Rafe asked the question Roxy was thinking. Shaving cream in the gloves sounded funny, until it was your gloves.

"Not at first, but he meant well."

"Meant well?" That was usually code for he got pretty pissed. But how pissed?

"Michael doesn't like his work stuff messed with. But he used his spare gloves, and he was fine by the time he got home from work."

"Is that where Michael is today?"

"Yeah. He works over at North Valley Metal Supply. He's pulling some overtime." She sniffled. "We could use the money."

Roxy sat down on the far end of the couch, next to Rafe. They needed to get back to talking about Cliff. "Any other jokes Cliff played recently?"

"Just on his friend Davis."

When Sarina had called Davis, he'd mentioned they'd had a falling out. But he'd also mentioned they hadn't seen each other in months—except for that group clubbing trip. "What did he do to Davis?"

"Oh goodness. Cliff released a bag full of crickets in Davis's house. Well, not Davis's house, his mother's house." Celeste laughed, a deep throaty laugh. "Apparently, it was quite the sight. Crickets chirped all day and night for two weeks. Davis found one in his shoe. He even found one in the cereal."

"And Davis thought that was funny?" Roxy would have burned her house down if anyone let creepy-crawlies loose—preferably with the cricket-releaser still inside.

"Not really. Especially when his mom kicked him out of the house."

Another piece fell into place. He'd mentioned living with Cliff's mom for a bit. "Is that why Davis was living here for a while?"

"Yeah, I took him in until he could find his own place."

"That was nice of you. Was Davis mad?"

"He hasn't talked to Cliff in a few months."

"Well, except for that club they went to a couple weeks ago, right?" Roxy had heard all about how those friends were bad news and Cliff had stayed out all night with them.

"I don't think they went anywhere together. Davis would have told me. I thought that was sad. Best friends for eighteen years, and it all fell apart for a little prank."

So Davis wasn't lying when he'd said they hadn't talked. He must have been covering for Cliff when he said he'd gone out with him the other night. Even angry, Davis had Cliff's back.

"Getting kicked out is a pretty big deal. Maybe Davis was madder at Cliff then he let on?"

"Oh no, they did things like that to each other all the time." Celeste stared at Roxy, eyeing her up and down. "Weren't you at the police station with that girl?"

Roxy smiled—or attempted one. She had no idea what to say. Yes? No? That was my twin?

"You need to leave." Celeste pointed at the door. Apparently, having a hot associate wasn't enough distraction for her.

"Ms. Foster-Robbins, I could really use your help." Rafe broke out the weaponized smile and fluttering lashes. Hot associate powers activated.

Celeste's eye lids dipped as a grin crawled across her lips. "What can I do for you?"

"I just have a few questions."

"Sure." Celeste's eyes bored into Roxy. She didn't say that she'd happily answer questions from him and not Roxy, but it was implied in the glare.

"We're looking into Cliff's enemies. Did he have any?"

"Not that I know of."

"Had his behavior changed at all?"

"No." Celeste was not offering anything. No matter what Rafe asked. They weren't getting anywhere.

Roxy turned to Rafe and he nodded. He leaned toward Celeste.

Rafe reached across and rested his hand on Celeste's. "I know this a tough topic, but what was Cliff's relationship with Sarina?"

Celeste grabbed onto his hand like it was the last pair of heavily discounted Louboutins in her size. "That girl was his stalker. She followed him everywhere. We didn't know this would happen. We all thought it was funny."

While the blood boiled in Roxy's veins, Celeste stared off in the distance. Roxy's hand curled into a fist. Sarina was not a joke.

"She wanted to be with him, but he had no interest. She couldn't take a hint."

"You do know your son spent a lot of time with Sarina?" Rafe seemed hesitant to ask the question. He probably didn't want to spook her.

"I know." Celeste nodded as tears poked through her lashes. "If I'd known it would end like this, I would have stopped him. I should have stopped him."

Rafe patted her hand, concern etched in the wrinkles bracketing his eyes. "Would he have listened?"

"Not a lick." Celeste laughed. "Ever since his daddy left, he's been rebelling against anything I say. That boy had his own mind."

"Like most children." Rafe grinned.

"Amen."

Rafe's eyebrows twisted in confusion. He was playing it up. "If he had no interest in Sarina, why would he spend time so much time with her?"

"He was too nice to that girl. He should have told her off long ago. But he didn't want to hurt her feelings."

Yeah, that Cliff—always worried about hurting feelings. He was so concerned with everyone else's feelings, he slept around and psychologically abused women. A real Good Samaritan.

"But wasn't he engaged to Kandi? Isn't that part of being faithful, saying no to other women?"

"I guess. He just had a soft spot for broken toys. And she is as broken as they come."

Roxy was about to enlighten Celeste on just who the broken toy was in this whole dang scenario when the front door swung open.

A big, burly boot stomped on the floor. A man banged a cooler-type lunch box against the door as he pushed it open. "I'm home." He stopped mid-enter when he saw Rafe with Celeste's hand in his.

She pulled her hand away and smiled. "I'm so glad you're home. Michael, this is Rafe and Roxy. They're looking into Cliff's... situation."

"Ain't the cops taking care of it." Michael dropped his lunch cooler to the floor. The sound reverberated through the house and amplified the tension. He didn't seem to want them there.

"You know them cops are messing it up."

"True." Michael looked to Celeste and nodded. "You deserve some closure on all this mess."

"No way!" Jared yelled from the other room. "You killed me."

"Hey there, boy!" Michael's face morphed from attentive husband to angry father in the blink of a screen—a video game screen to be exact.

"Sorry," Jared called out before talking into his headphones.

"Don't you got homework to do? Them damn schools ain't teaching you nothing."

Jared dropped his headphones and clicked off the television. "I'm going to do homework now." He got up to retrieve a thick book and went back to the leather chair. He opened the book and pulled out a folded piece of notebook paper.

"Shoulda been doing your homework from the start." Michael shook his head. "What's for dinner?"

"I started a roast." Celeste smiled as she turned to Rafe. "I need to get supper on the table."

Roxy's stomach rumbled as her nose registered the roasting meat.

"Of course." Rafe handed Celeste a card. "Please reach out if you remember anything."

Celeste took the card and handed it to Michael before heading toward the door that probably led to the kitchen and the heavenly smell.

"I'm sure she told ya everything." Michael ushered them to the front door. "No need to talk about this anymore."

"Thank you." Rafe followed Roxy to the door. "But if you know anything that might help, we want to make sure the person who did this pays for it."

Michael slammed his hand on the open door. "Wait. Why do you think I'd know somethin'?"

The fire in the man's eyes had Roxy stepping back. That Rafe didn't seem to be moving back told Roxy they were about to fight. And he was worried she'd end up in jail today... *Crap.*

CHAPTER 19
THE WISE MAN CAN CHANGE HIS MIND; THE STUBBORN ONE, NEVER. ~ IMMANUEL KANT

RAFE GLARED.

Michael's arm still blocked the door. Roxy watched as the two men stared each other down. She felt helpless. If Michael moved his arm three inches, Rafe would be in a headlock and there wasn't much she could do to help. The man was immense. Maybe she could jump on his back to slow him down, and give Rafe a fighting chance to break free. But all of that sounded like trouble. And she was under strict orders to avoid trouble.

He'd have to forgive her in this case, though. Right?

"Where were you stationed?" Rafe nodded to a tattoo on Michael's arm as Roxy thought of ways to use that arm to climb onto Michael's back.

Michael glanced at his arm. "Okinawa. Ghana. Iraq."

Rafe nodded. "Semper Fi."

Military talk. Roxy had been around enough ex-military to know that trash-talking and military-speak were about to ensue.

Michael looked Rafe up and down. "Where were you stationed?"

"Mostly Iraq. Operation New Dawn."

"That was a shit show."

Rafe nodded. "Try being boots on the ground."

Michael pulled his arm down and laughed. "Most of the operations were FUBAR."

Even Roxy knew that one. Fucked. Up. Beyond. All. Recognition.

"That's what you get when you have dumb-ass brass making decisions." Michael chuckled.

"Amen," Rafe said.

"Don't know if this'll help." Michael shook his head and checked the kitchen door before looking back at Rafe. "It's been a rough few days."

Rafe nodded, frowning a little. "Anything can help."

Michael leaned into Rafe. "Cliff was a good kid, but he had problems." He stopped. He seemed to be thinking about something. Maybe it was about his impending dinner. Or maybe it was just his next words.

"Like?" Roxy didn't have the patience to wait for his thoughts to coalesce.

The wheels seemed to turn. Like he hadn't heard Roxy speak. His eyes stared off into the distance. Those darn wheels were obviously still turning.

Finally, Michael's eyes unclouded and he ran a hand down his face before speaking. "He had a sex addiction."

"Cliff did?" That explained so much. Roxy knew he had issues.

"He'd been seeing a therapist for a few months." Michael sighed. His attention on Rafe.

"For sex addiction?" Roxy asked another question that she figured Michael wouldn't answer.

"It wasn't right. The way he slept around." Michael crossed his arms and leaned against the door frame. "I tried to talk to him about the birds and bees and wearing a condom. The usual. But mostly I tried to get him to stop putting it out there. I was so glad when he proposed to Kandi. I thought she'd get him to stop all the shenanigans."

Rafe nodded. "When did he propose?"

"A little over a year ago."

Roxy nearly gagged. Over a year ago. He'd done so much with Sarina over the past year. Proposing hadn't calmed him down at all.

"Have you noticed any improvement since he started seeing the therapist?" Rafe asked, like he didn't know the answer.

Roxy did. That would be a big HELL NO.

"At first, he seemed to relax a bit. We knew where he was most of the time. That was an improvement. But then he was at it again. He'd be missin' for days."

"Didn't you worry about him?" Roxy couldn't imagine anyone from her family being gone for a few days without a full search and rescue team getting called in.

"I can't believe he's gone for good." Michael ignored her questions. Again.

Roxy checked her hands to see if she was still visible.

Rafe asked the question Roxy wanted to ask. "Did you try to find him?"

"Why? It was his way. He'd shack up with a woman he barely knew for a few days and then come crawlin' back."

But he didn't barely know Sarina. He'd stayed with her a lot over the last year or so. Unfortunately, it didn't change anything—maybe made it worse for Sarina. But this whole thing sucked for her, no matter how you looked at it.

"Do you know any of the women? Do have a name?"

"He spent the most time with that Sarina." So they did know he was with her— at least Michael knew.

"Do you think she killed him?"

"I'm not sure. I met her once."

"You did?" Roxy couldn't remember Sarina ever mentioning that she had met any part of his family.

"I saw them both at the Luxor one night. He introduced her as his friend. She didn't seem to like that." Michael shook his head. "That's when I knew that therapy wasn't workin'. She obviously thought they were more than friends. The way they'd been holdin' hands before Cliff saw me, they were more than friends."

Rafe kept him talking. "When was that?"

"Two months ago."

"Did you ever talk to him about it?"

"Affirmative. I told him he needed to stop that shit

right now." Michael shook his head. "But he never listened."

"Did you tell the therapist?"

"I told his mother, but she didn't want to believe it. He was happy and treating everyone so nice, she thought he was fixed. So I doubt she told the therapist."

"Do you have the name of the therapist he was seeing?"

"No. Government watches over our shoulder and is in all our business, but I can't find out the name of my son's therapist. Years of his disappearing and then this, and we can't find out who he was talking to."

"Dinner's ready." Celeste walked into the front room wearing a "World's Greatest Mom" apron. Her smile morphed to a frown. "Did you say something about the doctor?"

"I didn't say nothin' that didn't need sayin'."

"But..." Celeste began, but stopped as she watched Michael put his foot down. Literally.

Roxy had heard the expression a million times, but honestly, she'd never actually seen it in action.

Celeste lowered her head, her shoulders slumping in on themselves. "Dinner's on the table."

Something about the way he talked to Celeste rubbed Roxy the wrong way. Not that she was about to say anything to him. They barely got past the first almost-fistfight.

"Thank you for your help." Rafe nodded to Michael as Roxy slipped out the front door.

"Yep." Michael turned and closed the door.

Roxy made her way to the truck and got in as

Rafe held open the door. "So that was interesting. I thought you were going to go all smackdown with the guy."

"Smackdown?" Rafe laughed as he closed the door and walked around to the driver's side. He opened the door and slid inside the truck.

"Like the wrestlers, but without all those pesky muscles to get in the way."

"Are you saying I'm weak?" Rafe started the truck.

Maybe she had chosen the wrong words, because there was no way the man on her left was weak in any way. "No. I know just how strong those arms are. My ass has the wall-rash to prove it."

"That was a good night." Rafe smiled. "I can't help I love spending time with you. I get excited."

Roxy's cheeks burned as her lips quirked up. He was so sweet. "I like spending time with you too. I get excited too."

He pulled away from the curb and headed out of the subdivision. She didn't know what to say next. So many emotions passed inside of her. Happiness. Elation. Love.

That last word scared the heck out of her. The L word always ended in pain or divorce— well, one divorce, but she really didn't want to start collecting them.

And she really didn't want to keep travelling down this line of thinking. Time for a topic change.

"What did you think of Michael?" She thought it was pretty obvious he was a tool.

"Do I think he's a killer?"

That was probably a better question. "Yeah." As it was, the man was at the top of her list.

"He could be, but he didn't have a motive. He seemed to care for Cliff."

Roxy stared at Rafe's profile waiting for something—a punchline maybe. "He was a controlling jerk."

"Yeah, but he seemed genuinely worried about Cliff and his choices."

"He literally put his foot down when Celeste tried to speak. He was a jerk to Jared and I'm sure he treated Cliff the same way. Heck, he even ignored me, and my questions were thought-provoking."

"Thought-provoking?"

"Whether they were or not, he could have acknowledged that I spoke."

"Yeah. I noticed that he was ignoring you. I was going to ask for pointers."

"On how to ignore me?"

Rafe nodded as he laughed, a gut-bunching guffaw. She had something she'd like to do with his gut, and it included her fist.

"That was for the muscle comment." Laughter crimped the sides of his eyes as they sparkled. He looked pretty darn cute, even if that happiness was at her expense.

She would own that she started it. "So can we agree Michael is on the list?"

"Yeah." Once out of the neighborhood, Rafe pulled the truck into the local fast food parking lot.

"Are we stopping to eat?"

"Not here. No. We're regrouping." Rafe shifted the truck into park. "Where to now?"

"We need to figure out the therapist's name so we can talk to them."

"Patient confidentiality might make that hard."

"But we have to try." She knew it was a long shot, but she had to try every avenue.

"What about the manager?"

"Fissure?" Roxy stared at her phone. "I tried to call him, but he didn't answer. I can't believe you were able to get his number with just the name Fissure."

"I have talented staff."

"I better watch my back. They could come after my job."

"I'll watch your back for you." He looked her up and down. "I like to watch you."

Roxy's cheeks warmed. The way he was looking at her made her body sizzle. *He could watch her any day.*

Rafe smiled and leaned his head back. "We need to focus. We don't have enough to go on."

"I know." Roxy dialed the number for Fissure and he picked up.

"Hello?"

"Hello, is this Fissure?"

"Who wants to know?"

"My name is Roxy Horne. I want to talk to you about Cliff Foster."

"Why should I talk to you, since they found the person who did it?"

"Because we're trying to make sure that the charges stick." She was lying through her teeth, but she didn't think he'd talk to her if he knew she was searching for the real killer.

"Fine." Fissure blew out a breath. He sounded annoyed. Get in line. This whole trying to make sure her best friend didn't rot in jail was annoying to her too.

"I'll be at my office for the next two hours. If you want to talk, come meet me."

"Where are you?"

"My building's in North Las Vegas." Clicks and clacks came through the phone. "Are you on your cell?"

"Yeah."

"I'll text you the address."

Roxy looked over at Rafe for any indication they wouldn't be heading to North Las Vegas. There was nothing. "Okay. We'll be there in thirty."

Fissure ended the call, and a few seconds later an address pin came through from his number.

"I got it." She turned the phone to Rafe as his phone began to ring. The name Gabe Martin scrolled across the screen on the dashboard.

"It's my team, I have to answer."

"Hey Gabe, what's up?"

Gabe was the first responder at the hotel when Roxy got into a bit of trouble last year. He was a nice enough guy, and he seemed to be loyal to Rafe.

"We got a problem, boss. Jeannie was hurt during an altercation with a pickpocket. Saul took her to the emergency room, so we're running short. Can you come in?"

"Why is he with her?" Rafe's words were clipped.

"It's his wife."

"I don't care. We have a policy. What does the policy say?"

"To call an ambulance." Gabe's voice went soft. "It's his wife, Rafe. We couldn't stop him.

"I get it, but there's a reason we have rules." Rafe sighed. "We'll talk about it when I get there."

"Sure, boss."

Rafe ended the call. "I have to go in."

"I figured." Roxy looked at the address of Fissure's office. This was going to be a fifty buck Uber ride. She hated not having a car.

Rafe pulled out of the parking lot and headed toward the Las Vegas strip. "This should take me about an hour or two. I'll try to get one of the night guards to come in early."

An hour or two was not going to give them enough time to get to Fissure's office. "I'll call Fissure and see if he can meet tomorrow."

"Why?"

"I really don't feel like cabbing it all the way to North Las Vegas."

"Take my truck. Just make sure you drop it off when you're done."

"Take your truck?" That he trusted her felt really good.

"You still don't have a car, right? I don't think that bike will get you to North Las Vegas."

"You'd let me use your truck."

"Just don't hurt it."

"I won't." It wasn't like she'd ever hurt a car before.

Hopefully that wasn't an omen.

CHAPTER 20
THE QUESTION THAT HAUNTED EVERY INVESTIGATION WAS "WHY". ~ LOUISE PENNY, THE INSPECTOR GAMACHE MYSTERIES

ROXY DROVE the car-clogged streets of Las Vegas Boulevard until she could grab I-15 toward North Las Vegas. Rafe's truck was so much bigger than her car. She felt like she was hovering over the cars on the road. If only she could drive over them. That would be awesome.

After thirty minutes of pretending to monster-truck her way through Vegas traffic, she pulled up to a shopping center on Nellis. She parked in front of the door with *Fissure Talent and Recording* on the front.

She stepped out of the truck and onto the gray concrete walkway leading to all black windows. She tugged on the glass front door. Nothing. Locked. If she drove all this way only to have been stood up by Fissure, she was going to eat her weight in ice cream.

Although, that actually sounded like fun whether he was here or not.

She placed her cupped hands against the dark glass and peeked in. It was too hard to see inside. She tapped on the door. Maybe they were closed. The building didn't exactly post hours of operations.

A lock clicked and the door swung open. A black man, about six feet tall, wearing bright pink spandex leggings and a red sequined top stood on the other side. "You're late."

She didn't realize they had set a time. "I came right over."

"Mmm-hmmm." Spandex scrunched up his lips, like he didn't believe her. His judgey fists were adhered to his narrow waist. "I'm Dinky."

"Dinky?" Roxy tried not to look, but you find out a person's name is Dinky and you look at...well, what might have earned him that moniker. He was skinny. Long arms. Longer... Nope. The pink spandex left very little to the imagination. And what was left was not little.

"It's ironic." Dinky winked, his tongue lodged in his cheek. He definitely saw her checking him out. And he didn't seem to mind at all. "Come on in."

Roxy followed Dinky inside the dark building. The front area held a table and chair. All lights were off, but she could see remnants of some sort of work. Papers were strewn about the surface. Boxes lined the floor next to the desk—a cardboard filing system, maybe.

She was tempted to send Rafe her location, just in case she disappeared. She'd seen movies. She knew how following people into creepy empty buildings led to your picture on a milk carton.

"Fissure was about to leave. They don't like to be stood up." Dinky opened a door that led to a back area.

Two leather recliners sat against the side wall, duct tape holding them together. A soundboard sat across from the recliners.

Past the soundboard was another room. Gray quilted blankets were taped to the walls and ceiling. Microphones stood in the center. It was what Roxy expected to see in a recording studio, except for the duct tape holding everything together.

Another person sat at the sound board. Graying brown hair pulled back into a ponytail. Manicured fingernails with red nail polish. Headphones over their ears, head bobbing to a beat only they could hear. Lights danced on the board as they moved switches up and down with the bright red talons.

"Fizz." Dinky walked over to the person and tapped them on the shoulder.

"What?" Fissure tipped up the earphones.

"Your one o'clock is here."

"It's after one o'clock." Fissure glared at Roxy.

"I came as soon as I could. I'm sorry. I didn't realize we had a set time to meet." Roxy had no idea why she was apologizing. Just because they decided to assign a time didn't mean she was late.

"I had work to do. No harm." Fissure dropped the headphones onto the board and stood up. Where Dinky was six feet, Fissure was not. They had to be two feet shorter. "Dink, can you make sure everything is locked up before you go?"

"Sure." Dinky waved with a flick of his fingers and disappeared through the door to the front.

"So, what can I help you with?" Fissure pressed some buttons and the lights on the board shut down.

"I want to talk about Cliff."

Fissure walked into the soundproof room and turned off the light. "Tragedy. My boy was on his way up."

"Was he?" There might have been a tad too much surprise in her voice. But they were talking about Cliff.

"Did you ever see him mix?"

"Yeah. He was okay." Roxy hadn't been all that impressed. He wasn't a bad DJ. He just wasn't all that good.

"He could get a crowd on their feet."

"So does a fire alarm." Roxy didn't mean to say that out loud, but apparently she did.

Fissure laughed. "A fire alarm can get everyone moving, but it takes a special person to get a group of twenty-somethings to dance not ironically."

"Do they dance ironically?" And what was the difference? She had so many questions.

"It's not just getting them on the dance floor, it's getting them to come back again. It's making them want to spend the money to party with you over and over again. Cliff had that gift."

Even Roxy could admit he was good at getting people to party with him. Davis had said that Cliff had the best drugs. But that wasn't all. Cliff had a way of getting people to love him. He did it over and over again with Sarina and Kandi and many other women of Vegas. It probably did help his career to be so easily loved.

"I can see that."

"People don't seem to get it. It's not just about spinning records and compiling music. I mean, that's a big part. But there's another part. A human component that needs to be met. If people don't want to hang out with you, they'll find something else to do. I've tried to get Pauly to understand. He's good looking, the girls would fall at his feet if he wasn't such a cardboard cutout on the mike."

"Is that why Cliff got the Luxor job over Pauly?"

"Cliff got Luxor because I'm an amazing manager." Fissure sat on one of the recliners. "I took the club manager to lunch and worked my magic."

"That must have pissed off Pauly." Although Roxy still wasn't convinced the doting father was a murderer.

"That's an understatement. He passed pissed and landed in disturbed."

Roxy's hopes rose. "Disturbed enough to hurt Cliff?" She needed to find anyone to replace Sarina. She hated it might be a father, but if he was a killer, he needed to be put away.

"Didn't they already find the person who killed him?"

"They have someone, but we want to make sure that the charges stick." Roxy was so tired of the lie, but she didn't know where anyone stood. So far, they all thought Sarina was guilty.

"Really?" Fissure's eyebrow raised in the universal sign of skepticism.

Whatever. He could be skeptical all he wanted.

She had questions. "What about you? What were you doing the night Cliff died?"

"As I told the cops, I was in LA with one of my clients. She got an invite to try out for a new band. And before you ask, Dinky was with me. There were at least twenty people who can vouch for me."

"So you didn't kill Cliff?"

"Why would I? He was making me money." Fissure shook their head and then ran a thumb under their eye. "And the guy was my friend. I miss him." Fissure stared at the wall, like they were looking for something.

"I hear he was looking at other managers."

"Let me guess, Kandi." Fissure laughed. "She tried to pull Cliff and I apart over and over again. But I just got him a residency at the Luxor. Why would he leave me?"

Roxy hated to admit it, but that made sense. It also took another person off the potential killer list. "Why would Kandi lie?"

"I don't know if you talked to her much, but she's a liar. That's why they fought all the time."

"They probably fought all the time because he was constantly cheating." Roxy wasn't sure she'd stop at fighting if she found out her fiancé was banging anything that moved.

"Well, there was that." Fissure nodded. "But he wouldn't have needed other women if she wasn't such a horrible nag all the time."

That wasn't exactly how cheating worked, but what

would anybody named Fissure know about women and relationships? "So, did you meet the other women?"

"Most of them. I met that Sarina a few times. She was a stage-five clinger but she was harmless."

Stage-five clinger? Roxy wasn't sure what that meant, but it didn't sound good. The harmless thing sounded okay though.

"I talked with Destiny a few times," Fissure added.

"Destiny?" Cliff was dating a Destiny. Why did all the women he was with have stripper names? With the exception of Sarina, naturally.

"The new one." Fissure smiled. "She was pretty hot."

Of course she was.

"Was Destiny the sex worker he drove home the night he died?"

"Yeah, they were celebrating his new contract."

"Why wouldn't he celebrate with his girlfriend or his fiancée?" Roxy had enough trouble juggling life with one boyfriend. Why would she want two?

"He was going to get rid of the excess—the girlfriends and fiancées."

Wait, what? "There was more than one fiancée?"

"Nah, I just wanted to see your reaction." Fissure leaned over in laughter. "Your eyes about popped out of your head."

Funny. Not.

"Cliff was sick of the drama. He wanted things to be simple. Juggling three women was weighing on him."

"Is that why he went to the therapist?"

"He went to the therapist because his mom made him go. He couldn't stand that chick. She gave him that crappy ADHD medicine that messed with his rhythm. He was always tired when he took it."

That was new information. "He was on medication for ADHD?"

"Nah, he hated the stuff, it interfered with his creativity."

"So he just stopped taking it." Roxy wanted to be clear on this.

"If you couldn't do your job, wouldn't you stop?"

She'd welcome a reason to not knock on strangers' doors and give them court summonses. The things she'd seen—ugh—could not be unseen. The man who answered his door wearing only a pump came to mind. The rubber bulb swaying in the wind. No one needed to see that.

"Are we done?" Fissure was standing by the front door. At some point they must have gotten up.

"One more thing. Did the medication help?"

"Maybe. He was calmer on the meds, but it was just more tired than anything. He'd stop seeing the extra chicks for a bit. But it wasn't worth it. He lost his spark. He couldn't do his job like that. He couldn't be the person he needed to be."

All those times Cliff would disappear or break up with Sarina. They were probably him on the meds. He should have stayed on them, if those meds were keeping him from hurting all of those women. Not that it mattered now.

"Thank you for your time." Roxy walked toward the door and left as Fissure held it open.

She crossed the parking lot to Rafe's truck and climbed in. She watched Fissure lock up the building and slide into a minivan. A nuclear stick figure family lined the back window. Maybe they did know what it was like to be in a relationship.

She should probably work on not judging books by their covers.

CHAPTER 21
STUBBORNNESS IS A POSITIVE QUALITY OF PRESIDENTIAL LEADERSHIP— IF YOU'RE RIGHT ABOUT WHAT YOU'RE STUBBORN ABOUT. ~ DOUGLAS BRINKLEY

LATER THAT NIGHT Roxy sat at the white granite breakfast bar in Rafe's condo. The scent of meat cooking filled the air. She'd thrown together some beef, potatoes, and a bunch of other ingredients into the crockpot that morning before they'd left. She was feeling so domestic.

"So, what did Fissure have to say?" Rafe stirred the stew in the crockpot. "Did he mention why he has such a ridiculous name?"

"They didn't." Roxy laughed. That was a missed opportunity. She should have asked them about the name. "They did mention that the sex worker who was with Cliff that last night was named Destiny. Oh, and get this, Cliff was on medication to help with his ADHD. When he would stop dating Sarina, it was probably when he took the medication."

"Does that actually work?"

"I don't know, he stopped taking the medication."

"The world may never know." Rafe put the lid back on the crock pot. "Soup's on."

"I'll grab the bowls." Roxy's stomach growled as she walked around the island and opened a cabinet. She wasn't sure if it was the rich scent of the food or just Rafe announcing it was done, but she was starving.

The doorbell rang.

"Are you expecting someone?"

Rafe wiped down the counter with a towel. "No."

Roxy set the bowls down and turned toward the door. "I'll get it."

"Look through the peephole. If it's my neighbor, pretend we're not home." The bowls clinked, so Rafe was probably getting the food together.

Roxy's stomach gurgled in agreement as she walked down the long empty hall. Well, it was mostly empty. Now that Roxy was hanging around a bit more, pictures of Rafe and Roxy lined the space. She was doing her part to warm the place up.

Roxy checked the peephole. She peeped a cop. "It's MacAuley. Should I pretend we're not here?"

"I can hear you," MacAuley growled from the other side of the door. Although Roxy wasn't positive that's what he said. It was a bit muffled with a door in the way.

"Never mind. He knows we're here." Roxy turned the knob and smiled at the officer. Last she'd checked, Sarina was still at home. So he shouldn't have any news. However, MacAuley didn't make a habit of showing up at Rafe's very often.

There had been an incident back in the day, due to

ancient history where MacAuley failed to mention Rafe's ex-wife of one year was banging Rafe's boss—for two years. And MacAuley knew before the wedding. Apparently, it wasn't his secret to tell. Rafe disagreed, and their friendship had taken a toll.

"To what do we owe this pleasure?" Roxy asked.

MacAuley's eyebrow arched. "Didn't I just hear you say you were going to pretend you weren't here?"

"I'm hungry." Not a lie. She was still starving, and meat fumes were still hanging in the air.

"I won't take too much of your time then." MacAuley nodded inside the condo. "Can I come in?"

"Sure." She opened the door and MacAuley strolled in. He made his way down the hall to where Rafe was setting steaming bowls on the breakfast bar.

"It smells good."

"I'm sure you didn't come here to compliment Roxy's cooking. What's up?" Rafe leaned against the counter.

"Right to it then." MacAuley turned to Roxy. "I heard you talked to Fissure." He sounded mad.

"Yeah. Nice person. Dumb name." Those were the highlights of the conversation. Well, the highlights she was willing to share.

"I thought I told you to stay out of it."

She could do a mean voice too. She slammed her fists onto her waist. "And I thought I told you this is Sarina."

MacAuley sighed.

Roxy dropped her hands. She wasn't even that mad at him. This was their game. He'd tell her to do one thing, she'd do the other. But in this case, she was right. She would do anything for Sarina.

Rafe rearranged the silverware next to the bowls. Smart man. Stay out of it.

"You know why I can't let this go." Roxy shouldn't have had to say it. He knew.

"Look I get it, but..." MacAuley sighed again. "Sarina is the main suspect."

"And she shouldn't be. Why are you focusing on Sarina? You know she didn't do this." Roxy's blood pounded in her ears. She shouldn't have to remind MacAuley of this over and over again.

"That's not how the evidence is stacking. She had motive, we found her prints on the murder weapon and there is a period of time where she is unaccounted for." All of which sounded damming on the surface, if you didn't know Sarina.

"Come on, MacAuley." Roxy felt the plead in her voice. "You know she couldn't..."

"No. I don't know. I have to listen to the evidence."

Evidence? Was he for real? There was an easy fix for that. "Find new evidence. Do your job."

"Fine I'll do my job if you do yours and stay out my investigation." MacAuley's voice was eerily steady. The calm before the storm.

"If you'd do your job, I wouldn't have to."

"Enough. We're all on the same side." Rafe stood between them, which was probably a good idea as she was inches away from catching a case.

"Stay out of my way," MacAuley growled.

"Then get Sarina out of this."

MacAuley turned, his shoes slapping against the hallway floor. He slammed the door and left silence in his wake.

Roxy sat at the breakfast bar and brought a spoon full of meaty goodness to her lips. It did taste good, or she was just really hungry and anything would taste good.

Rafe stood next to Roxy's chair. He wasn't moving. He looked at her like she was a wild animal about to be let loose in an enclosure. "We're not staying out of his way, are we?"

"Hell no." She took another bite.

"Didn't think so." Rafe shook his head and sat next to Roxy. He took a bite.

"Do you think we should?" Not that she was going to stop if Rafe said to stop, but she might actually think about it before she... nah. She wasn't going to stop until Sarina was out of the hotseat.

"Stay out of it? Hell no." Rafe smiled as he brought another spoonful to his mouth. "This is delicious."

She nodded. She wasn't sure if she nodded because she couldn't trust her voice or if she didn't want to stop eating. Either way, there was no way they were letting up.

MacAuley practically had Sarina working on the chain gang without finding the real culprit. And Roxy was going to find that culprit, or die trying.

CHAPTER 22
PREGNANCY IS THE ULTIMATE EXCUSE FOR BEING LATE, FORGETFUL, AND EMOTIONAL. ~ AMY POEHLER

FINDING DESTINY HAD BEEN HARDER than expected. Maybe being a call girl was a good way to eliminate your online presence. Not that Roxy was thinking of switching careers, but a girl had to keep her options open.

The Monday morning sun beat down on a meticulously neat newly built two-story tan home on the edge of North Las Vegas. The front yard was an untrodden mix of grass within a swirl of rock. Tiny baby bushes were spaced along the front of the home, leading to the front door on the right side.

Roxy didn't know much about sex-working, but it must pay well because the house was pretty darn nice.

Rafe barely knocked on the front door before it flew open. A woman whose beauty rivaled that of the house stood in the doorway. Her black hair was pulled back in a long ponytail. Her skin was a smooth dark brown. She wore a baggy sweatshirt over slim leggings.

Roxy could almost see why she was able to afford a place like this. She was hot.

"Destiny Warren?" Roxy smiled at the woman, who smiled back. She was just so pleasant.

"You must be Roxy."

"Yes, and this is my associate Rafe."

"So nice to meet you." Destiny stepped to one side of the doorway. "Please come in."

This was so different than all the other interviews. She was sweet and actually seemed to want them there. Well, wanting them there might be a bit much, but she wasn't hostile.

The bar was set a little low these days.

"You have a beautiful home." Roxy looked around the wide-open first floor. Everything was brand new. It even smelled brand new—like paint and plastic.

Destiny led them into a large open-concept living area. On one side there was a matching set of extra-deep oversized cream couches flanking a massive big-screen TV. The other side held a kitchen worthy of a Michelin chef and a large eight-seater table. Boxes sat on the kitchen table. Maybe she was moving in.

Destiny motioned to the couches. "Please, have a seat."

Roxy sank into one end of the couch and looked around. It was so soft. She fingered the soft material and melted.

"May I get you anything to drink?" Destiny stood over Roxy and Rafe. Apparently he'd sat too. She hadn't noticed while she was fondling the texture. But to be fair, it was some good texture.

"What type of fabric is this?"

"Velvet."

"Really?" Roxy ran her hand over the pillowed seat. Her parents were old Vegas. She knew velvet. Intimately. Every holiday dress from birth to fifteen was some sort of velvet monstrosity. Her father even owned multiple velvet smoking jackets in various hues—and he didn't smoke.

But she could honestly say none of them felt this good. Or fluffy.

"Ahem." Rafe's voice cut through Roxy's thoughts. "Do you want anything to drink?"

"Um...no?" Roxy looked to see that Destiny still stood over them both.

A smile played at Destiny's full pink lips. Yeah, she had to be popular at the office. "I'll be right back. She turned around and headed to the kitchen.

Rafe leaned in. "Are you okay?"

"Yeah, why?" She slid her hands under her thighs to stop from petting the couch. She had no idea why the darn thing fascinated her so much. Her fingers inched back and forth under her lap. If her bed was made of this material, she'd never leave. It was comforting and soft.

"You're paying more attention to this couch than you did to me last night. And I even did that thing you like."

That thing she liked. Oh my, would that feel good on this couch. She was almost getting excited thinking about it.

"Roxy." Rafe looked over at her with horror on his face. "That was the look you gave me."

"I was just thinking of our time together." True. She was just also thinking of that time together happening on the smooth velvet. Her cheeks warmed. Both sets.

She had to stop. She placed her hands in her lap. Far away from fabric temptation. She needed a distraction. She turned her attention to Destiny's place.

Live, Laugh, Love signs hung on the wall above the front door. A wooden sign said, "God Bless America". A plaster duck sat in the corner wearing a frilly little dress. It looked like something out of Country Living.

The manners. The house. Roxy might be stereotyping, but TV did not portray streetwalkers accurately.

"Here you go." Destiny placed a bottle of water and a coaster in front of Rafe and opened the one in her hand before she took a drink. "What can I help you with?"

Roxy knew she shouldn't do it, but she had to know. "I have got to ask. How do you afford this place?" She was pretty sure Rafe just spit out the water he had started to drink.

"I'm sorry." Rafe looked at Roxy like she'd tossed his toothbrush in the toilet.

"That's okay." Destiny lowered the water bottle in her hand and placed it on a coaster she'd laid out for herself. She was so sweet. She was way too sweet to be working the streets of Vegas. Although wasn't it a tale as old as time, nice girls came to Vegas to make it as a showgirl and ended up with the wrong crowd.

Although that might be in Los Angeles, but whatever. "What do you mean?"

"I mean, do you live with your business manager?" She couldn't live with her boyfriend. He was the reason they were both there.

"Um... no." She rolled her eyes. "What do you think I do for a living?"

What was the politically correct verbiage? Working girl? Call girl? Sex Expert? None of that. She could go with sex worker, but that didn't feel right either. "Woman of the night?" She really should have looked up the proper way to ask a woman who boinked her way to tax evasion.

"So you think I'm a sex worker?"

It was sex worker. Darn. She'd messed that up.

"Is it because I'm black?" Destiny looked confused. Not angry.

Crap. Roxy would be beyond mad if she was Destiny. She'd messed that up immensely—in so many ways. She didn't mean to be racist. "No, it's not because you're black. That would be horrible to think that way. I know people do, but I would never." Oh please make her stop talking. Roxy's mouth wouldn't stop. "I can't even imagine how terrible that would be for you." Her mouth kept moving. STOP! Roxy took a breath. "I was told."

"By Kandi?"

"Yes. And the cops."

Destiny shook her head. "Who were told by Kandi."

You probably couldn't trust the jilted fiancée for

accurate job titles. Roxy probably should have had that thought before she'd opened her mouth.

Destiny shook her head again. "She's just evil. She's been telling anyone that'll listen I'm some sort of floozy. I have a doctorate in Physical Therapy and I'm a licensed masseuse. I work at the Golden Palm Spa."

"She didn't mention that."

"Of course not. She takes joy in defamation of character." Destiny grabbed her water bottle. "I'm just glad I'll be rid of her soon."

"Rid of her?" Was this her way of confessing to Cliff's murder and the future murder of Kandi?

"I'm moving to LA." Destiny motioned to the boxes on the kitchen table. She was moving out then. Her eyes brimmed with tears. "Kandi threatened him, you know."

"Threatened who?" Roxy knew Kandi was awful, and she was hoping this was the smoking gun she needed to get Sarina out of this trouble.

"Cliff."

Bingo. Roxy refrained from dancing a jig. "Why did she threaten him?"

"He told her he was leaving her."

"He was?"

Destiny shrugged. "We were going to move to LA together."

"You were?" Roxy tried to hide the skepticism in her voice, but she had a feeling she failed as Destiny's eyes narrowed. At this point, Roxy wasn't sure what to believe. One woman thought she was his girlfriend, one thought she was his fiancée planning a big wedding, and woman number three thought they were moving to LA.

"Kandi didn't believe me either—not that I care. I'm starting a new job at the Ho'omaha Spa in Beverly Hills next month." Destiny picked up some papers and handed them to Roxy.

It was a rental agreement for an apartment in Pacoima, California. Signed by Destiny and Cliff. The paperclipped copy of the check used for the down payment even had his name at the top.

"What about his DJ career?" Roxy hated to admit that Cliff had actually made a career out of being an average DJ.

"He was looking to get into the LA scene, that's where the real money is. And he'd come back here for the Luxor gig till he made it."

Roxy handed the papers to Rafe. "Did Kandi know that he was leaving?"

"Yeah. He told her a couple of weeks ago, when he sold his motorcycle."

"Then why is she still wearing his ring?" Roxy couldn't see wearing the ring of a man who was planning on leaving, but Cliff had some weird hold on them. And what about Sarina? There's no way she knew he was three-timing her and was planning to move to LA.

"That's what everyone wants to know." Destiny sighed. "I personally think she was hoping he'd change his mind. But we were in love. He wasn't going to change anything but his address."

That was a plausible answer for Kandi, but what

about the manager? "Why didn't his manager know he was moving?"

"He was looking for new representation in California. He didn't want to upset Fissure." Destiny took another drink of water. "Fissure had just got him that Luxor deal. He felt disloyal bailing, but he'd gotten as far as he could go with Fissure."

"Wasn't the Luxor thing big? Why would he want to leave?"

"It was big for Vegas, but he wasn't going to make a living there. Anyway, he was looking to branch out globally. Manchester, Berlin, Ibiza… He wanted more, and Los Angeles was going to be the steppingstone."

"What's this?" Rafe separated a sheet of paper from the stack and handed it Destiny.

"Oh, That's a referral for a new psychiatrist." Destiny traced a finger over Cliff's name. "I guess he won't be needing that."

A new psychiatrist. "Was he taking his medication?"

"He was."

"Didn't it ruin his creativity?"

"It did, but we wanted to build a family." Destiny rested her hand on her stomach.

Oh no. "Are you pregnant?" Please be no. Please be no. That would kill Sarina.

"Yes. Three months along."

Roxy felt her heart crack. And she was pretty sure Sarina's would be breaking into a million pieces. How much more could Sarina take before she just lost it?

"And it's Cliff's baby?" Roxy didn't need an answer. She just knew.

"Yes. I'm not sure how I'll do this alone, but I guess we have to take the challenges God gives us."

Now Roxy could see it. Her cheeks were filled out and her waist showed a little bump. "Very true. We should let you get back to your day."

"I'm just packing."

Roxy put her hands on the couch to lift herself up, but before she stood she swirled her palm over the fabric. "Are you taking this couch with you?"

"I was planning on it."

Roxy felt the bubble burst in her chest as she stood up. Not that the couch leaving was the worst thing she'd heard today, but it would have been a nice consolation prize for dealing with all this crap. "If you change your mind, I'd be happy to buy it off you."

"I'll keep that in mind." Destiny led them back to the door and opened it. Sunlight poured inside.

Roxy squinted as she stepped outside. They'd gotten information from Destiny, and now she had to tell Sarina. She had to be the one to break her heart. Roxy was not looking forward to any of it.

CHAPTER 23
I'VE BEEN POOR AND I'VE BEEN RICH.
RICH IS BETTER. ~ SOPHIE TUCKER

AFTER THAT, Roxy dropped Rafe off at Pura Vida. Apparently, they were missing him, or maybe they just needed the boss around to keep things in line. She stopped and ate some food that was fast and hot, and then drove Rafe's truck to the Golden Palm and Wellness Center.

When she'd originally called Sarina and didn't get an answer, she'd thought the worst. But a quick chat with Sarina's mother and she found that Sarina was taking a few days to relax. What better way to relax than a ridiculously expensive spa.

Not that Roxy was knocking it. If her parents could afford it, she'd be getting her feet massaged and her body pampered. But alas, no such luck for her. The closest she'd get to pampering was a visit with Jessica at the Nawty Nail Emporium—which usually included bacteria.

The Golden Palm wasn't that type of place. It was where celebrities rested after their face-lifts and Botox.

Roxy drove back roads toward the end of the earth, or at least the end of the Vegas valley. The spa was located in Mount Charleston, over twenty miles northwest of the city. She passed huge mountain-retreat style homes, finally turning onto a curved tree-lined road carved into the mountains. Sunlight sliced through the gap in the bluffs, shimmering off the white building just beyond the red brick wall surrounding the property. It had to be at least ten feet tall. There was no getting over that—which was probably the point. Keeping the celebrities inside and the riffraff out.

Roxy half expected the metal gates to clang shut, but she drove though without even a guard questioning her. She pulled into the parking lot in between a gold Porsche and a cherry-red Aston Martin. Thank goodness she didn't have her old Camaro. It would wither next to these expensive cars. Rafe's truck was practically sputtering in embarrassment, and it was fairly new.

The building was beautiful, even without any windows. The red leaves of desert paintbrush, planted in beds all along the front, glowed against the white stucco. An impressive arched doorway trimmed in taupe sat underneath a brown tiled roof. Roxy walked up to the building, through the arch, and down a long stone entryway ending at a pair of heavy wooden doors. She pulled one open.

Holy...

She'd found all the windows. Sunlight streamed in through a wall of glass. Trees spread along the mountains that jutted and dipped in the distance. The scene was calm and tranquil—perfect view for people trying to relax.

Her attention left the view and wandered inside. Another ode to tranquility. A white couch surrounded by mint green chairs sat in a large front area. Pink roses and pink and white calla lilies in large vases covered black marble end tables. A large golden chandelier hung over the seating area.

Roxy walked under the chandelier and up to a high white counter with a young man standing behind it. His smile was contagious. Gorgeously straight teeth. Dark hair hanging over sunflower blue eyes. "Welcome to the Golden Palm Spa and Wellness Center. I'm Jacob. How may I help you?"

"I'm here to see Sarina West."

"Your name?" He smiled and tapped on a touch screen.

"Roxanna Horne."

"Ah, yes." He continued to tap away. "She's expecting you."

She was? Sarina never answered her phone, so Roxy didn't think Sarina knew she was trying to talk to her. Apparently, she knew. Either she was channeling that ESP they'd told Daisy Plimpkin they'd had in grade school, or maybe Sarina's mom called.

"Please follow me." He gestured to a hallway behind the desk.

Roxy followed him. The room beyond was more white and mint green. The black marble was, again, covered in colorful flowers. But this time the ceiling was see-through, allowing the sun to warm the room.

There were also live trees, with small bistro tables and chairs positioned underneath them.

People dressed in yoga pants and T-shirts that probably cost more than all the clothes Roxy owned sat at the tables enjoying coffee. At least she assumed it was coffee, as there was a coffee bar in the far corner with a sign that announced a "plant-forward culinary journey".

A couple sat on a far bench snuggling. They both wore a ring on their left hand, so either they were married to each other and both needed relaxation, or they had somehow adopted corporate rules and they were work spouses—with benefits.

With the exception of the couple, everyone stopped talking and watched Roxy follow her new friend Jacob through the coffee area and out a door in the back. More tables and chairs sat on a large stone patio. Past the patio was a path leading to a collection of wooden chaise lounges covered in white cushions. Mint green pillows and light blue towels sat on the cushions and a small wooden table sat next to each chair.

Roxy passed a woman with gauze covering most of her face. Her cream robe was pulled tight and cream sherpa slipper-boots crept up her legs. The only thing left uncovered were her eyes. She looked like a remnant from a mummy movie. She was leaning back in her chaise, unmoving.

Like, not moving at all. Her chest didn't appear to have any rhythmic movement. Ummm...

"Is she okay?" Roxy leaned into Jacob and nodded toward the hopefully sleeping mummy.

He smiled. "Of course. She's sleeping."

"Are you sure?"

He nodded and followed the next path toward another set of chaises.

She kept staring. Her body twisted backward as she walked forward. She was waiting for something—a blink or a twitch. Anything. Unless she wanted to walk backward, she was going to have to give up. Darn it. "Can you go check on her when we're done?"

Jacob smiled again. "We're not allowed to disrupt her."

"Is she famous?" Roxy did a full about-face and stopped. But there was no way she could see any face through that dressing, even if she squinted her eyes. And she'd tried. It didn't help.

"I'm not at liberty to talk about our guests." Jacob motioned in the direction they had been walking.

Roxy nodded and continued to follow her guide toward a wall of trees with another grouping of chaise lounges in front. Only one was occupied.

Please don't be Sarina. Please don't be Sarina.

The woman on the chair had her knees drawn up to her chest. Blond hair piled on top of her head in a messy knot. Her head was propped on one hand, elbow on the arm of the chaise. Her other hand held a tissue. Used tissues surrounded the chair.

"Sarina?"

"Roxy?" Sarina's head flew up. Her eyes were rimmed in red. "You got here early."

This wasn't the first time this week she'd been

expected at a certain time and didn't quite make it. "Do you want me to leave?"

Sarina angled herself up into a sitting position, tossing the tissue on the ground.

"Can I get you anything, Miss West?" Jacob started picking up the tissues.

"I'll take care of that, Jake." Sarina leaned forward and reached for a tissue underneath the chaise. Unfortunately, gravity was not on her side. She toppled sideways. Fortunately, Jacob was right in front of her and caught her hand before she kissed the stones.

Roxy knelt, and began picking up the used snot-rags—trying real hard not to think about the snot that was lurking in each tissue.

"Are you okay, Miss West?" Jacob was no longer holding her up, but he looked like he was worried he should be. "Would you like me to get your doctor?"

"No, thank you." Sarina forced a smile. "I'm good."

Jacob looked from Sarina not falling over to Roxy crawling around the chair. He nodded. "You look like you're well taken care of." He turned away and headed back toward the building.

"Don't forget to check on the mum... the lady over there." Crap. Roxy almost called her a mummy. That felt like prejudice of some sort.

"I will." He kept walking. Maybe he wasn't going to check on anything or maybe he was, but Roxy had done everything she could without invading a celebrity's personal space with a mirror under her nose.

Roxy crawled under the chaise to retrieve the last few tissues.

"I have a garbage pail." Sarina picked it up and held it out to Roxy.

Roxy looked at the snotty rags in her hand and the empty garbage pail. "You have a garbage pail?"

"Yeah." Sarina's face lowered and a small smile flitted across her lips.

"Let me show you how this works." Roxy took the handful of tissues and dropped it into the pail. "See, you take the snot rags and you place them into the opening."

Sarina rolled her eyes.

"Now, it might be confusing. So let me show you again." She then grabbed another handful from the chair. "I get the opening is not very big and you may miss. But if you keep trying, I know you can do it." Roxy dropped the new handful into the awaiting pail.

"I'm having a bad day and you're really giving me crap about tissue?"

"We're never too busy to learn something new."

"I have something new for you." Sarina scooped up a stray tissue and shoved it in the pail. "It includes this pail and your ass."

"Wow." Roxy couldn't help but smile. This was her Sarina—feisty. "I hate to tell you, but that's not new for me."

"Liar. You've never shoved a garbage pail up your ass."

"Okay, fine. I haven't, but that would be so funny if I had."

Once the chair was empty, Roxy set the pail aside

and sat on the ground. "I'd ask how you're doing, but looking at the remnants, I think I get the picture."

"It's been so hard." Sarina's spark faded as she pulled her legs into her chest again. "I miss him, but I think all of this is my fault. I actually wished for him to die."

"No, you wished for him to get beaned with a turntable, big difference."

"But it happened. Maybe I wished it into existence."

"I don't think that's a thing. If it was, I'd be married to Harry Styles and we'd be recording our latest album together." Roxy would love to wish that into existence, but given the warble she called singing wasn't appealing to anyone with working ears, she didn't think her daydream would come to fruition.

"But everyone thinks I killed him." Sarina dropped her head. "I couldn't kill anyone. Not like literally."

"I know, sweetie." Roxy leaned over Sarina and grabbed her hand. "Not everyone thinks you're guilty."

"I guess. It's just so hard. I want to be allowed to mourn, but I can't. Everyone here looks at me."

"They look at you?"

"Like I'm a monster." Sarina's eyes teared. "Like I'm some murderer."

"These people don't know you."

"They act like they do." Sarina's tone hardened as woman walked past, watching Sarina like she might jump up and stab her with the garbage pail. It would have to be, because Sarina didn't appear to have anything pointy on hand.

Once the woman disappeared, Sarina swallowed hard. "I mean, why would I kill him. I loved him." Tears appeared in her eyes again.

Roxy hated to do it. But she had to pull the Band-Aid. Sarina deserved to know. "He was leaving."

"What do you mean leaving?"

Roxy's heart cracked. There was a literal pain in her chest. And now she had to explain.

Maybe she had time to run, because this was not going to be easy.

CHAPTER 24

I THINK MY HUSBAND IS HAVING AN AFFAIR WITH HIS SECRETARY, BECAUSE I WOULD FIND LIPSTICK ON HIS SHIRT, COVERED WITH WITE-OUT. ~ WENDY LIEBMAN

THE SUN PIERCED Roxy's eyes as she looked around the spa. She didn't want to have to tell Sarina any of what she was about to say. Taking in the environment allowed her to procrastinate.

"Roxy?" Sarina glared. "You said Cliff was leaving. What did you mean?"

Roxy couldn't put it off any longer.

"Sarina." She reached out with both hands and grabbed Sarina's hand. "I really hate to have to tell you, but he was going to move to Los Angeles."

"Why?"

"Well, you know the girlfriend they mentioned?"

Sarina's eyebrows arched in confusion. "Kandi?"

"No, not the fiancée. He had a girlfriend. The one he drove home the night he was killed."

"The hooker?"

Roxy winced. "Yeah, she doesn't like being called that. She's a massage therapist. Like, with a doctorate and everything."

"Oh."

"He was serious about her." Roxy could do this. She knew that. But every reveal felt like another dagger.

"Who told you that?"

"She did."

"She could be lying." Sarina didn't have any conviction in her voice. She knew the straw she was grasping was flimsy.

"She's not."

"How do you know?" Sarina's voice rose. She pulled her hand from Roxy's and waved it around. "She couldn't know him like I did. He was with me for years. You know that. I knew him. I was there when his mom met Mike and all the crap he lived through. I was there when he was kicked out of the house, when his brother ran away... I was there."

"Honey." Roxy pulled Sarina's hands back to hers. "Destiny and Cliff were moving to LA. I saw the rental agreement with his signature."

"That can be faked."

"He sold his bike to pay for the down payment on the apartment." Roxy rubbed her thumbs along the back of Sarina's hand. She wanted Sarina to know that Roxy was here for her. This was the only way she knew how.

"He sold his bike because he was tired of riding." Sarina's voice was barely a whisper.

"Maybe that's the part that was faked. He didn't know how to tell you."

"Why wouldn't he know how to tell me? We talked

about everything. We had that trip to Rachel, and we were talking about going to New York next year. We had plans. Why would he make plans with me if he was moving in with someone else?"

"I don't know, sweetie. But— Destiny's pregnant." Roxy already hated the words coming out of her mouth, but seeing the color drain from Sarina's face made her hate herself for having to say them.

"Oh."

"She's having Cliff's baby." Roxy didn't know if a paternity test was needed or anything, but she believed Destiny. She didn't seem like a woman who would lie.

Sarina didn't say anything. She just stared straight ahead.

Roxy didn't know what to do. Did she push to get her to talk? Did she let her digest what she'd just heard? She knew the one thing she wanted to do, she couldn't. The jerk went and got himself killed, so now Roxy couldn't beat the crap out of him. She just wanted to hurt him for hurting Sarina.

"Can we walk?" Sarina's stare was gone, but misery was coating every slow movement.

"Sure."

"Do you know why I'm here?" Sarina started walking down a path that led away from the chaises and the building into a forest of Joshua trees.

"To get away?"

"I needed quiet so I could work with a therapist." Sarina pulled a leaf off a tree and kept walking. "Cliff was so hot and cold. He'd build me up and then tear me down."

"Part of the reason might have been because of the medication he was on."

"He was on medication?"

"For ADHD, and when he was on it he tended to be more faithful. I guess. I don't know if that's how it even works, but that's what his family thinks. When he was on the meds he claimed he was foggy and couldn't create music. So he would stop. That can't be healthy for anyone."

"Oh." Sarina continued walking along the path toward the mountain range, Roxy beside her. They didn't talk. Sarina was obviously processing. Heck, Roxy found out hours earlier and she was still processing.

Finally Sarina said, "I think I knew he wasn't being faithful. Deep down I knew he wasn't a good person. I just kept hoping he'd be the person I first started dating. I figured he'd change back if I just helped him."

The path was white concrete. Smooth and even. It wasn't the type of place where you'd get lost or you could hide. But it was quiet. It was a good place to think.

"That doesn't make sense, you know." Roxy frowned. "You can't change someone who doesn't want to change."

They walked a little farther without words. Roxy had pushed it. She'd been too hard on Sarina. There was a nicer way to say that it didn't make sense, but she hadn't thought about it. She was so used to being blunt.

Before Roxy could stop their forward momentum and beg for forgiveness, Sarina broke the silence. "I know." Sarina smiled, a brittle lift of her lips. Her fingers twisted the leaf in her hand. "I just kept hoping. That hope kept me going. I don't even know how to live without it anymore. But something you said does make sense."

Roxy smiled. "What does?"

"That Cliff was on medication." Sarina shook her head. "He would get different. Sometimes better, I guess. Sometimes not."

"He obviously had problems. It had nothing to do with you."

"I know." Sarina really seemed to believe that. "It just hurts. I would have done anything for him. I just don't think he wanted me."

"I don't know what he wanted. I'm not sure he even knew." Roxy followed the path as it made a turn that seemed to head back toward the spa.

"Probably not. I didn't even meet his family. How can a relationship be serious when he won't even introduce you to his family?"

"But you did meet his stepdad, Michael."

Sarina stopped and tilted her head to the side. She seemed to be thinking. "I don't remember that."

"He said he met you at Luxor two months ago. Cliff introduced you as his friend."

"I remember that night. We got into that huge fight and broke up. He'd been sleeping at my place for over a week, but called me a friend. A friend. But then again, Cliff didn't tell me that was his stepfather. He said he was an old boss."

Roxy might have questioned that one. "Has he ever had a job?"

Sarina laughed. "That should have been the first indication he was lying. I don't think he's worked a day in his life."

"Well, he worked my last nerve."

Sarina laughed. It was practically musical and it warmed Roxy's heart. She'd been so worried about her friend, that hearing Sarina laugh actually made her think it all might be okay.

Roxy shrugged. "I mean, if he got paid for annoying the heck out me, he'd be hanging at his yacht on the water."

Sarina laughed again. The sound trailing off.

They walked for a bit in silence—the only sound Sarina's slippers and Roxy's shoes scuffing along the ground.

"I'm not looking forward to going back." Sarina stared at the building getting closer and closer. Roxy grabbed onto Sarina's hand and gave a squeeze. She might not want to be here, but this was the best place for her right now. Sarina knew it. So there was no point offering false platitudes.

But she could offer distraction by way of gossip. "Do you know who the mummy is?"

"The mummy?"

"There's some celebrity wrapped up in gauze. I swear her chest wasn't moving. But Jacob swore she was alive. Not quite sure how he knew that."

"Maybe he saw her eyes move."

"I looked, those eyes weren't moving an inch. It was

like Zach Simpson from summer camp. Remember him? His eyes didn't move. It was creepy."

"Didn't you have a crush on him?"

"Yeah, but he was still creepy." Roxy couldn't control what her heart wanted. And apparently in fourth grade she was into creepy.

"Didn't you let him feel you up?"

"Well, yeah, we kissed and he played with the girls. But that was before I realized he was an idiot. After he got all gropey and slobbery, he told me that if I got knocked up he'd lie about kissing me."

"You never told me that." Sarina laughed. "He thought kissing equaled babies?"

"It was embarrassing. What nine-year-old thinks kissing causes babies? Or worse, he thought fondling boobs did." Roxy felt the laughter bubble out of her chest. "I had no idea how people in *his* world created babies. I just realized I didn't want to live in that world."

"Come on, now." Sarina giggled. "Don't you want alien boob babies?"

Roxy mock-glared at Sarina. "None of those words belong together." She truly didn't care what made Sarina smile—even if it was at Roxy's expense.

Sarina's giggle morphed to a guffaw.

"I mean, It wasn't even a good kiss. The grope was like he was tenderizing meat." Roxy lifted her hands and made a honking move.

"Stop." Sarina's chest shook as she stopped and crossed her legs. "I can't. I just can't. I need a bathroom."

Roxy laughed as Sarina snorted.

"Crap." Sarina slammed her hand over her mouth. "We need to get back before I have an accident."

"Just pop a squat and water a tree."

"Uh, no." Sarina wiped at the tears in her eyes. But these were tears of joy, not misery. She uncrossed her legs and headed toward the building. Luckily they were only a hundred feet from the back door. "They only let guests in the back."

"Okay. I'll head home." Roxy slid her arm through Sarina's.

Sarina squeezed Roxy's arm. "I'm so glad you came. I really needed that."

"That's what I do. It's in the best friend contract." Roxy bumped Sarina's shoulder. "Should I come back to visit?"

"I'm probably going home this weekend. I'm starting with a grief counselor next week. But I'll keep you posted."

Sarina and Roxy left the path and weaved through the tables on the back patio.

"So you'll answer my phone call?"

"Sorry. I was having trouble getting out of my head."

"Well, stay out of there. It's scary." When they reached the door of the building, Roxy turned to Sarina and wrapped her in a hug. "I love you, sweetie."

"I love you, too." Sarina squeezed back.

"I won't stop looking."

"I know," a muffled voice that sounded like Sarina said.

"If you start to get sad or miss me, just think about alien boob babies."

Sarina laughed. "Okay. I have to go now." She waved a medallion on her wrist over a sensor and the door clicked. She threw open the door and ran inside.

"Do the pee-pee dance run." Roxy felt the smile deep in her soul as she yelled to the closing door. Part of her wanted to follow Sarina inside and see what all the fuss was about. But she didn't want to get Sarina thrown out or earn herself a stint with Metro.

Roxy headed back through the coffee shop. A woman stood at the counter pouring milk into a steaming mug. A woman Roxy recognized.

"Destiny?"

Destiny turned from the counter—all smiles. She looked even more beautiful in the light from the skylight. Or maybe it was that she looked professional in her mint green scrubs. "Roxy, right?"

"Yep." Roxy approached Destiny, looking at the steaming mug in her hand. Were pregnant women allowed to have caffeine? Wasn't pregnancy all about getting rid of all of life's pleasures?

Destiny must have seen the direction of her attention, because she said, "This is tea. I'm not drinking coffee. Sometimes I forget, but I'm really trying."

"I forgot you mentioned you worked here."

"For the next week anyway. What brings you to the spa?" Destiny's smile withered as she swirled a spoon in her drink. "Did you interview Sarina?"

"I did." Roxy didn't feel like getting into to the specifics. She probably should have told her that she was Sarina's best friend yesterday, but she hadn't wanted to have her shut down the conversation. And who would have thought they'd run into each other in the wild like this? "Have you worked with her while you've been here?"

"Oh no, I generally work with the hospital rehab patients. It's rare they have me work with the fragiles."

"The... fragiles?"

"Sorry. It's what we call the ones that are here for something other than medical necessity." The fact that Destiny had a condescending word for that made Roxy like her a little bit less.

Sarina was somehow fragile because she needed to get away after her boyfriend was murdered? To be fair, Destiny's boyfriend was murdered as well, and she was back at work. But Sarina was also the prime suspect. That would put a lot of stress on anyone.

Destiny rested her open hand on her stomach and winced.

"Are you okay?" Roxy couldn't not care, not when Destiny was obviously in pain.

"The baby's moving."

"That must be exciting."

"Here, touch it." Destiny grabbed Roxy's hand and rested it on her stomach.

Roxy didn't have the heart to say she didn't want to put her hand on someone else's belly. Especially when something was moving inside. It felt more like an alien than anything else. Destiny's eyes watered. Roxy pulled her hand away like the baby bit her. "I'm sorry. Did I hurt you?"

Destiny flashed a watery smile. "No. I just don't have anyone to touch my belly anymore with Cliff gone."

"What about your parents?"

"It's not the same." Destiny pulled out a tissue and dabbed her eyes.

"What about Cliff's mom?"

"She doesn't know."

"Aren't you going to tell her?"

Destiny shook her head. "I've thought about it, but I don't know what to say."

"Just tell her the truth. She might be glad to know that part of her son lives on. Jared might be excited to be an uncle."

"Jared knows. He was going to move with us to LA." Destiny rubbed the tissue under her nose as she shook her head. "I guess that's one more thing that won't happen. That poor kid is stuck with his parents." Destiny smiled. "I should get back to work. Thank you for being so kind."

"It's easy to be kind." Roxy smiled as a woman came in the front door waving. "I should get going."

"Yeah, I have a client." Destiny tipped her cup to Roxy. "It was nice seeing you."

"It was nice seeing you too." Roxy turned and headed out the door. She walked toward Rafe's truck and the fancy cars lining the lot. But off to right, surrounded by all the fancy, was Sarina's pink Jeep. She must have missed the car earlier when she'd walked in.

Roxy wanted to leave her something. If she had a

Post-it, she'd write her a note. She looked around. At the edge of the pavement was a bed of marigolds. She went over and picked a few, walked over to Sarina's Jeep and tucked flowers underneath the windshield wiper.

Roxy smiled as she headed to Rafe's truck. It was good to see Sarina smile again. It made her feel like everything was heading the right direction.

CHAPTER 25

JUST WHEN I THINK I HAVE LEARNED THE WAY TO LIVE, LIFE CHANGES. ~ HUGH PRATHER, NOTES TO MYSELF: MY STRUGGLE TO BECOME A PERSON

ROXY WOKE up the next morning feeling good. She'd managed to sleep in past ten. Rafe was lying naked next to her. Sarina was going to be okay—Roxy was going to make sure of that. And she'd had a good night sleep because of all of that.

"What are you thinking about?" Rafe leaned on an elbow and ran his hand along her arm.

"How we're going to solve this, so life will be back to normal—where my biggest concern is how to get Karan to train me while trying to avoid her." She turned toward him, trying not to drool at the gorgeous chest in front of her. "What are you thinking about?"

She knew that was a loaded question as his fingers lazily lingered along her skin. If his gaze said anything, he was thinking about something to do with her being naked.

"Pancakes."

"Pancakes?" This was so not the direction she thought the conversation was going.

"I have a taste for pancakes, and I need to make sure you eat." He leaned over her, his bulging arms keeping him levered over her body. He grinned in the most deliciously wicked way and then whispered in her ear, "You'll need energy for what I have planned this morning."

She looked at the clock. Ten fifteen. "Don't you have to work today?"

"I'm heading in after lunch. I have a management meeting tonight." His lips found their way to her neck as he talked. Warm breath tickled along her collarbone.

Her eyes closed as her brain stopped functioning. All she could do was feel. And the feeling was good...

... until it wasn't. His mouth was gone. The warmth of his body gone.

"Get up!" Rafe slid a T-shirt over those abs before pulling on a pair of basketball shorts.

Bummer.

"I'll start breakfast." Rafe left the bedroom, and the whoosh and gurgle of coffee percolating wafted from the kitchen. Soon the smell of sugar and flour would be hitting her square in the taste buds.

Roxy smiled. How could she not? Things were good.

Her cell phone rang. She stretched over to the nightstand on her side and grabbed the device. Sarina's mom. *Shit*.

She accepted the call. "Hi, is Sarina okay?"

"No honey, there was an accident."

Wait.

What?

"She's in Summerlin Hospital."

Thank goodness. She's alive. Roxy never thought that the idea of Sarina being in the hospital would be comforting. "What happened?"

"Get here when you can."

Roxy clicked end on the call. None of that sounded good. Tears threatened to poke at the back of her eyes, but she held them back. She didn't have time. She threw off the covers and jumped out of bed.

She tossed on jeans and a sweatshirt—although she did put on a bra and underwear, after she'd actually considered skipping them both.

Roxy sat on the side of the bed and pulled on a sock as her phone dinged. *Please let Sarina be okay. Please let Sarina be okay.* She picked it up and said a silent prayer that nothing had changed for the worse.

Don't forget to schedule your annual physical. Contact your doctor to schedule your appointment now!

She slammed the phone down. She normally appreciated her doctor's office being proactive and telling her about her upcoming appointments. She'd never remember to schedule anything without these little reminders, but she didn't need it now. She had more pressing issues. She pulled on her other sock.

"Breakfast is almost ready." Rafe walked in the bedroom. "You're dressed?" He must have seen her face, because he kneeled down and rested his hands on her knees. "Roxy, what's wrong?"

"It's Sarina." Roxy felt a tear break free. "There was an accident. We have to go."

"I'll get dressed." Rafe jumped to his feet. "Pour us both some coffee to go while I get ready."

Roxy nodded. She walked into the kitchen. At least she thought she did. The past few minutes were a fog, and she wasn't all that upset about it. If she actually thought about what was going on, she'd lose her shit. So it was better if she just turned off her brain. Turned it all off.

CHAPTER 26
NO ONE EVER TOLD ME THAT GRIEF FELT SO LIKE FEAR. ~ C.S. LEWIS, A GRIEF OBSERVED

ROXY WALKED the sterile hallway of Summerlin Hospital. Men and women in scrubs sat at computers in the cubbies lining the hall. Everyone was smiling and working, like it was just another day. But it wasn't another day.

Rafe led Roxy toward the corner room and knocked. The front desk had told them the room number, but Roxy hadn't been able to concentrate. She'd let Rafe take control.

The door opened and Sarina's father stood there. Long, curly golden hair mixed with gray pulled back into a ponytail. His face was normally lined with wrinkles. Those lines were exacerbated with worry for his daughter. "I'm glad you could come." He wrapped Roxy in a hug.

"Who is it, Onni?"

"Roxy." He pulled away, a ghost of a smile on his lips. Then he leaned in. "She'll be so glad you're here."

Roxy didn't have the heart to ask whether his wife

or Sarina would be glad she was there. She tried to walk into the room, but was met with Sarina's mom's arms.

"I'm so glad you're here," Valentina cried as she let Roxy go. She dabbed a tissue at her eyes as she looked Rafe over. "And you are?"

"This is my boyfriend Rafe," Roxy told her.

"I've heard so much about you from Sarina." Valentina smiled as she hugged him. She pulled away and went to the other side of Sarina's bed and sat down. "Thank you so much for coming."

"How is she?" Roxy shuffled into the room, following Valentina. She looked over at the bed when Valentina sat down on the far side of it—and she wished she hadn't.

Sarina was so small. Her skin was so pale against the stark white sheets. She had a cut along her hairline and bruises on her face. Her right arm and leg were both in a cast, and tubes and wires were attached all over her body.

"She's in a coma." Valentina shook her head and turned as a tear streamed down her cheek.

"What happened?" Rafe asked the question that Roxy wanted to ask but she just couldn't seem to find her voice. Sarina was in a coma.

"They think someone cut the brakes on her car." Sarina's father shook his head as he moved to the window across the room. "Who would do that?"

"What?" This just kept getting worse and worse. Roxy didn't know what to do to make it right.

"When she left the spa this morning, she didn't get very far. Her car wouldn't stop, and the angle of that hill... She couldn't stop." Her father choked on a cry. "Her car crashed into a tree."

"Will she be okay?" Roxy fought to get the words past her closed throat. She was terrified of the answer.

Valentina grabbed a tissue from the table next to Sarina's bed. "They're hopeful."

"Hopeful?"

"Her airbag didn't fully inflate. Her head—" Valentina put one hand over her mouth, clearly fighting a sob. "She was cut and bruised. We don't know the extent of the injuries."

"When will we know?"

"When she comes out of her coma." Valentina wiped her eyes with a tissue. "It's up to her now."

"What are the cops saying?" Rafe looked as devastated as Roxy felt, but he also looked ready to kill. He wanted someone to pay.

Roxy would get there too. She was too busy sorting through the emotions at seeing her best friend like this.

"Nothing yet. We haven't seen them."

Typical. When she didn't want Metro in her business, she couldn't get them out. But when she wanted information, they were nowhere to be found.

"She can hear you." Her father turned from the window and smiled. "You should talk to her."

Roxy nodded, and walked to the edge of the bed. She wrapped her hand around Sarina's, careful to avoid the IV. Her hand was cold, limp. It took everything in Roxy not to drop to the floor in a crying heap. But she had a job to do. And Sarina's parents didn't need to see Roxy lose her shit.

She held her bestie's hand and stared at the heart monitor. Up and down. Up and down. She looked to Sarina. She'd know the perfect thing to say in this situation. Even if she didn't, she'd say something funny and make everyone laugh. Roxy had no idea what to say.

She wanted to yell at her to fight. She wanted to beg her to be all right. She settled for "I love you. We still have things to do. We haven't seen a Broadway show in New York. We haven't gone skinny-dipping in Lake Tahoe."

Her father cleared his throat as a deep chuckle came from where Rafe stood. Valentina smiled from across the bed. "I can't picture Sarina skinny-dipping."

"That was my addition to the bucket list." Roxy was having a hard time remembering the rest. "There's another one, we haven't gotten a tattoo. There are so many things on our list that we haven't done. So you can't leave me yet."

Another throat-clearing stopped Roxy in her tracks. Detectives MacAuley and Geary stood in the open doorway.

"Good morning, Mr. and Mrs. West." MacAuley greeted Sarina's parents and nodded to Roxy and Rafe. She guessed they were past words. Or he was still mad at them for the last time they talked. She didn't care if he was mad as long as he did his job and got Sarina out of this mess.

"Do you have a minute? We wanted to talk to you about what happened." MacAuley focused his attention on Sarina's parents. Like Roxy wasn't going to listen in on this.

"What happened is someone tried to kill my daughter." Sarina's father's face was red with anger.

"We'd like to get more information, Mr. West."

"Why? So you can pin it on my daughter without doing your job?" The red was almost purple and his face was practically pulsing. Not that Roxy would argue. She'd had the same discussion with MacAuley. "Let me guess, my daughter killed her boyfriend, the man that she loved, and then cut her own brakes before driving home."

"Mr. West..." Detective Geary said, but her father was having none of that.

"She had plans to see a grief counselor today. They had talked while she was away, and the counselor was helping her realize it wasn't her fault. It wasn't her fault that he cheated or that she knew nothing about it. It wasn't her fault that someone else hurt him. She was finally optimistic that maybe she'd get over losing the love of her life. But yeah, she cut her own brakes."

"Onni." Valentina had gone to her husband during his onslaught of words. "Let the officers do their job. Please calm down before you give yourself a heart attack. I can't be visiting you both in here. I need you."

"Fine."

Valentina led her husband to the chair she had vacated and motioned for him to sit. "I'll stand for a while."

MacAuley nodded. "I have the file from the Metro officers on the scene of the accident. Have they gone over it with you?"

"No." Valentina shook her head. "We've only heard what the doctors have told us."

"Sarina left the Golden Palm Spa at six AM this morning. An employee saw her walk to her car and get in."

"What about the flowers?" Roxy thought Sarina would at least get a smile from them.

"What flowers?"

"I put flowers under her windshield wiper yesterday when I went to visit."

MacAuley looked confused. Join the club. "There's no mention of her doing anything outside of getting into her car. Why did you put flowers under her windshield wiper?"

"I thought it might make her smile."

MacAuley nodded. "After she got in her car, she pulled straight out of the spot and onto the road. That was the last anyone saw her, until another spa employee found her and the car against a tree on the side of the road. The police on the scene got her medical attention, but they felt something wasn't right. Something about the way the car was angled, and they found brake fluid where her car had been parked. They knew her involvement in our case, so they sent the file to me."

"Was her brake line cut?" Rafe joined the conversation.

Detective Geary nodded. "Yes. We had someone check it out this morning when he got in."

"So what do we do?" Valentina's voice rose. Almost frantic.

"There's nothing you need to do," Macauley said. "Stay with your daughter. She'll need you. We'll take care of the investigation."

Roxy wasn't satisfied with that answer. Neither was Valentina, because she snapped, "What if they come back and try to hurt her again?"

"There isn't any indication that someone will try again." Detective Geary didn't look remorseful or anything as he gave that news to a crying mother.

Valentina ran a tissue under her eyes. The poor woman couldn't get the tears to stop. "Is she still a suspect?"

Detective Geary shook his head. "Unfortunately, this doesn't change anything with the Foster investigation." Still no remorse.

Valentina nodded as tears streamed down her face.

Roxy's hand curled into a fist. She so wanted to use it on these cops.

"We should go." MacAuley followed Geary out the door.

Watching Sarina's mother cry was the last straw. Roxy had been nice. She hadn't said a word when they didn't assign an officer to her room. She didn't say anything when they didn't remove her as the primary suspect.

She couldn't sit still. She couldn't keep quiet.

CHAPTER 27

BUT WHEN IT IS DARK ENOUGH, THE STARS SHINE OUT.... ~ AMELIA EDITH BARR, ROMANCES AND REALITIES: TALES OF TRUTH AND FANCY

ROXY WALKED into the hallway and saw the detective's retreating backs. "MacAuley!" She ran toward them and they both turned toward her.

MacAuley looked a little less annoyed than Geary. But Geary got annoyed with everything, so he didn't count.

"Why is she still a suspect?" Roxy's blood pressure rose. "Her brake lines were cut."

"We're looking into it." MacAuley nodded to an open door. "Let's talk in here."

Roxy walked into the empty room. The bed was stripped. The medical equipment didn't beep. There was no noise. The smell of antiseptic permeated the air. "Fine. Cliff was killed and Sarina was almost killed. That should tell you she didn't do it."

Detective Geary stepped closer. "No, it tells me no such thing."

"So her previously functioning car all of the sudden has a cut brake line while she's being wrongly accused of a murder, and you're saying it's a coincidence. What happened to not believing in coincidence?"

"That's why we're looking into it." MacAuley put his hand on Geary's arm. "I got this. Why don't you go wait in the car."

"Are you sure?" Detective Geary looked at Roxy like she was going to cop-nap his partner.

"I'll be fine." MacAuley nodded toward the exit, probably so Geary would know which way to walk.

Geary nodded and left, leaving them alone. Well, except for a nurse holding a chart and staring into the room like it was his favorite telenovela.

Roxy pushed the door till it clicked. "Do you see how insane this is? Sarina is the sweetest person we know." Roxy knew she was begging. She didn't care. She was begging. "You have to know she didn't do this."

"It doesn't matter what I think..."

"Don't give me that crap. You get paid for what you think. You rely on your gut for a lot of your decisions. Don't tell me about the evidence."

"My gut only gets us so far. The evidence is what drives the investigation."

"Did you investigate anyone else?"

"Of course I did." Fire burned in MacAuley's eyes as his voice rose. "And I'm sick and tired of you questioning me about doing my job. I get enough of that shit from Geary. I don't expect it from you."

The injured look on his face was almost too much. Roxy was being a jerk. He didn't deserve it. He'd busted his butt a few months ago to prove her innocence. He'd do the same for Sarina. He was that type of cop. A good one. "I'm sorry. I don't know what else to do. She'll never survive in there. I can't lose her."

"You won't."

"Did you see her face? They beat the crap out of her in jail. What happens in prison?" Terror shook down her spine with just the thought of sweet Sarina in the prison system. Tears slid down Roxy's cheek just thinking about Sarina's shiner from the joint. That was after one day. One day. Multiple days would kill her.

MacAuley shook his head. "That person has been dealt with. It was a case of mistaken identity. Sarina's stronger than you think."

Roxy wanted to believe that was true, but she wouldn't survive in lockup. Sarina's kind spirit would get destroyed. "I know she's strong, but this is too much for her. I'm so glad you're on the case. If anyone can figure out who really killed him, it's you."

"About that." MacAuley ran a hand over the back of his neck and winced.

"What?"

"The investigation is done. I know you don't want to hear that."

"She's going to trial?"

"You need to let the process play out."

"I can't wait. That can't happen. We have to do something."

"I'm sorry." MacAuley did actually look remorseful.

Roxy leaned against the edge of the bed as her head swam. Darkness danced at the edges of her vision. This couldn't be happening.

She wished she could change places with her. She might not be prison material but she could handle it better than Sarina. She'd learn how to make a shank out of a toothbrush and make the best toilet wine they'd ever seen. She watched television. She knew how it went.

But Sarina didn't, so she couldn't end up on the other side of the bars.

There was only one way.

Roxy raised her hands to waist height, wrists together. "Take me. I did it. I killed him. Slap the cuffs on me."

"Don't be ridiculous. The..."

She blocked out the rest of what he said. Not on purpose, her brain just couldn't wrap around the words. She blurted, "But I hated him."

MacAuley rolled his eyes. "Get in line. We found plenty of people who hated him, but that doesn't mean they killed him. Stop panicking. Sarina is out on bail. That hasn't changed." MacAuley walked toward the door and paused, his hand on the knob. "Are you okay?"

No. She was definitely not okay. But instead of telling him what he already knew, she simply nodded and watched him open the door and walk on through.

The timeline just moved up. She didn't have time to wait around. When Sarina woke up— and she would wake up— she needed to have a life to come back to.

Roxy had to get hold of Cliff's therapist. She stared at her phone, but she'd already left two messages. She needed to focus on finding the person who cut Sarina's brakes. If that person tried to kill Sarina, they probably did something to Cliff.

There was only one person who knew Sarina was at that spa, and Roxy was going to talk to her.

After checking on Sarina, who was flexing her hand when people spoke to her, Roxy needed to get back to work. She didn't have time to sit at the hospital.

When they reached his truck, Rafe pulled a fob out of his pocket and handed it to her.

"What is this?"

"This is for the truck. Keep it until you can pick up your car."

She'd forgotten her car was out of commission. Probably because she needed the money to pick it up. With her not putting in the hours at work and focusing on getting Sarina out of this predicament, she might never see her car again.

Small price to pay to make sure Sarina got out of trouble.

Rafe held open the passenger door. "The door code is eight-two-nine-seven."

Eight-two-nine-seven. She'd never remember that, if the status of her car was any indication.

Rafe paused. "Her parents understood why you left, but I don't."

"I can't let this go to trial."

"I know, but Sarina is in a coma. Nothing is going

to happen until she's ready to be released from the hospital."

This was the first time she was ever thankful someone she loved was in a coma. If only Sarina could stay that way till Roxy fixed all of this.

"Rafe." Roxy got into the passenger seat and Rafe waited in the open door. "I need to make sure she has a life to get better for. She can't fight to live only to end up in prison. Not when she doesn't belong there."

He nodded and closed the door, going around to the driver's side and sliding in. "You're right. We have to figure this out."

Roxy nodded. Not that she knew how to figure it out. "What do you suggest?"

"I'm sure you already have a plan, but we need to know who tampered with Sarina's car."

"There is only one person who knew she was there. She works there."

Rafe's eyebrows arched as he tried to figure out who they'd interviewed that worked at a spa. "Destiny?"

"Destiny. We need to head to Golden Palm Spa."

Rafe nodded and headed toward I-11.

Thank goodness Rafe was going with her. This way Roxy wouldn't hit a pregnant woman. Probably.

CHAPTER 28
HALF OF THE PEOPLE LIE WITH THEIR LIPS; THE OTHER HALF WITH THEIR TEARS. ~ NASSIM NICHOLAS TALEB, THE BED OF PROCRUSTES: PHILOSOPHICAL AND PRACTICAL APHORISMS

THE GOLDEN PALM Spa was as beautiful as she remembered. Even Rafe couldn't stop rubbernecking. The sunlight lit up and split through the large golden chandelier. Slices of light twisted and bent along the white marble floors and furniture. New flowers were arranged in the large vases.

The reception area was empty, except for one person on the white couch in the center of the next room. From the back, it looked like a woman. All Roxy could see was the hood of a white robe and the drape of silk over narrow shoulders.

"Where do we go now?" Rafe asked.

At the sound of his voice, the person on the couch turned. The mummy! It was the obviously famous person, wrapped like Brendan Frasier should be chasing them.

Straight teeth and blue eyes appeared behind the front counter. "Welcome to the Golden Palm Spa and Wellness Center. I'm Jacob. How may I help you?"

"We need to speak with Destiny Warren."

"She's with a client." Jacob frowned. "Do you have an appointment?"

"No." Roxy wanted to scowl right back, or maybe throat-punch him. Was she that forgettable? She leaned over the counter and rested her elbows on the black granite. "Do you remember me? I was just here to see Sarina West."

Rafe must have sensed Roxy's short fuse, because he reached out, pulled her back and asked, "When will she be done? It's important that we talk with her today."

"I'm sorry, but who are you?"

"We're friends." Roxy didn't think *we're the ones that are going to kick her ass for messing with Sarina's car* would go over very well. "Friends" sounded much more pleasant.

"Well, *friends*, Destiny is working. Perhaps you should reach out to her during her off hours." He turned away and thumbed through paperwork behind the counter. "Where does she get these friends?" he muttered under his breath.

"I'm sorry?" Roxy was seriously going to hurt this guy. Why was he judging them?

"Look, we can't have another scene," Jacob whispered. "Destiny's friends aren't welcome here."

Rafe rested a hand on Roxy's arm in the universal *I got this* move. "This place is really nice. I'm head of security for the Sonutoso Entertainment Group, so I know how hard it is to secure a place of this size."

"Yeah. You would be surprised the crazy stuff that happens."

"I get it." Rafe leaned in like he was sharing a secret. "Last week we had a man smuggle his iguana into the hotel and then lose it."

Jacob laughed. "No."

"Yeah, I had all my security staff checking rooms and opening vents for this two-foot lizard that apparently had PTSD after a traumatic upbringing, so he liked to bite first, ask questions second. That was all per the owner." Rafe's voice rose a bit as the story unfolded.

"Did you find him?"

"Yeah." Rafe smiled. "He was hiding in a pile of used towels in another guest's bathroom."

"Did the guest complain?"

"Luckily they were out, so we were able to tell them after the fact. The terror of a loose iguana loses something if you don't actually see it."

"Whoa. We haven't ever had anything like that."

"That's good. It's hard to get access to rooms without causing a panic." Rafe lowered his voice, back to secrets mode. "You mentioned Destiny's friends. When did they make a scene?"

Jacob looked around, like he was trying to decide if he was allowed to share the information. He must have made a decision because he leaned closer to Rafe and smiled. "Yesterday, Destiny's boyfriend's fiancée came here with the boyfriend's mom. We had to drag the fiancée out the door and threaten her with the cops. It was a nightmare. And then…"

Destiny's voice came from the hall next to the counter. "Make sure you drink plenty of water."

Wait. Jacob said, "and then". What came after that?

"I'm going to miss you, honey," a woman said.

"You can always visit me when you're in LA," Destiny replied.

"I will." A woman wearing a robe and slippers ambled past the front counter and headed to a door at the far side of the next room. She waved to mummy-lady. "Hi, Jen."

Jen. Her name was Jen. There were so many famous Jens.

Not that Roxy had time to think about that now.

"Destiny, your friends are here to talk to you."

Roxy could tell when Destiny noticed her and Rafe standing there because a look of confusion passed across her face. Whether she was confused that they were there or that they were introduced as her friends, who knew. Probably both.

"Hi." Destiny didn't actually question any of it as she pointed toward the door Roxy had followed Jacob through just two days before. "Would you like to talk outside?"

"Sure."

Destiny attempted a smile toward Jacob. "Thank you. I'll be right outside when my next client checks in." She walked through the large family room and out the door. Roxy and Rafe followed.

"I'm at work." Destiny turned to face them, arms crossed. She wasn't as pleasant today. Maybe because they interrupted her at work... or maybe because she had something to hide.

"You are." Roxy nodded. "We wanted to know if you were here yesterday when someone tampered with Sarina's car."

"I was here."

"Did you tamper with her car?" Straightforward tended to work.

"Why would I touch her car?" Destiny uncrossed her arms and rested one hand on her stomach. "Even if I wanted to mess with it, I don't know anything about cars, and there was no bad blood between her and me."

"Really?" Roxy leaned in. Close enough to slap her —and wouldn't that be amazing. Rafe pulled on the back of Roxy's shirt till she was back at his side. No fun. "She's currently the main suspect in your baby-daddy's murder. That gives you a motive."

"I guess." Destiny sighed. "This is all getting out of hand."

"What is?" Rafe angled himself between Roxy and Destiny. Like Roxy was actually going to hit her. She wasn't going to hit a pregnant woman. That would be wrong. Wouldn't it?

"Look, I just want to finish my time here and get out of town. I wasn't going to tell anyone, but then you mentioned his mom should find out about the baby."

To be fair, Roxy only asked if she'd planned on telling her. It wasn't exactly advice. "So you told his mom. How did that go?"

Destiny sighed. "I showed up at her house and told

her about the baby. She held my hand and we laughed about Cliff and she talked about how she wanted to see her grandchild once he or she is born."

Rafe nodded. "It sounds like it went well." He was definitely playing good cop.

"It went great. I was going to have Cliff's family in my life, even if I couldn't have Cliff." A tear glistened in Destiny's eye. "We cried together. We laughed at all the funny things he did. I couldn't have asked for better."

"What happened?"

"The next day, Celeste showed up with the fiancée. Kandi. They started screaming about how I was a liar and how they wanted me to take a paternity test. The fiancée knocked down one of the vases and kept yelling about all the women trying to ruin her relationship with Cliff. I even offered to show her the lease that we signed for Los Angeles."

"That didn't convince her?" Even Roxy had been on board at that point.

"No, Kandi said I made it all up to steal his mother's money." Destiny sighed. "I don't want a dime from them. I don't even think they have a dime to give. I just thought it would be nice to have her in the baby's life."

"So, Kandi broke a vase and was yelling. What happened next?" Rafe was obviously trying to get the story back on track.

"Jacob and the security guards escorted them out of the building, and told them if they didn't go away, they'd call the police."

"Did you call the police?"

"No. They left and we didn't see them again."

"Did security watch them leave?"

Destiny shook her head. "I don't know. Security said they got in their car, so I'm thinking they left."

"You weren't worried they'd come back?"

"Oh, I was. Security walked me out to my car that night and watched me pull out. If I could have taken one of the security guards home, I would have. I practically ran into my house when I got there."

"So you didn't tamper with Sarina's car? Do you know who did?"

"No. I don't know who did, but I'd bet money on Kandi. She was unhinged. She kept yelling about how all these sluts kept messing with her happiness. And she was tired of all the gold-diggers coming after Cliff's money."

Roxy couldn't have heard that right. "Did he have money?"

"Apparently he did." Destiny shook her head. "There was a fifty-thousand-dollar life insurance policy."

"On... Cliff?" Roxy didn't believe it.

"It was through his stepfather's job."

"How did you find out about that?" Roxy asked her.

"His mom let it slip when we talked the other day. I told Celeste I didn't want her family's money. But they still came here ranting and raving."

Jacob stuck his head outside. "Destiny, your client is here."

"Thanks, Jacob." Destiny sighed. "I have to get back to work. Are we done here?"

"For now." Roxy was pretty sure Destiny didn't have any more information. And Roxy still wanted to know what happened after "and then..."

"Can you make sure they find their way out?" Destiny asked Jacob once they were all back indoors.

"Sure," he said. "Time to go, Destiny's friends."

Oh no it wasn't. "I'm not leaving until you finish your story," Roxy told him.

Jacob's eyebrow arched. "My story?"

"After you dragged the fiancée out the door. You said something else happened."

"Oh yeah, we dragged the fiancée outside and watched as they got in the car. She continued to scream as they drove around the lot and pulled away.

"So you watched them leave." Any hope Roxy had was dying in her chest.

"We did."

"Did they come back?"

"I don't think so, but I was back at the front desk." Jacob waved toward the exit. "Speaking of, I need to get back to my post."

"Sure." Roxy headed toward the exit.

"Thank you for your time," Rafe said from behind her. "If you think of anything else, please call the number on this card."

"I will."

Back out in the bright sun, Roxy crossed the parking lot to Rafe's truck. They had a fiancée and a mother to see. They'd start with the mother. Celeste would still be on the ground if she'd gone underneath the Jeep to mess with the brakes. No. It had to be Kandi, and Roxy needed to get the new grandma to roll over on her.

So Roxy could roll over Kandi with Rafe's truck.

CHAPTER 29

WHEN YOUR EARS HEAR ONE THING, BUT YOUR EYES SEE ANOTHER... USE YOUR BRAIN. ~ FRANK SONNENBERG, SOUL FOOD: CHANGE YOUR THINKING, CHANGE YOUR LIFE

RAFE DROVE them to Celeste's house. Roxy doubted he'd let her use the truck to run over Kandi, so that might not be in the cards for the day. With the afternoon sun beating down, there was still time for Roxy to make it happen later—if she ever had the money to pick up her car.

Kandi cut the brake lines. Roxy could feel it in her bones. And given the woman tried to kill Sarina, that wasn't too far off from killing Cliff—in Roxy's mind, anyway.

Roxy didn't bother waiting for Rafe as she walked up to the front door and knocked. Instead of Celeste, it was the brake-cutting lunatic herself.

"What do you want?" Kandi was so delightful.

"We're here to talk to Celeste." Roxy nodded to Rafe as he walked up the sidewalk.

"Oh, hi Rafe." Kandi's tone changed, but the look of annoyance was still on her face.

"Hi." Rafe smiled, all charm and machismo. He did

everything but lean down and kiss her hand. "It's so good to see you."

Kandi preened. Literally preened. Her chest lifted and her shoulders snapped back. She looked like a demented peacock, if the peacock had bleachy hair in a ponytail.

"We stopped by to see Celeste. Is she home?"

"Come on in." Kandi opened the door wide and stepped to the side for Rafe to walk in. Roxy slid inside before Kandi could close the door on her.

"Mama, there are people here to see you."

Celeste waddled into the living room, a soda in one hand and a cane in the other. "Hello. I'm surprised to see you here." She walked to a chair and sat down with a groan.

Kandi took the cane and leaned it against the back of the chair.

"Surprised?" Roxy could think of a million reasons for them being there.

"Well, since they got all the proof they need to make that girl pay for killing my son."

Right. That. "Well, we're looking into the attempt on her life." Roxy did not add "And the fact that the proof the cops have is circumstantial at best since Sarina couldn't have done it."

"She deserved it," Kandi snapped.

"What?" Roxy could feel the fire burning in her eyes.

"That homewrecker deserved it. It's just too bad she lived."

"Say it again! I dare you." Roxy lunged for Kandi.

Kandi jumped toward Roxy. "You bitch!"

Rafe got between them, elbows and hands out, blocking both woman's forward momentum. Roxy lunged around Rafe to grab bleached-out hair. She yanked. Blond hair stuck between her fingers. Kandi twisted, screeching, Rafe pivoted to block her, and Celeste sat on her throne and yelled, "Enough! I'll kick y'all out if you can't behave."

The fire burning in Roxy's veins simmered to a dull roar. She couldn't get kicked out—not without information. She pulled away from Rafe's restraining hand on her arm.

"Yeah, we'll kick you out." Kandi glared at Roxy.

"I'm talking about all y'all." Celeste waved at everyone in the room. "I'm too old for this shit."

Kandi glared at Roxy. "She started it."

"You started it." Roxy glared back. She could be childish, too.

"Sit down over here." Rafe led Roxy to the couch and watched her sit down. He didn't tie her down, so she could easily get back up. Miscalculation on his part. But she really did need more information.

"I'm sorry, Celeste." Rafe used his eyes and soothing voice, and the woman smiled at him. "It's been a very stressful time, as you know."

"I know. Things have been rough lately." Celeste's smile melted into a frown. She seemed to be inches from crying.

"Then you get it." Rafe moved closer. He sat on the table across from her.

"I do." Celeste wiped her arm across her eyes as the tears started to flow. "This has been the hardest week of my life."

"Has it only been a week?" It felt more like a month. Roxy wanted it all to just end. Everyone seemed to ignore her question. Roxy wasn't sure she even said it out loud since no one so much as turned her way.

"Have you spoken with Destiny?" Rafe asked.

"Yeah." Celeste's tears started falling in earnest. "She told me she's pregnant with Cliff's child."

Kandi huffed. "She's lying."

"Why would she lie?"

Kandi glared at Roxy. Apparently Roxy actually said that out loud. She had no idea why Kandi got so cranky. It was just a question.

"I have no idea why she'd lie," Kandi snarled. "I just know that the bitch lied."

"You don't like her much, do you?" Rafe asked. A completely redundant question, In Roxy's opinion. He was usually so much better at this.

"Of course I don't like her. She was sleeping with my husband and she lied about getting pregnant."

Roxy didn't know if Destiny was a liar, but that belly and her cheeks said she was knocked up. "She appears to be pregnant."

Kandi rolled her eyes. "Fine. She's pregnant. Then she lied about who got her pregnant. She sleeps around with married men, and we're supposed to believe my Cliff is the father. Where was she when he was alive?"

Roxy didn't think she should remind Kandi that Destiny was sleeping with him while he was alive. Or that Kandi was the one lying, calling Cliff her husband. She didn't think that would go over very well.

"Do you know anything about them renting an apartment in Los Angeles?" Rafe redirected the conversation. See. Good at this.

Kandi turned her head, avoiding Rafe's question. She didn't bother calling Destiny a liar again. Maybe she realized she wasn't lying or maybe she got sick of saying the word liar.

"She told me about that." Celeste's red-rimmed eyes were conflicted.

Rafe raised an eyebrow. "You don't believe her."

"He never would have left Jared and me. He liked to think he was a protector," Celeste sobbed.

Rafe rested a hand on hers. "Who was he protecting?"

"Me and Jared."

"From?"

"Michael." Celeste squeezed Rafe's hand. "He gets angry."

"That sounds hard." Rafe put his other hand on hers. "Did he get physical with you?"

She nodded.

"How about the boys?"

Her lips quivered. Her shoulders shook. She didn't speak, only nodded through tears. "He'd— he'd throw —" she gulped air "—things and hit..." She couldn't continue. Her body heaved as air fought for purchase in her chest.

Rafe dropped to a knee and wrapped her in a hug. For a good five minutes, she cried, and he held her. Finally, Celeste slurped a big gulp of air and the convulsing stopped.

Rafe sat back and let her gather herself. "Are you okay?"

She nodded. "It's hard to think about."

"It must be so hard to live through."

"It is."

"Maybe Cliff wanted to get you away from here. She showed us a rental agreement."

"That can be forged." Oh look. Kandi found a new word instead of liar.

Rafe ignored her. "Do you think Michael would have hurt Cliff?"

"He was an angry man, but he wouldn't kill anyone." Celeste didn't say that with conviction, but she was probably afraid. Michael didn't seem like the type of guy who would like his wife talking about how he was a killer. A sound came from outside the house. Celeste checked her phone. "Michael will be home soon. You should go."

Rafe nodded and stood. "Please call me if you need anything. You shouldn't have to live that way."

Celeste turned her head and didn't say anything. The pride that she had was palpable. She didn't want help, but she couldn't seem to get away on her own. It was sad.

Roxy angled up from the couch and followed Rafe out the door. Something told her they weren't done with this family. Michael was an evil man. And even though Cliff wasn't an angel, he hadn't deserved living in fear for his family.

No one did.

CHAPTER 30
GETTING OUT OF THE HOSPITAL IS A LOT LIKE RESIGNING FROM A BOOK CLUB. YOU'RE NOT OUT OF IT UNTIL THE COMPUTER SAYS YOU'RE OUT OF IT. ~ ERMA BOMBECK

AN HOUR LATER, Roxy was back at the hospital. Sarina's mother had called to say Sarina was not only moving her hand, she was talking, and Roxy knew she had to see her friend. After she dropped Rafe at work, she drove right over.

Roxy walked down the hall, passing nurses and patients. Outside Sarina's door stood a uniformed Metro cop. Roxy was tempted to throw a donut down the hall and see if he'd chase it, but just the thought felt offensive. So she kept it to herself.

She smiled at the officer as she walked past and into the room.

Roxy's heart glowed—she could actually feel the warmth in her chest—when she walked in and saw Sarina's eyes open and alert. Her cheeks were rosy and her face wasn't sallow and gaunt.

"Mom, I don't need another blanket."

"You look cold." Sarina's mom dragged a blanket over her feet.

"Valentina, let the girl be." Her father shook his head.

"Onni, she could catch something if she's cold."

"Would you both stop." Sarina smiled when she saw Roxy. "You're embarrassing me in front of Roxy."

"That's silly. Roxy knows what we're like."

Roxy laughed. She did know how Sarina's parents were. She knew they were fiercely protective and loyal, and they loved their daughter and anyone their daughter loved whole-heartedly.

"That doesn't mean you can't work on yourselves," Sarina grumbled. "Not argue over blankets."

"But how will we make up if we don't argue?"

"Mom!" Sarina groaned and laid her head back on the pillow.

Roxy didn't need an instruction guide to know what Valentina meant when she said, "make up". It made Roxy giggle. Her parents couldn't be in the same room without removing all the weapons. So watching Sarina's parents was like heaven—all love and kindness and innuendo.

Sarina's dad held out his hand. "Valentina, let us get some coffee. Let the girls talk."

"Fine." Valentina pulled the blanket up to Sarina's chin and kissed her forehead. She turned to Roxy and rested a hand on her cheek. "Please watch over my baby."

"Of course." Roxy leaned into the touch. It meant everything. It meant Sarina's mom was trusting her with her daughter. It meant she trusted her with her whole world. Roxy understood.

Once her parents left, Sarina turned to Roxy as she shoved the blanket onto her lap. "Can you help me get this darn blanket off?"

Roxy nodded and took the blanket. She folded it and placed it at the bottom of the bed. "So, how are you feeling?"

"I'm achy, but overall okay." And she looked okay. She looked better than okay—with the exception that she was sitting in a hospital bed with a cop posted outside.

"That's good." And it was good to see her looking so healthy. "What are you going to do?"

"About all this?" Sarina pointed to the doorway where the cop stood guard.

"Yeah." Roxy took the chair next to her bed.

"My parents are freaking out. They've spent hours with the lawyers." Sarina shook her head. "It's a mess."

"I'll figure this out."

"Thank you for everything you've done, but it's over." Sarina sighed. "Either way, it's up to the lawyers now."

Roxy rested her hand on Sarina's. "I'm so sorry."

Sarina wiped her eyes. "Enough of this pity party. The lawyers will figure it out."

Roxy wished she had the same faith in the lawyers.

"You should go home. My parents will be back here in a minute. I'm just going to go to sleep. I'm tired."

"Okay." Roxy sat back. She'd leave when Sarina's parents got back, but Sarina didn't need to know that. "If you need anything, just ask."

Sarina rested a hand on Roxy's arm. "Actually, can

you get my lip gloss from the apartment? My mom bought me this stuff from downstairs and it's awful." Sarina showed her a tube of lip balm. "My lips are so dry, and this is not helping."

"I'll get it to you tomorrow after work." Roxy could do that for her friend. Heck, she'd do anything.

"Thank you." Sarina patted Roxy's arm and turned over.

"Good night, honey." Roxy ran a hand down the back of her hair. "I love you."

"I love you, too," Sarina mumbled as her breathing evened out.

Ten minutes later, Sarina's parents tiptoed in the room, and Roxy slipped out past the cop playing on his phone.

Even though Roxy wanted to be happy, the idea of leaving everything up to the lawyers—and the cops—made her chest tight. Tears slid down her cheeks. Roxy needed to clear Sarina's name, because no one else seemed to care.

CHAPTER 31
RUN LIKE THERE'S A HOT GUY IN FRONT OF YOU AND A CREEPY GUY BEHIND YOU. ~ UNKNOWN

THE NEXT AFTERNOON, after showing her face at work and thankfully not bumping into Karan, Roxy parked Rafe's truck in the lot of Sarina's apartment building. She had a key for Sarina's place on her key ring, just like Sarina had one for Roxy's place. It just made it easier in situations like this. Not that they'd had many situations like this.

Roxy walked into the building and held the door as someone walked up behind her.

"Jared?" She stepped to the side as he walked through the door.

"Hi." Jared carried a large duffel bag on one shoulder. He looked at Roxy like he'd seen a ghost, all big eyes of terror. Although one of those eyes was circled in dark blue and purple. The telltale sign of a fight or abuse. She had a feeling she knew which it was.

"Do you remember me? We met at your house a few days ago. We had questions for Celeste."

"Yeah, what are you doing here?" Recognition or something must have struck, because he smiled—albeit strained. Maybe he didn't remember her but was just being nice.

"I'm here to grab something for a friend." She couldn't remember if they knew she was friends with Sarina. Roxy didn't think it was something she should announce to the world. It would just upset the kid. And he already seemed pretty upset.

"Oh." He nodded as he hitched the duffle bag on his shoulder higher. "I'm seeing my buddy, Adrian." He pointed at a door down the hall. "He lives here, well, down there."

The kid was nervous, if his death grip on the bag was anything to go by. Although it also could be the strained grin and darting eyes. He wanted to be far away from her. She'd be offended, but she wasn't even sure if he remembered her. "What happened to your eye?"

"I walked into the door at school." His free hand touched his face. "I wasn't paying attention."

Upon closer inspection, he also had a bruise on the arm holding the duffle bag.

"That is some door. It got your arm too."

He laughed, a nervous chuckle without humor. "I'm clumsy."

"Yeah." She smiled, but deep down she wanted to find his father and beat him with a bat. Although, the last time her and Sarina had talked about violence it came true so she might just keep that to herself. "Well, it was good seeing you again."

"You too." He turned on his heel and walked to the door he'd pointed to earlier. Adrian's.

She walked the opposite way, toward Sarina's door, but stopped when she reached the corner. She turned around just in time to see Jared run down the hall toward the exit.

What the...?

Roxy took off after him. Why was he running?

Roxy made it out the side door just as Jared jumped in a run-down Volkswagen Beetle. She raced up to the passenger side and opened the door. She slid in. "So, where are we going in such a hurry?"

"I forgot to get pizza." He pulled the bag closer.

"We always have pizza."

"Who?" She wanted to trip him up. He was up to something, and she didn't think it had anything to do with Adrian who lived here. She wasn't even sure he had a buddy in the building. But why would he be here?

"My friend Adrian. I told you he lived here."

"Ah." A knock on Jared's window made both Roxy and Jared jump in their seats.

"Dude. Where are you going?" A kid about Jared's age stood there. Jeans, T-shirt, acne. "Who's your friend?" And leery.

Just what Roxy needed today—to be leered at by a teenager.

"She's a cop," Jared said.

"Really?" Leery grinned. "Hey, cop. How are things at Metro?"

"I'm not a cop." She sighed. "Who are you?"

"I'm Adrian." He tipped his head and winked. "I'm the good-looking one."

The good-looking one of what? she wanted to ask, but was afraid of the answer. Some things were just better left alone.

"Is she why you're blowing me off?" Adrian leaned into Jared and whispered, "I'd totally blow you off for a piece of that."

"I was just going to grab snacks. It's my turn to bring pizza."

"No it's not." Adrian's eyebrows fused together. "I got pizza and cinnamon sticks. Like always."

"Oh." Jared shook his head. "I forgot. It is your turn." He turned to Roxy. "I don't have to leave."

Roxy nodded and slipped out of the car.

Jared followed Adrian into the building, Roxy trailing behind. Adrian rambled about CIA agents, Pantheon and evidence boards. Roxy got bored and stopped listening. She didn't have time to figure out what all that was about. Maybe Jared was just embarrassed that she saw him with a black eye. Maybe he didn't want her to meet his friend. Adrian was a little creepy.

Either way, she didn't have time to deal with teenage drama.

The door where Jared had stood earlier was closed. No teens were in the hall. She headed to Sarina's apartment.

Once she unlocked the door and went inside, it was obvious the door hadn't been opened for a few days. The air was stale and everything was a mess. Sarina would have a meltdown if she saw her place like this. She was neat and tidy. This was tornado-with-flying-monkeys-level destruction.

Finding a lip balm in a haystack was going to take forever. Her stomach growled. She should have stopped for something to eat before she came, but she was in such a hurry to help Sarina with... anything... she didn't think about herself. It wouldn't hurt to pause a minute and take the edge off her hunger.

Roxy went into the kitchen and checked the fridge. It wasn't like Sarina could eat anything from home right now. Why let food go to waste?

A package of string cheese sat on the top shelf. Roxy could do string cheese. She pulled a piece from the bag and peeled the plastic wrapper. She tore a piece off. Her stomach rumbled as she ate. She hadn't realized how hungry she was.

After finishing off her snack, she pressed the pedal on the garbage can and tossed it in. She looked inside. A ball of police tape sat in the center. Great.

In Sarina's bedroom, Roxy found the makeup bag right away. The insides were dumped out on the dresser. Roxy sifted through the pile and pulled out a Mango Madness lip gloss. Thank goodness. She slid it in her pocket and looked around the room.

What were they going to do with all of Sarina's things if she wasn't here? Roxy could store it at her place, or Sarina's parents would take it. They had more room. But this was Sarina's home.

Hell. It was Roxy's home away from home. There

were times that she'd spent as much time here as she did at her own apartment.

She sat on Sarina's bed and ran her hand over the dark blue comforter with white squiggles. If you looked close enough, you'd see the squiggles were alien heads and UFOs and moons. How many times had Roxy made fun of Sarina for this bedspread? How many times had she laid in this bed comforted by Sarina and this very same bedspread? How many times had Roxy worn Sarina's clothes because she forgot to bring her own?

Sarina's perfume calmed Roxy. Sarina calmed Roxy. It felt like her heart was on the verge of being ripped from her chest. She'd been the steadiest part of Roxy's life for over twenty years. When her parents got divorced, Sarina was there. When Grayson Williamson III dumped her, Sarina was there. When her father came home with a woman Roxy's age and knocked her up, Sarina was there with Ben and Jerry's.

What was she going to do without Sarina?

She could barely function with Sarina around. Without her... She couldn't imagine. And the fact that she might have to made Roxy want to hurl.

Roxy got off the bed and opened the closet. She wanted... no, needed, something of Sarina's. She didn't care that it made her a stalker. She didn't care how weird it was. She needed her around in any form she could find.

Taking the lid off the wicker laundry basket, Roxy pushed aside a pair of socks and underwear— because she wasn't that weird— and found Sarina's Aliens are

People Too sweatshirt. Roxy brought it to her nose and inhaled. Sarina's perfume stuck to the edges.

That would have to do.

She slung the sweatshirt over her shoulder and went to put the lid back on the basket. Something deep red was inside the basket. It was a familiar red. Roxy recognized it because she had to throw out an entire outfit when she'd fallen into a pool of blood a few months ago.

It was that same color.

A color she should not be seeing in Sarina's laundry. Something Roxy couldn't touch unless she wanted to be an accomplice to all this.

She needed gloves or a hook or something.

Roxy found a pair of tongs in the utensil drawer in the kitchen. Those would have to do. She ran back into the bedroom and pulled out a shirt. Sarina's shirt. Caked with blood.

Sarina did it?

No freaking way. Why would she lie about it? Roxy would've moved heaven and earth to clear her name, even if she was guilty. So why didn't Sarina tell her?

Roxy took the T-shirt into the living room. She had to destroy it. They couldn't have any more ammunition.

Or, she could just throw it in the garbage and dump the bag somewhere no one would think to look. She headed for the kitchen and opened the garbage can.

Great. She was throwing away the shirt with the police tape. It was a like a Vegas billboard saying "I'm evidence. Please find me."

Her brain whirled as she debated if she should toss

the shirt and the tape. Would anyone look? Would anyone care? Maybe if she threw the bag in a restaurant's dumpster? As she stared at the ball of police tape, a thought had her running back to Sarina's bedroom.

The police had already been through the apartment. And the laundry basket. How could they have missed this?

Roxy dropped the sweatshirt and the bloody shirt back in the basket. She pulled her phone from her pocket and dialed Rafe.

"Everything okay?"

"I don't know. I found a bloody shirt."

"Where?" Rafe's voice held an edge of incredulity. Like he couldn't believe she found something else to involve herself in another murder. It's not like she chose to find things. They just happened.

"At Sarina's apartment."

"Why are you in Sarina's apartment?"

"I'm grabbing her lip balm."

"Lip balm?" More incredulity.

"Her lips are dry."

"That seems important at a time like this." Sarcasm was not a pretty look on Rafe.

"You're missing the point. There's a bloody shirt here. In the laundry basket. How could the police have missed it?"

"They wouldn't have. Call McAuley."

"Are you sure? I don't want to get her in more trouble."

"Is it her shirt?"

"Yes. The house looks like a tornado hit. Everything dumped on the floor, but somehow there are clothes in the laundry basket, with the lid on, and one of them is Sarina's bloody shirt."

"I still say call McAuley."

"Fine." She said her goodbyes and hung up the phone. It was time to get Metro involved.

CHAPTER 32
LIES DON'T END RELATIONSHIPS, THE TRUTH DOES. ~ SHANNON L. ALDER

THE TALK with McAuley didn't go as bad as Roxy thought it would. He only yelled at her once for being in the apartment. When she explained there hadn't been police tape on the door, he quit yelling. Either he was out of breath or really surprised.

When she told him about the shirt, he seemed more than surprised, maybe even a little angry. He told her to wait, he'd be there as soon as he could.

She wasn't quite sure how long that would be, but it sounded like she might be here awhile. She returned to the kitchen for more food. That gnawing hunger was still a thing. She opened the fridge. She didn't think more cheese would help. She checked the cold cut drawer. All expired. That wouldn't work.

If only she'd had the foresight to bring a pizza...

Part of her wanted to go down the hall and grab a slice from Jared. It was the least he could do after being so weird earlier.

He had been weird.

What if he had something to do with the shirt? Or he knew something?

Maybe that was why he was so acting so odd. And why would he just leave when he was going to his friend's place? His car was parked by the door nearest Adrian's apartment, so why was he coming from the direction of Sarina's apartment?

All of a sudden she needed a piece of pizza. Now.

Roxy walked down the hall and stopped in front of Adrian's apartment. She knocked.

Nothing.

She couldn't hear any sounds coming from inside. No gunfire. No bombs. Maybe they left.

She knocked again. Louder.

Still nothing.

She leaned against the door and sighed. No sound. Then she heard it. Laughter. They were in there. Ignoring her.

Across the hall, on the wall, was the fire alarm. That would get them out of the apartment. Before she could change her mind or worry about the ramifications, she pulled the lever.

Nothing.

For cripes sake. She jiggled the lever up and down. Even tried pulling it. Not one beep. Holy safety violation.

Knocking it is. She crossed the hall and knocked. When no one answered, she tried the handle. It was open. She probably shouldn't just walk into a room with two teenage boys, being she was an adult and all, but desperate times.

Roxy opened the door and a wide grin spread across Adrian's face as he got up. He pulled the headphones from his ears, sauntered toward her and licked his lips. "Hey. Miss me?"

"No." Roxy pushed him out of the way and walked inside.

"Hey, you can't just come in," Adrian whined.

Roxy pulled the headset off of Jared's ears. "I need to talk to you."

Jared didn't look up. He kept his eyes on the split screen in front of him.

"He's busy." Adrian sat next to Jared and unpaused his part in the game.

"Now, Jared." She tossed the headphones on the floor. "Unless you'd like to do this here."

Jared paused his game and stood up. "I'll be right back." He picked up the duffle bag he was carrying earlier.

Adrian nodded and went back to slaying zombies or terrorists or whatever.

Following Jared out the door and into the hall, she wished she had a leash. Just in case he tried to make a run for it again. He was going to run. She just knew it.

But instead, he walked out the back door and turned around once they were outside. He didn't look at her, just leaned against the wall of the building.

"Do you know why I want to talk to you?" Roxy asked.

Jared shook his head.

"What's in the bag?"

He shrugged. She was going to have to treat him as

a hostile witness. But beating this kid wasn't going to get the answers she needed. Michael did enough of that. She needed another approach.

"Let me guess." She went with fear of jail. "You have the tools you used to cut Sarina's brakes. You tried to kill her."

Jared's eyes rounded to saucers. "No. No. I wouldn't..."

"Then what do you have in the bag? Why would you hurt Sarina?"

"I didn't."

"Then who did?"

"My father!" Jared burst out.

Roxy was so confused. "Why would he hurt her?"

Tears slid down Jared's cheeks. "He was protecting me."

"You?"

"I didn't mean it. It was an accident," Jared cried. "He promised. He promised to take me with when he moved to LA. He promised to get me away from my dad."

"Did your dad do that to you?" Roxy pointed at his black eye.

Jared nodded as he swallowed hard.

"Why couldn't Cliff take you with him?"

"He said that he didn't have the money. He said I should stay back and protect his mom. Why? She chose to marry that monster. I didn't have a choice. I couldn't choose who my father was. I deserved to get out." He sniffled. "I need to get out."

Roxy's heart broke. This poor kid was abused and

neglected and something awful happened. She still wasn't sure what, but she hoped he'd keep talking. "What happened that night?"

"I didn't mean it." He slumped down and sat against the wall, the duffle thumping onto the floor.

Roxy sat next to him and leaned her shoulder into his.

"It was an accident. We were talking about the baby and how we'd move to Los Angeles. Then he said that things changed and I couldn't go. He'd send for me." Jared slammed his fist on his knee. "I knew what that meant. He was going to leave Vegas and never come back. I begged him to stay. I begged him to take me with him.

"He told me that he couldn't do it. He had a family to take care of. Like I wasn't his family anymore. I tried to get him to listen to me, but he wouldn't. He turned around and started messing with his damn turntable. Just dismissed me. Wouldn't talk about it."

"That must have hurt."

"I was so mad. I just wanted to hurt him like he hurt me. But I didn't want to ..." Jared gasped. Choked. "I didn't mean to."

"I get it. It was an accident." Roxy tried to help him keep going. She needed to know what happened next.

"I just... pushed him. He fell back and hit the table. The legs just...broke. The turntable slid off and fell on his head. There wasn't anything I could do. I was covered in blood. There was so much blood."

"Why didn't you tell Metro? It was an accident."

"I know, but when I called my father, he said

they'd lock me up. He said, 'no son of mine is going to jail like some common criminal'. He came to the apartment and fixed the table. I found one of Sarina's shirts and I used it to clean myself up and when she used her key to come into Cliff's place, we hid in his bedroom closet."

"Didn't she see him on the floor? Weren't the lights on?"

He shook his head. "The lights were on, but she didn't go into the living room. She walked down the hall and checked the bedroom, and then she went into the kitchen."

"Did she say anything?"

"She just kept complaining about Cliff and his demo tape. Dad thought that was the perfect motive." Jared shook his head. "Dad wiped down everything, took the demo, and the shirt I used. He didn't tell me what he was going to do with it. I didn't know."

"We showed up to talk about Cliff. Why didn't you tell us then?"

"My dad told me he'd kill me." Tears streamed down Jared's face.

"Oh honey." Roxy wrapped an arm around his shaking shoulders. "You know you have to tell Metro. They'll help you."

"I killed him." He leaned into her. "They're going to lock me up forever."

"Not forever. If you get a good enough lawyer, it won't be long at all. It's manslaughter, at best." She wasn't totally sure about that, but she needed to talk him into doing the right thing. Sarina deserved it and

Cliff's family deserved it—even Jared deserved it. "How are you feeling since this happened?"

"I can't sleep. I'm barely eating. I feel awful and I don't know what to do."

"Honey. It was a mistake. They happen."

He ran an arm under his nose and eyes. "Have you killed someone?"

"Not technically." Vegas Metro thought she did once. "But I've hurt people. I've done things I didn't mean to do. And if you don't own it, it will eat you alive."

"Roxy?" She heard the voice, but she couldn't see who it was with the ceiling fluorescent light shining in her face. She lifted her free hand and shielded her eyes.

MacAuley stood in front of them. She wasn't sure how long he'd been there. But the look on his face said he was mad at her.

What did she do now?

CHAPTER 33
NOTHING MATTERS BUT THE FACTS. WITHOUT THEM, THE SCIENCE OF CRIMINAL INVESTIGATION IS NOTHING MORE THAN A GUESSING GAME. ~ BLAKE EDWARDS

"HEY, MACAULEY." Roxy didn't move. She kept one arm around Jared's shoulders and used the other to shield her eyes from the sun. The kid needed a friend and a bit of support and she needed a shield from MacAuley's glare. "Do you remember Jared?"

MacAuley nodded. "I do. What are you doing out here?"

"Chatting." Roxy nodded toward Jared. "Want to join us?"

"On the ground?"

"Yep. It's comfy down here." Roxy tilted her head again. This time she added a glare of her own.

MacAuley must have understood, because he sat down next to Jared. "So, what's the topic of conversation?"

The three sat in silence. Roxy waited for Jared to say something. Anything.

Silence.

"We were talking about the night Cliff died." She watched Jared's reaction. He didn't appear to be ready to run, but she kept her arm on his shoulder just in case. Dual purpose. Provide support and keep him grounded.

Nothing.

"Jared, do you have anything to add?"

He dropped his head to his knees and mumbled, "It was an accident."

"I'm sorry, I couldn't hear that." MacAuley looked at Roxy, but it wasn't her story to tell.

"It was an accident. I didn't mean to kill him." Jared lifted his head. His voice a hollowed-out shell.

"Kill who?"

"Cliff." Jared's eyes welled with tears. "We were fighting and I pushed him. He fell, but it was an accident."

"Did someone put you up to telling me this?" MacAuley's stare hit Roxy like an anvil. She wouldn't con a child to admit to murder. Who would do that?

Jared shook his head. "No."

"Then why didn't you say anything sooner?"

"My father threatened me."

MacAuley nodded. "Maybe we should continue this at the station. We have soda and air conditioning."

Jared nodded as he wiped his face with his sleeve.

"I'll drive." MacAuley stood, and reached down to help Jared stand. Jared waved him off and got up on his own. MacAuley offered his palm to Roxy. A peace offering.

She took his hand and let him lift her. Not because she was accepting his peace. She was going to have words with the man for accusing her of coercing a confession. "I'll follow."

"Okay." MacAuley nodded and led the way to an unmarked dark green Ford Explorer in the parking lot.

Roxy ran ahead and stopped when she reached Jared's side. "Hey, kiddo." She bumped his shoulder with her own. "You okay going with him? I'll follow right behind you."

"Can you come with me?" Jared looked ready to cry again.

"I don't think he'd let me, but I promise to be right behind you. I'll be there when you get out of the car."

"Thank you." Jared wrapped her in a hug and she hugged him back. The kid was going to be going through a lot if all this panned out to be true.

When Jared pulled away from Roxy, MacAuley took the duffle bag from him and helped him get in the back seat of the SUV. MacAuley closed the door behind him. He then set the bag on the ground before pulling out a pair of plastic gloves. He knelt down and zipped the bag open.

"What is in there? He was guarding it with his life earlier." Roxy could admit the curiosity was killing her.

MacAuley sifted through the bag, pulling out a brimmed hat and a pair of socks. He stared inside and sighed. "Shit."

"That doesn't sound good." Roxy leaned over his shoulder, trying to see inside the bag.

He pulled out a piece of paper covered in blood. "I'll need to get that shirt you found from Sarina's apartment."

"Yeah, the blood probably matches." Part of her was so happy to get the spotlight off of Sarina. But another part felt her heart broke. Jared was a kid who'd made a mistake.

"He said it was an accident."

MacAuley put the items back in the bag. "That doesn't explain why he didn't say anything."

"His father told him not to come forward. He also said his father cut the brake line on Sarina's car."

"Do you believe him?" He opened the back of the Explorer and set the bag inside before he pulled off the gloves.

"Are you sure you want my input? I apparently am capable of coercing a confession out of children."

MacAuley sighed. "I had to ask the question and yeah, I want your opinion."

She wanted to be angry, but it did feel good that he trusted her judgement. "I've seen him a few times, and each time he's had a new bruise. His dad is bad news. Cliff was supposed to take him away from all this."

"Poor kid got a raw deal."

"Yeah."

"On brand." MacAuley shook his head. "Cliff was a terrible person."

"Did you know him?"

"You get to know people on cases like this. When you get past all he did to Sarina, the guy jerked around his fiancée and his baby-momma. Why not jerk around the kid he considered a brother." MacAuley just shook his head as he shut the hatch. "I'll meet you at South Central."

"Okay." She wasn't sure exactly where that was, but that's why God invented Waze.

CHAPTER 34

NOBODY'S EVER BEEN ARRESTED FOR A MURDER; THEY HAVE ONLY EVER BEEN ARRESTED FOR NOT PLANNING IT PROPERLY. ~ TERRY HAYES, I AM PILGRIM

AN HOUR LATER, Roxy sat outside the interrogation room. She'd tried to slide into the observation room, but the cops had obviously figured out her methods. They locked the door.

She couldn't believe it either.

She was sitting outside like a peasant. She had no idea what Jared was telling the cops. Celeste had shown up half an hour ago. They were finally getting down to the questioning part of the day. Roxy wanted to know what was being said, but there were too many people sitting around, so she couldn't exactly put her ear to the door.

It hadn't stopped her before, but this time it wasn't Sarina inside. She decided on showing a modicum of decorum.

Michael stormed into the precinct, his face red with rage. "Where the hell is my son!"

"Sir, we'll get you to your son." The officer tried to stop him, but Roxy had a feeling only a stun gun would break his stride.

"I want to see him now!"

"Slow down, Mr. Robbins."

"Is there a problem?" The commander did his own version of storming into the room.

She was assuming he was the commander since he had added stripes on his lapels and his tone said he'd pulverize Michael into the ground.

Michael didn't seem intimidated. "Your officers are interrogating my sixteen-year-old son without a parent present."

"His mother is with him."

"His mother is dead."

"Mr. Robbins, we're going to have to ask you to sit down. Jared's stepmother is in the room with him." The commander indicated a vacant bench. The bench across from Roxy.

Michael looked around, and then those eyes found Roxy. Even though cops flanked him, the murder in his eyes didn't make her feel all warm and fuzzy.

"You!" He pointed at Roxy as the officers grabbed him. "You will pay." Michael shook off the cops. "I'll leave." He glared at Roxy before turning around and stalking out of the station.

"Are you okay?" one of the officers asked Roxy.

"Yes, I'm fine." Roxy smiled.

The cops dispersed. All attention went back to reports and cell phones.

MacAuley walked out the door of the interrogation room. "What's going on?"

"Jared's father was here."

"Was that the yelling?" MacAuley eyed the room, probably noticing nothing was out of place. Everyone was back to hushed chatter and paper shuffling.

"Yeah."

"Where is he now?"

"He left."

"Shit." MacAuley shook his head. "I wanted to talk to him."

"Jared told you about how he covered everything up, huh?"

"The kid was terrified."

"You can't send him home to that house."

"Child and Family Services is on the way."

"Good." Roxy waited, watching as MacAuley fingered the folder in his hand. "Jared needs you to go easy on him. It was an accident."

"It was, but that doesn't change the fact that they framed Sarina for this. I would think you'd be less understanding since your best friend almost landed in prison."

"Does that mean you've dropped the charges?"

"It's looking hopeful, but we'll need more to make that stick."

"Jared told you he planted the evidence."

"But we need to talk to his father first."

"Fine." She needed Sarina to be completely out of the crosshairs. "Did he say anything about what happened to Sarina's car?"

"He said he didn't know."

"That's what he told me." She nodded. "Do you believe him?"

"Yeah, I think he's a kid that got in over his head."

"It doesn't help that his father is an abusive jerk."

"Yeah."

"Are you okay?" Rafe walked up behind Roxy. "Everyone is talking about what happened."

"Yeah, Michael was here."

Rafe put an arm around her shoulders. "I take it Sarina is no longer a suspect."

"We're working on it, but it's looking less likely. Jared admitted to planting the evidence we found and to the murder."

"Good. Then we can put this behind us." Rafe guided Roxy toward the door. "We should get you home."

Roxy turned to MacAuley. "Thank you."

MacAuley nodded before heading back into the interrogation room.

Following Rafe out the door, Roxy took in a deep breath of Vegas air. Her lungs expanded and contracted, freedom bursting through every exhale. Having Sarina out of trouble was like a huge block of granite removed from her shoulders.

Rafe escorted her to his truck. Even her feet felt lighter. "How did you get here?" She just realized his truck was here with her.

"I had Gabe bring me." Gabe Martin. One of his minions at the hotel.

"How did you know I was even here?"

He opened the passenger door and didn't say a word. The ghost of a smile flitted across his lips.

Of course. "MacAuley."

He checked to make sure she was inside and then shut the door. He walked around to driver's side, opened the door, and angled in.

"For two people who hate each other, you gossip more than the hens at the country club."

"It's not gossip." He smiled. "He knows I have a vested interest in keeping you safe. He keeps me in the loop."

"And what do you do for him?"

"I don't kick his ass." Rafe pulled the truck out of the parking spot and headed out of the lot.

"He's got the short end of this stick."

Rafe laughed as he turned onto Las Vegas Boulevard. "Well, we have an understanding."

"I get it." She watched the scenery passing her by. "Where are we going?"

"North Vegas."

She knew Sarina was out of the hot seat, but part of her needed to see this thing through. "Why North Vegas?"

"Because your car is ready and I talked Romeo into knocking a few bucks off the bill. I also talked him into a payment plan."

"How did you manage that?"

"He owes me a favor." Rafe smiled.

"We'll unpack that later." Roxy sighed. She wanted to be mad because it was her responsibility, but it was really sweet of him to get her a deal from Romeo. "Can we do one thing before we get my car?"

"What thing?"

"I want to head to Michael's house."

"Why? Sarina's out of danger. We can just stay out of it."

"But he's not sure yet. MacAuley said they had to talk to Michael. After he ran out of the police station... I just have a feeling he's going to run. And then what?"

"And then Jared will take the fall. Not Sarina."

"That doesn't make it better. Neither one of them deserves to take a fall at all. Jared deserves to be punished, but not for the parts Michael forced him to do." She rested her hand on his knee. He needed to see that this was important to her. "We need to follow this through. It's the right thing to do."

Rafe sighed. "We'll find him and call MacAuley."

"Let's head to Michael's house." She smiled. They were so close to getting Sarina out of this.

CHAPTER 35
THE MORE OFTEN A STUPIDITY IS REPEATED, THE MORE IT GETS THE APPEARANCE OF WISDOM. ~ VOLTAIRE

TWENTY MINUTES LATER, Rafe pulled into the driveway of Celeste and Michael's home. The place hadn't changed. The bars still covered the windows. Roxy walked up to the door and knocked on the screen.

Rafe leaned into the window, cupping his hand above his eyes. "I see someone inside."

"Is it Michael?"

"I don't think so."

Roxy heard rustling behind the door. The door flew open and Kandi stood there. Her straight blond hair was pulled back with a headband. She scowled when she saw Roxy. "What are you doing here?"

"Hello to you too." Roxy smiled. Just because she was awful didn't mean Roxy had to be. "We're here to see Michael Robbins."

"We?" Kandi took a step forward. A grin broke out when she saw Rafe. "Oh, hi."

"Hi, Kandi."

Kandi giggled. "It's nice to see you again."

Roxy couldn't stop her eyes from rolling. Not that she was trying. Kandi was a pile of goo every time she saw Rafe. Not that it bothered Roxy all that much, but melting around Rafe was her job.

Rafe smiled and stepped in front of Roxy. This again. "I was hoping you could help me."

"Sure." Kandi giggled again.

"I'm looking for Michael."

"Oh, he was here a few minutes ago, but he left."

Rafe leaned against the door jamb. "Do you know where he went."

"I don't know. Maybe back to work?" She flipped her hair over one shoulder. "He grabbed a bag from his room before he left and shoved a bunch of clothes inside."

Probably not back to work. "I doubt he's going to work unless he's planning on moving in."

Kandi rolled her eyes. Apparently she could do that, too. "He said he needed to grab something from his locker at work. I have no idea where he's going after that." Kandi made sure to glare at Roxy.

Roxy didn't have time for her attitude. They had to find Michael before he hurt someone or he ran away and they never found him. After all, it sounded like Michael was running.

"Do you know where he works?"

"North Valley Metal Supply over on Cheyenne Avenue in Vegas."

"We should probably go." Roxy pulled on Rafe's arm, but he wouldn't budge.

"Look, Kandi, if Michael comes back, don't let him

in the house." Rafe nodded to the door. "Keep this locked."

"What's going on?" Kandi frowned, complete with a pout.

"You know how Michael abused Jared and Cliff," Rafe said.

Kandi nodded, and Roxy wanted to smack her.

"They think he covered up Cliff's murder," Rafe continued. "You know what he's capable of."

Kandi gulped. "Yeah, he's horrible. I know he cut the brake line on Sarina's car."

"You knew that?" Roxy was proud of not screaming.

"I was the decoy." Kandi's face drooped. "I went inside to keep security busy."

"You knew what he was doing?" Rafe asked.

"No." Kandi made a surprised face. Roxy didn't believe that for a second. "He said he was going to mess up her car like she messed up our life. I thought he was going to key her car or something. I just wanted to make her life miserable."

"By ending it." Roxy's fists dangled at her waist, but they wanted to hit Kandi right in the face.

"No!" Kandi shook her head, whipping her fake blond hair back and forth. "I swear I didn't know. I wouldn't do that to her. I wouldn't do that to anyone. I might be angry, but I'm not crazy."

Roxy wasn't sure she believed her about the crazy, but she did believe about her involvement in Sarina's sabotaged car.

Rafe slid his fingers through Roxy's fisted hand.

Apparently, her hand hadn't received the memo that Roxy believed Kandi. But his touch made her hand open like a lotus flower.

"We have to go. Make sure you lock the door." Rafe walked toward the car, dragging Roxy. He turned to make sure Kandi shut the door.

"Why did you tell her about Michael?" Roxy opened the passenger door.

Rafe rested his hand on the top of the door. "She should know what could be coming her way."

She leaned into Rafe. "You're a good man, Rafe." She kissed his cheek. He was such a thoughtful guy.

She angled into the truck and waited as Rafe closed the door. She pulled out her phone and opened the internet. She needed to get the address for North Valley Metal Supply.

CHAPTER 36
UNLESS I'M WRONG, WHICH, YOU KNOW, I'M NOT. ~ ADRIAN MONK (TONY SHALHOUB)

RAFE'S TRUCK tires pinged and crunched on the gravel parking lot of North Valley Metal Supply. He parked on the far side of the lot and they walked toward the oversized white brick building. The whirring of a humongous HVAC unit drowned out all of the silence.

Two cars sat in the lot. Seemed like that was weird for a weekday afternoon. There should be more cars. "Shouldn't people be here working?" Roxy asked, looking around.

Rafe nodded. "You would think. Maybe they're all at lunch."

"Maybe."

Rafe and Roxy made their way to the front door, and she knocked on an ornate steel front door. No one answered, not that she expected anyone to, but a girl could dream. She turned the knob and the door squeaked open.

"Hello," she called into the silence. No one said anything back. No noise. "Anyone home?" She opened the door all the way and held it for Rafe. "I don't think anyone is here."

A scuffed counter sat by the door. Behind it, a red forklift sat on the concrete floor waiting for someone, anyone, to lift something.

Rafe followed her inside and turned left at the forklift. She turned right. Divide and conquer. Good plan.

Roxy passed rows of cubbies holding all sizes and shapes of steel. Circular rods and square tubes of various thicknesses. She followed what she guessed must be an outside wall until it ended at another wall. There was a door. She opened it.

Inside was a typical office with multiple desks. On the nearest one sat a pile of job applications. She could see what they were even from a few feet away. Seemed like a privacy violation of some sort.

She closed the door. It was weird that the door was left open, when there was clearly a lock on it.

Behind her, the front door squeaked and she turned to see what made the noise.

A tall man with a scar along his jaw, wearing jeans and a T-shirt, came in the door. "Who the hell are you?" He looked right at Roxy as he walked toward her.

"I'm, um." She knew why she was here, so why that reason wasn't flying off her tongue, she had no idea. But the size of the man and the anger in his eyes made her nervous. "I'm looking for Michael Robbins."

"Why?" He stopped about six feet away.

"I just want to talk to him about his son."

"Is Jared all right?"

A little arrested, but who was counting. "Yeah. Just some school issues. I'd rather talk to his father."

"Well, he ain't here. He didn't show up today." Jaw-scar didn't look all that happy that Michael wasn't here.

But then again, when one of Roxy's coworkers ditched work, it left more work for her, so she understood. "Is that normal?"

"Why do you care?" Jaw-scar didn't seem to be the sharing kind of guy. He was also very mistrustful. Someone must have hurt him. She thought about asking who, but that would be sharing. So, one, he wouldn't answer the question, and, two, she had a feeling his punch would pack a wallop. She had no desire to find out how hard his fist was.

"You need to leave," he said.

She agreed. She didn't want to stay where she wasn't wanted, but she needed Rafe. Her head swiveled, hoping Rafe would appear from the shadows. She edged to one side and tried to get past him. "I just..."

"You just what? Get out." He grabbed at her arm and pulled her to the front door. Fingers dug into her skin. There was definitely going to be a bruise. But if she got out of this with just a bruise, she was calling it a win.

He pushed her out the front door and she tripped on some loose gravel. Her purse slid down her shoulder and tumbled to the ground. Thankfully she didn't fall, but her stuff was all over. She picked up her lockpick set, ChapStick and wallet and shoved them back into her bag.

She needed Rafe. He had the fob for the truck. Jawscar stood in the doorway with his large arms crossed.

She wasn't going to be able to get back in. Hopefully, Rafe would know to come out. She walked to the truck and looked inside. No Rafe.

Not surprising. He was probably slinking around all stealth-like checking out the company. She hadn't been stealthy at all. Mostly because she hadn't thought that she needed to be.

She figured she'd wait a minute before she went back inside to find him. She really didn't want to go back in, so she hoped Rafe would come sneaking out. Any minute.

Roxy pulled out her phone to see if he'd texted or called. Nothing from him. Nothing from anyone else. She started to text Sarina, but Sarina didn't have her phone. So that wouldn't do much good. She decided to text Rafe. His phone should be on silent.

I'm outside

And just in case bad guys had access to his phone:

with the cops

The building stayed silent, so she crept up to a dusty window and peered inside. It was dark and quiet. No one appeared to be in the front. But she knew Jawscar was inside. A light glowed from an object in the center of the floor. A cell phone. Rafe's cell phone? She wasn't sure without getting a good look.

Calling the cops seemed like a good idea right about now. She dialed MacAuley.

"What's up, Horne, I'm in the middle of something right now."

"I'm not sure, but I think Rafe is in trouble."

"What do you mean? What did you do?"

"I didn't do anything. Rafe and I went to Michael Robbins' work to talk to him." Roxy swore she heard a sigh come across the line, but she wasn't sure.

"Send me the address."

She texted him the address. "It's North Valley Metal Supply in North Las Vegas."

"It's going to take me twenty minutes to get there. Don't move."

"I don't think he has twenty minutes." She really didn't. If that was his phone and he wasn't near it, he was in trouble.

"I'll hurry. I mean it, Horne. Stay put." MacAuley hung up and the line went dead.

Dead. Hopefully Rafe wouldn't end up like the line.

CHAPTER 37
MURDER IS LIKE POTATO CHIPS: YOU CAN'T STOP WITH JUST ONE. ~ STEPHEN KING, UNDER THE DOME

ROXY WENT BACK to the front door and slowly turned the knob. Jaw-scar had locked it. She shouldn't be surprised, but somehow she was. That meant they had something to hide. Rafe.

She took out her lockpicks. She needed to get in there. Quickly and quietly. Quickly and her lockpicking skills weren't exactly synonymous. But she didn't have a choice.

Taking a deep breath, she got to work, listening hard for each click. Without any warning, the door popped opened with a small whine from the hinges. She grabbed for the knob to keep it from opening further and waited. Nothing.

She put the lockpicks back into the bag and shifted the strap over her head, making it into a crossbody. She held her breath and pushed the door open till she could slide inside.

Still nothing.

She tiptoed to the flashing rectangle on the floor

and touched the screen. A picture of her and Rafe at Lake Las Vegas popped up. So sweet. She really did look good in that picture. Rafe chose a good one. She picked up the phone and made sure the ringer was off.

Yes. Good boy.

She slid his phone into her bag and checked the room. No sign of Rafe. Whispering came from a hallway to the left. The way Rafe had gone.

She needed a weapon if she ran into Jaw-scar. In front of one row of cubbies sat a plastic bin filled with metal rods. She pulled out a thick square one, wincing at the slight scrape of metal.

Roxy crept to the left and down the hall. The whispers grew.

"I still don't understand why you hit him." That was Jaw-scar.

"What was I supposed to do? He was here to take me in."

Roxy couldn't see anyone yet, but she was sure that was Michael. The menace in his tone matched from the Metro station.

"The same thing I did with her. Escort him out of the building."

"He's military. It's not like he's some trollop you can just threaten with a scowl." Did Michael just call her a trollop? Who called anyone a trollop without wearing a frockcoat and breeches?

Roxy slipped closer to the door where the voices were coming from. She peered around the corner, trying to keep herself hidden. Rafe lay on the ground.

Two men stood over him. One was Jaw-scar and one was Michael.

"Well, what are we going to do with him now?" Jaw-scar kicked at Rafe's leg. Rafe didn't wake, but his chest appeared to move up and down. He was alive.

"We leave him here and get the hell out." Michael walked over to a desk and whipped open a drawer. He pulled out papers and a metal box. When he opened the box, Roxy saw stacks of money. What was going on? How was any of this related to Cliff's murder?

"He saw me here with you." Jaw-scar shook his head. "He can't stay here."

"Then what do you want to do with him?"

"Take him with you. Use him as collateral if you need to, and kill him when you're gone."

Michael seemed to think about it before he nodded. "Not a bad idea. We don't need any loose ends. But what about the chick?"

Oh goody. Roxy had graduated from trollop to chick. Or was that a demotion?

"She's nothing."

Michael shook his head. "She saw you here."

"But she didn't see you."

"I'll take care of him." Michael motioned to Rafe. "You take care of her."

Take care of...? Roxy had no desire to be taken care of in any sort of way by these guys. She had a feeling it would be a very painful and miserable death.

"Do you need help carrying him to the car?"

"Yeah, might as well." The men leaned over to pick up Rafe.

Roxy had no idea what to do. MacAuley wasn't going to be here for another ten minutes. If she stood up to them, they'd kill her. It was on Jaw-scar's list of things to do today. Why make it easy?

But she couldn't let Michael drive away with Rafe.

She needed to keep them busy. Ten minutes. That's all she needed. There was an office on the other side of the building. It had a lock. Hopefully it worked. Hopefully her plan worked.

She tucked the rod between her thighs. There were so many jokes she could make, but she didn't really have time. She pulled out her phone and aimed it at the men carrying Rafe. "I can't wait to share this picture with the cops." She slid the phone back into her pocket and took the rod from between her legs.

She waited while the men registered that she was there. She had to make sure they were following her and then run. Really fast.

"What the fuck?" Jaw-scar stalked toward Roxy, but he must have forgotten he was carrying Rafe, so he didn't get very far.

Roxy felt like Kevin from *Home Alone*. She thought about winking and telling them they couldn't catch her. But she hadn't set booby-traps, and angering these two anymore than she had already felt like overkill. Or something she'd get killed over.

"Go get her!" Michael yelled. "I got him."

Roxy took that as her cue to leave. She ran through the building, the bar in her hand. She could see the door to the office. There was a lock. She heard Jaw-scar panting behind her. His shoes slapped against the concrete.

Seven feet. She just had to make it seven more feet. She kept running. Her thighs burned. Her breath rushed in and out of her lungs. One shoe crossed the threshold. Her free hand rested on the door as she ran inside the room and went to slam the door.

A large hand curled around the edge, stopping her from closing it. She jammed her body against the door and pushed. Her arms strained, jamming her shoulder against the wood. Her feet slipped as the man on the other side pushed back. Harder and harder. She just needed to get it closed so she could lock the door.

But she couldn't push any harder.

Her muscles whined.

Her shoulder screamed.

But ten minutes hadn't passed. She hadn't heard sirens.

If she didn't hold the line, they were going to kill her. And Rafe. She couldn't let them.

The door moved. Roxy slid back further and further.

A hand grabbed at her arm, pulling her away from the door.

The door closed, with Jaw-scar on the wrong side of it.

"You shouldn't have come back." He turned the lock with a click.

She was in so much trouble.

CHAPTER 38
I THINK PERHAPS ALL OF US GO A LITTLE CRAZY AT TIMES.
~ ROBERT BLOCH, PSYCHO

ROXY SAT DOWN HARD on the floor, using her hands and feet to scrabble away from Jaw-scar. Her purse cut at her neck, but she didn't care. She didn't care that she'd lost the metal bar at some point. Her heart hammered in her chest and her pulse surged through her ears in a dull roar.

"You made this too easy," Jaw-scar said.

"You don't have to hurt me. I just want Rafe and we'll leave you alone." Her back hit a desk.

End of the line.

"Like that would happen." Jaw-scar ran a hand along his chin.

"Did you have anything to do with Cliff's death?" Roxy was hoping this was just a misguided man who was trying to be loyal to his friend. Not the kind who'd hide a body for him, but the kind that would turn on his friend when he realized his friend was insane.

"What are you talking about? Of course not." Jaw-scar moved closer.

She pushed back against the desk, bracing her feet under her, but there was nowhere to go. She had only one option. Reason. "Then why are you helping him? You didn't do anything wrong. This is all on Michael."

"Just shut up." He said the words, but he wasn't moving closer. He was listening.

She needed to keep it up.

"He was there when Cliff was killed. He covered it up. He cut the brakes on my best friend's car. She almost died."

"I don't believe you."

"What do you think is going on? He's trying to get away because he knows he's going to jail. You don't want to go with him."

He shook his head. "You're lying. Anyway, I owe him my life."

He moved. All conflict gone. He was going to kill her. She moved her hands, getting ready to push to her feet. Her right knuckles brushed something cold and hard that wasn't the floor. The metal bar.

If she didn't kill him first.

She curled her fingers around the bar. She figured she'd only get one shot at this. "You don't have to do this." She just needed him a little closer so she could hit him.

She raised her left hand, palm out. One last try at logic. "We can just walk out of here and let the cops handle Michael. They're on their way."

He laughed in a maniacal I'm-not-going-to-do-the-right-thing way. "The cops aren't coming. You didn't have time to call them." Another step.

Only a few feet separated them. Not close enough.

Another step. "Don't do anything stupid." He moved another step.

Now.

Roxy waved her left hand, distracting him, and swung the metal bar with her right as hard and fast as she could. There was no time to get to her feet. At the last second, she got her left hand on the bar and finished her swing, connecting with the side of his knee with a horrible crunch.

Jaw-scar howled and went over sideways, onto one knee and a hand. Roxy made it to her feet and didn't think, just took another swing. She wasn't aiming at anything, and still she managed to slam the rod into his jaw. Bone cracked. Blood spattered from his mouth as he dropped to the ground. She watched him, panting and sweaty. He didn't move.

She leaned down and checked his pulse. He was alive. For now.

She had to go after Rafe.

She switched the rod from her right hand to her left and unlocked the door. She checked behind her to make sure Jaw-scar was still down. He was. And that hit she gave was going to leave more than a scar.

She moved the rod to her right hand again. She was going to need it if she wanted to save Rafe.

She could only hope he was still here. And that he was still alive.

CHAPTER 39
I CAN'T BELIEVE I BROUGHT A PIPE TO A GUN FIGHT. ~ ROXY HORNE

ROXY RAN THROUGH THE BUILDING, back to where she'd last saw Rafe. He wasn't there. She hadn't thought he actually would be, but she'd hoped. Michael had plenty of time to get Rafe out of the building and drive away by now.

She headed to the front door and ran outside. There was Michael, with Rafe over his shoulder, carrying him to the car at the far end. She opened her mouth to yell for him to stop, but noticed what was in his left hand.

A gun.

She'd brought a pipe to a gun fight. That was never going to work.

Michael swore and grunted as he lugged Rafe closer and closer to his getaway vehicle.

She just needed a gun. Rafe's truck. He had a gun. She jogged over to the driver side of his truck as quietly as possible. She needed the element of surprise. But she also needed to do this fast, before Michael got away.

Rafe had given her the code. She just had to remember what it was. There was a nine. Maybe. A five. There were at least two odd numbers. She needed in. She didn't have time to figure this out. He was not going to like this, but she felt he'd like being killed a lot less.

She hefted the metal rod to shoulder height, steadying it with both hands, and rammed it into the side window. The glass cracked, but not enough. Again. Then one more time. The glass buckled, and she used the bar to poke a big enough hole to get her hand inside and unlock the door. She opened the glove compartment and pulled out his Glock. She leaned over to the console and found the magazine. She'd watched pretty closely when Rafe had slipped the magazine into the gun, and got it in without too much fumbling.

She had the gun, now she needed the bad guy. Well, she just needed to keep the bad guy busy for a few more minutes. MacAuley had to be close. Unlocking the safety, she peeked around the truck. Nobody was there. Both cars were still in the lot, though.

"Michael, there's nowhere for you to run." Roxy hid behind the truck and yelled into the empty lot.

"There's nowhere for you to go either if you want your boyfriend," Michael yelled back. He was hiding somewhere.

She just wasn't sure where, so she needed to stay down. "That's all I want. I just want Rafe, and we'll go our way and you can go your way."

"I saw you at the police station."

"Yeah, I was there for moral support when Jared starting telling the cops he killed Cliff." Roxy probably shouldn't remind him that there was another murder involved.

"Come out and I'll give you your boyfriend."

"I don't want to be shot." Her honesty was on point today. That might not be a good thing.

"I won't shoot you, but if you don't come out I will shoot him." Michael sounded about as sincere as those guys selling stuff on late night TV, but she didn't really have a lot of choices at the moment. She couldn't let him shoot Rafe.

Roxy slid her purse strap over her head and dropped the purse on the passenger seat. She slid the gun in the back waistband of her jeans. Then she walked out from behind the truck with her hands open and her fingers splayed.

There was still a chance Michael would let them go. At least that's what she'd like to believe.

"I just want to take Rafe and go home." She walked closer to the car on the opposite side of the lot. She couldn't see Michael, but she knew he was here. She kept hoping he'd listen and not just shoot. "You haven't done anything wrong. What happened with Cliff was an accident."

"Is that what the cops told you?"

"It's what your son said."

Michael laughed. "Well, that's a lie." He stepped out from behind the side of the building, gun in his hand. Rafe wasn't anywhere in sight.

"Where is Rafe?"

"Your boyfriend is fine. He's over by the sheds." Michael motioned back around the building, from where he came. Which meant she needed to get him back to talking. Rafe was out of harm's way, as long as Michael was telling the truth.

"What's a lie? It wasn't an accident?" She believed that little brat when he'd cried that he hadn't meant to do it.

"You don't understand. Cliff was leaving, after all me and his momma did for him. Las Vegas has gotten too expensive. Without his money, we were gonna lose the house." Michael shook his head. "Ungrateful brat."

"He made that much as a DJ?"

Michael laughed. "No, he had other talents."

"I don't understand." Maybe she didn't want to understand. "I take that back. As far as I know, Jared pushed Cliff and accidentally killed him."

Michael said, "That's—"

Roxy interrupted him. "And that's all I need to know. I can take Rafe and you can leave. Whatever happened here will be between you and the police. I won't say a word."

It had to be over twenty minutes by now. Where the heck was MacAuley?

"He couldn't leave well enough alone. We had a good thing going. He'd take the product to all those clubs he worked. They were going to do drugs anyway, might as well make myself a few bucks." He shook his head. "Stupid kid."

"So Jared didn't kill him?" She already knew too

much, might as well get the full story before he filled her with lead. Or the world's slowest cops showed up. She was hoping for the latter.

"He almost did. Cliff was hanging on by a thread when I got there. I just finished the job."

"How?" Roxy gulped. This man killed his stepson in cold blood, and she was possibly the next victim, if Rafe wasn't already dead.

CHAPTER 40
TO STOP A BAD GUY WITH A GUN, IT TAKES A GOOD GUY WITH A GUN. ~ WAYNE LAPIERRE

MICHAEL'S EYES WENT DARK. Vacant. Like no one was in there, just evil. "It wasn't hard. I covered his mouth and nose till he stopped moving."

"Didn't Jared notice you suffocating him?"

"Nah, I sent him to get wet towels." Mike scowled. "That boy is soft. Didn't see it coming. Apparently, still ain't seen it."

"He blamed himself."

"Well, he should've. The accident was his fault. I could've talked Cliff into staying. I just needed more time. Anyway, Jared was trying to leave me too."

"Did Jared sell for you?"

Michael laughed deep and hearty. "No. He tried, but he don't have that kinda reach. He ain't got friends or social skills. Video games made him weak. Kids today don't know how to live in the world these days."

Or maybe he just had an abusive father and didn't have the self-esteem to be social. Too be fair, the whole Covid thing probably hadn't helped.

The low hum of sirens wafted on the wind. MacAuley. Finally.

She had to keep him focused on her. Once he heard the sirens, all bets were off as to what he'd do. "When did Cliff start selling for you?"

"We couldn't afford the house. Our rent is twice what it was. I was laid off. Cliff wasn't DJing. We needed to be creative." The sirens were getting closer, but Michael was apparently too busy talking to notice.

"That must have been so hard."

"It was... what's that?" His head came up and he scowled. "Is this a trick?"

His left hand flew up to support the gun in his right hand.

"No." Roxy tried to make herself smaller, pulling her arms in, crossing her legs and turning to the side. Not that any of that would help if he decided to shoot, but she couldn't help herself.

She slid her hand to her hip. She just needed to grab her gun, but she couldn't exactly out-draw him. He was already drawn. She couldn't outshoot him. He'd actually shot a gun multiple times. He'd been in the military, for goodness' sake.

The only way for this to work was for his attention to be focused someplace else. Then she'd have an advantage.

"Change of plans. You're coming with me." He took a step toward her, gun never wavering.

"Where?"

"Or would you rather I just shoot you and take your boyfriend?" He didn't really offer a lot of options.

"Can't you just go your way and we'll go ours?" she asked. With the sirens closing in, he'd be desperate soon and she didn't want to know what that desperation looked like. She took one step toward him.

"Just keep your mouth shut and we'll get through this just fine."

She walked toward him, in no big rush to become a hostage.

"Hurry up!" he yelled.

She bounced as she walked, trying to give the impression of speed. At least she hoped.

Michael moved, grabbed her left arm and jerked her forward. She let her right arm swing around to her back with the motion until she could get a grip on the Glock. She kept her hand behind her, waiting for her chance.

"What the hell are you doing?" Rafe stood by the shed, one hand propping him up as he swayed. Blood dripped down his forehead. His body wavered. He was going down.

And there was nothing she could do to stop him.

CHAPTER 41
BESIDES, IF WE'RE THE MOST INTELLIGENT THINGS IN THE UNIVERSE... WELL, THAT'S JUST DEPRESSING. ~ REKHA SHARMA

WHAT WAS RAFE THINKING? He was standing there like a sitting duck. Or a standing duck. Whichever, he was in trouble.

Michael's gun veered toward Rafe. It was her chance.

Roxy swung her right hand up and slammed the butt of the gun into Michael's temple. He dropped her arm and staggered to the side.

She took a step back and raised the gun with both hands. Safety off. Pull the trigger. The bullet ricocheted off the ground and hit Michael in the leg. He fell to the ground, his gun skittering across the gravel.

She ran after it and kicked it further away from Michael, toward Rafe. "Are you okay?" She motioned to her own forehead, miming where blood trickled down on his.

"Just a scratch." He winced as he touched his head. "Is that my gun?"

She nodded as she handed it to him. He was so

much more effective with the thing. Her aim required bouncing.

"I'm proud of you." Rafe put an arm around her shoulder as he kept the gun trained on Michael. Michael seemed to be out. Rafe didn't seem to be doing much better. The gash was angry and red. The blood was now running down his face.

"Are you sure it's just a scratch?" She ran her right hand along the side of his chin. He smiled, but then a frown erupted across his face like a bolt of lightning.

Rafe shoved her to the side, to his left, and Roxy stumbled against him. Michael ran toward them, anger and murder in his narrowed eyes.

The loud explosion of a gun being fired rattled her ears. Michael jerked, his shoulder going red before he fell back onto the ground.

Rafe stumbled, gun dropping to his side. Roxy grabbed his left arm and steadied him. "You're okay." She pulled him close.

"Thanks for catching me." He wobbled as she held tight. She didn't want him to hit the ground. He might bang his head again. There was no saying whether he had a concussion but why give him another chance to catch one. Michael lay in a heap on the ground. His arm twitched, so he was still alive, but he didn't appear to be getting up.

Rafe leaned against her. His head resting on her forehead. He breathed in and out. His eyes shut. "I'm okay." After a moment, he straightened up and smiled at her. "Thanks for grabbing my gun. I'm glad I gave you my spare fob for the truck. Maybe you should keep it."

Roxy had the spare fob. In her pocket. The window. Ugh, this was bad.

Sirens whipped around the corner into the lot, followed by twirling lights. MacAuley's SUV stopped at the edge of the lot and he jumped out, followed by a legion of Metro cars and uniformed police.

MacAuley ran up to Roxy and Rafe. "Anyone hurt?"

"No, we're fine." Rafe didn't touch his head. He didn't seem to be showing any pain or weakness.

Roxy tattled. "He was hit in the head."

MacAuley rolled his eyes as he dialed his phone. "It's MacAuley. I need an ambulance." He rattled off the address.

"Why did you say that?" Rafe whispered to Roxy.

"Because it's true." She rolled her eyes. Boys. "MacAuley, there's another guy inside."

The next hour went by in a flash. Michael and Jawscar, whose name was actually Tony, were checked by the EMTs and released to Metro for processing. Rafe and Roxy were also checked by the EMTs and given the all-clear.

"We'll get your official statements tomorrow." MacAuley pointed to someone and yelled, "Don't forget to tape off the shed," before turning back to Roxy and Rafe. "Where were we?"

Roxy sighed. "MacAuley, let's just get this over with."

"Fine. Why were you here?"

"We wanted to talk to Michael."

"I told you to step back."

"You did. But to be fair, I never listen."

MacAuley sighed. "At least you acknowledge it. So what happened when you got here?"

"We went inside and got separated," Roxy said. "I was caught by Tony and thrown out. That's when I called you. Then I went back inside."

"Even though I instructed you to stay out."

Roxy shrugged. Did she really need to say that she never listened... again? Maybe he was the one that didn't listen.

"Keep going." MacAuley sighed. Again. He knew.

"I found Rafe's phone on the floor. I grabbed a metal rod, and then I found Tony and Michael standing over Rafe."

"Michael sucker-punched me," Rafe growled. MacAuley's lips quirked up and, given Rafe's scowl, he noticed.

She needed to keep this on track or Rafe would be going downtown for assaulting a police officer. "They were talking about taking Rafe hostage. I knew I needed to keep them here until the cavalry came, so I taunted them."

"Taunted?" MacAuley and Rafe said at the same time.

"I took a picture." She pulled out her phone and started to scroll. She found the one she wanted. "See."

She showed them the picture of Michael and Tony holding an unconscious Rafe. Rafe growled. MacAuley snickered. Roxy continued. "Then Jaw-scar, I mean Tony, followed me to the other side of the building. I hit him with the piece of metal and came out here to see Michael dragging Rafe out. Then I got Rafe's gun from the truck." She figured she should leave out exactly how she got in. He'd find out soon enough. "And while he was distracted by Rafe, I hit him with the gun."

"Did you discharge the weapon?" MacAuley asked.

"I did and hit Michael." Roxy added, "Well, the shot hit the ground and then Michael." If they needed to get specific. Which apparently MacAuley did.

"Did Michael shoot back?"

"I didn't give him a chance."

MacAuley waved a hand. "Then what happened to the window on Rafe's truck?"

"What's wrong with my truck?" Rafe walked over to his truck and said a few swear words. He started back. She figured she'd wait to tell the story so she didn't have to relive this twice.

Once Rafe came back, she continued. "Michael had Rafe and a gun and I only had a piece of pipe. So, I used the pipe to get into the truck."

"You used the pipe?" Rafe said slowly, like she'd said something incomprehensible.

"I broke the window and unlocked the door. That way I could grab the gun."

"Why didn't you just use the fob I gave you?" Rafe's tone said he didn't much like her story.

"Um. I forgot I had it?"

"What about the code?"

"I couldn't remember it. I was stressed." She wasn't lying. She had been.

MacAuley smiled. Rafe didn't.

"I figured you'd be so happy you weren't dead that you wouldn't mind that I had to break the window to get the gun."

Rafe narrowed his eyes. "But you didn't need to break the window. All you needed to do was stand near the driver's side and the door would unlock."

"But I didn't know that." Roxy was getting pretty frustrated. It's not like she did it on purpose.

Rafe huffed.

MacAuley held back a laugh. Poorly.

Roxy continued. "I gave Rafe the gun, since he's probably a better shot, and you showed up right after that."

"I don't know you hit a guy with a ricochet. Not many people can do that." MacAuley actually sounded impressed.

"I think it's called luck."

"Twice?" MacAuley smiled. "You hit your target last time too."

The fact that there was a "last time" was why Detective Geary didn't seem to like her. It wasn't normal. She acknowledged her gift. She also acknowledged a desire for a refund.

"Can we go?" Rafe was cranky. She'd like to think it was from all the excitement of the day and a head injury, but she had a feeling it was his mangled truck.

"We can help more if you need us." They could answer questions. Put up police tape. Sweep. She wasn't picky.

"No, You two go. We'll reach out if we have any questions."

Roxy followed Rafe to the truck. She walked up to the passenger side and stared at the lack of glass in the window. MacAuley must have cleaned up the jagged pieces. Which was good. But she could see pieces strewn on the front passenger seat.

Rafe opened the back door on the driver's side. "Ahem."

"I suppose I shouldn't sit in the broken glass?" Roxy should probably be happy he wasn't leaving her here.

"I suppose not." He waited till she was inside and closed the door. Given the anger on his face, she was impressed he waited and didn't just pulverize her with the door.

He climbed behind the wheel and the engine roared to life. They drove for about twenty minutes in absolute silence. The only sound her guilt beating a tune in her head.

She worried her fingers and just plain worried.

The click of turn signal.

The occasional honk from outside the truck.

The whir of asphalt as they sped down the 15.

But the absence of words was killing her. "I'm so sorry. You were being held at gunpoint. I had to do something. I didn't mean to... I mean, I forgot I had the fob and I was just so worried and I didn't know what to do. I love you and..." *Oh crap*. She'd never said that before. This wasn't the right time or place.

The silence that met those words told her everything she needed to know. She wanted to sink into the seat and disappear. Forever.

CHAPTER 42
LOVE IS A MISUNDERSTANDING BETWEEN TWO FOOLS. ~ OSCAR WILDE

SHE NEEDED TO SAVE THIS. Love was a word that could be used for so many things. "I didn't mean it like that. I meant I love spending time with you and being with you and there's so much to love about you…"

What was wrong with her mouth? The path between her brain and tongue must be on the fritz. "Um. I'm done."

Well, she wasn't done, she had to fix this. "One more thing. I'll get my car back and you can use it until your car is fixed, and it goes without saying I'll pay to fix the window." She'd have to beg her mother for the money to cover both and be in servitude to her for the foreseeable future. But it was worth it to fix her mess.

Rafe shook his head. He wasn't going to forgive her. Well, he'd see that she was persistent. She'd find a way to fix it. She stared at his reflection in the rearview mirror, trying to get him to accept her apology through ESP.

He broke the silence. "I'd do anything for you, too, if you were in danger. I get it." He slammed his hand into the steering wheel. "I can't believe I let that guy get the jump on me. I'm usually better than that."

"Didn't he hit you from behind?"

"It doesn't matter, I shouldn't have let my guard down. You shouldn't have even had to break the window. I should have been on top of things." He sighed. "But don't worry about your car. I texted one of my guys when you were being checked out by the EMTs and had him pick it up."

"But the money?"

"I paid for it." A small smile played at his lips. "And just so there's no confusion, I love you too."

Roxy felt her smile all the way to her toes. He hadn't said the words before, either. She could admit they made her feel all warm and fuzzy. "So where are we headed?"

"My place, to get cleaned up."

"Are we cleaning up together? To save water and all."

Rafe looked back at her and smiled. The wattage was on full blast. She was pretty sure her smile matched his. "To save water."

She sat back in the seat and smiled. Yes. There was a lot of smiling. And yes, she was pretty sure she looked like a lovesick teen. But he loved her—so—she was allowed all of that and more.

Bootylicious sang out from the truck's speakers. She'd paired her phone with the truck when she first started using it.

Rafe jumped. "What is that?"

"My ring tone. Isn't it fun?" Roxy reached into the front seat and accepted the call.

"I could've done that." Rafe lips quirked. "Shouldn't you have your seatbelt on?"

She put the belt on and lifted her arms to show she'd obeyed his demands with a flourish.

"Hello? Roxy?" the voice on the phone said.

"Hi."

"This is Gabe Martin at Pura Vida. Have you seen Rafe?"

"I'm right here," Rafe said.

"Where have you been? We've been trying to reach you for hours." Gabe sounded frantic, and if he was looking for his boss, something must have happened.

"What's going on?"

"The Meadsy painting is gone."

"What do you mean 'gone'?" Rafe's voice raised an octave before he reined it back in.

"Someone stole it."

Stolen painting at Rafe's casino. That wasn't good.

A couple hours later, Roxy left Rafe's room feeling refreshed. She'd had something to eat, taken a shower, and basked in the glow of the words Rafe had said earlier. She'd also heard from Sarina, and she was out of the hospital and on her way to her parent's house.

And MacAuley called, saying that Jared was let go since he hadn't actually killed Cliff. Child Services picked him up from Metro and was working with

Destiny so that he could go with her to Los Angeles. He was excited to help out with the baby while Destiny worked. Roxy couldn't help but smile. The kid had lived through quite a bit. He deserved some happiness.

So far, a good day. With the exception of Rafe's job. He hadn't had time to eat or bathe or anything. Hopefully someone checked the wound on his head. The EMTs had cleaned it up, but they told her to keep an eye on him. He wouldn't stop to let her do it when they got back. Apparently a missing painting overrode personal care.

Roxy's phone rang. Karan. *Crap.* She'd forgotten about her. And the fact that Karan wanted to kill her. Maybe she wouldn't make it hurt as much if she answered. "Hi, Karan."

"Where are you?"

"I was clearing Sarina's name."

"You have work here to do." Karan's voice was harsh. Angry. "Did you forget?"

"No." Roxy sighed. How could she forget when Satan's mistress was waiting for her? No matter how much she'd like to. "I'm heading back now." In her car. Which was fixed. With Rafe's help.

"Good. I'll see you within the hour."

"I don't think...." Roxy started but Karan ended the call. There was no way Roxy would be back to the office in an hour. She had to check on Rafe and get across the valley. Well, she might be able to do it if she hurried, but she wasn't going to do that. Not when the man she loved was going through so much.

She walked the mostly empty halls and made her way to the main floor. On the outside, the hotel looked and felt the same. People milled around drinking, gambling and enjoying all that the strip had to offer. As she walked behind the large reception desk to the office area, Pura Vida was a cacophony of noise. Normally she would not have been able to get this far into the inner sanctum, but today no one stopped her. Everyone was too busy dealing with the fallout.

She walked past a room where Gabe stood in front of a group of security guards, well, she thought they were guards, given their suits.

"...if you notice anything out of the ordinary, report it. Immediately! There is no reason for two banners to be up for over a minute in any hallway!"

"Get back to work." Rafe stood up from the side of the room. Exhaustion paled his skin and drooped his eyes.

Roxy passed the men and women in suits as she made her way to him. The good news was that the wound on his head was still covered and he looked coherent. "How's it going, or should I not ask?"

He shook his head. He waited for the group to leave. "Gabe, shut the door."

"Yeah, boss."

Rafe dropped to a chair and sighed. "I don't know how they did it."

"Didn't one of your million cameras catch anything?"

"Nothing of use." He must have seen her confusion

because he continued. "They put up two retractable banners, grabbed the painting from the storage room, and then disappeared. My staff went to take down the banners and the painting was gone."

"Was it expensive?"

"Estimated two million dollars." So that was a yes. "They're threatening to fire the staff on duty at the time."

"What about you?"

"They haven't mentioned me yet, but it's only a matter of time. I'll find something, but these people have lives here. They can't just up and leave the city."

"You have a life here, too." She kneeled down and grabbed his hand.

"I do." His lips tipped up ever so slightly and he squeezed her hand.

She felt all his exhaustion, confusion, and concern in that one movement. "What a mess."

"It is a mess." A woman with short brown hair in a meticulous bob must have opened the door, because she was click-clacking into the room. Her black dress and heels were catwalk ready. Her scowl said she wasn't here for anything that fun. Those red pouty lips set off severe cheekbones and a perfectly sized nose. Her blue eyes sparkled. She was gorgeous. "Hi, Rafe."

And she knew Rafe.

Roxy turned to the man in question. All color had drained from his face. If she thought he looked pale before, this was a whole new hue for him.

"Monique, why are you here?"

Monique. The ex-wife. Whoa. In Roxy's imagination, Monique was short and round, possibly bald. She never thought Monique would look like a goddess. Or maybe she just hoped she wouldn't.

"You don't sound happy to see me."

Rafe didn't say anything, just scowled.

"Well, that's no way to treat your wife."

Wife? Roxy turned to Rafe. "You mean ex-wife." Roxy pulled her hand away from him.

Exhaustion. Guilt. All of his emotions appeared on his pale, sweaty face.

"I'm sorry he's so rude." Monique click-clacked up to Roxy. "I'm Monique De La Rue. I'm Rafe's wife."

"De La Rue?" Shouldn't she have Rafe's last name? So obviously they were divorced, like he said.

"I kept my maiden name. And you are?"

"Roxy Horne." Her voice wavered. She was pretty sure of it. But since she just found out her boyfriend was married, she'd give herself some grace. He wasn't going to get any of it, though.

"Enough, Monique." Rafe found his voice. "Tell her why we're still married."

They were still married. That meant she was an adulterer— or at the least the other woman. Shouldn't that mean she was younger, prettier, and had better hair? That was how it was supposed to work, in her experience.

"We're married because we love each other," Rafe's wife said. We just work in different countries."

"Monique?" MacAuley stood in the doorway and stared at the brunette bombshell that was currently imploding Roxy's life.

"Detective. Look at you. You get better-looking with age." She walked toward him and wrapped him in a hug.

"What are you doing here?"

"I'm the insurance investigator assigned to this case."

"I thought you were in Paris." MacAuley looked over at Rafe. Concern furrowed his brow. Old friendships died hard. Then he looked at Roxy. More concern. She must not be hiding her shock and awe very well.

Monique kept talking. Roxy stopped listening as she got to her feet. Her head swam. Her blood pooled in her feet. She couldn't move. She couldn't think. All she wanted to do was run, but she couldn't remember how to move her feet.

How could he have a wife? He'd said they were divorced. But apparently his wife hadn't gotten the memo, the way she was looking at him.

Roxy inched back toward the door. She needed to leave. She couldn't be here anymore. Her eyes wanted to cry. Her ears wanted the rushing sound of an erratic heartbeat to just go away.

"Roxy?"

She didn't want to talk or hear any explanation. She walked out the door and didn't look back. She swore she heard Rafe get up, which made her walk faster.

"Roxy, wait."

"Rafe." That was Rafe's boss. Good, he'd be too busy to give chase. "Any news?"

"No, sir," Rafe answered and the voices slowly dissipated as she put more and more space between her and the headache. Thank God her car was fixed.

She did get the irony that the person she should be thanking for that was the same person she needed to use the car to get away from.

CHAPTER 43
LOVE STINKS. ~ J. GEILS BAND

A HALF HOUR LATER, Roxy walked into Sarina's parents' house.

"Where are your parents?" Roxy dropped to the couch next to Sarina's feet.

"They went out. Finally." Sarina was laying on the oversized couch, a blanket covering the lower half of her body. Her arm was still in a cast and, given the bulge under from the blanket, so was her leg, but the bruising had subsided. She didn't look like a complete punching bag, only partially, with patches of yellow across her face.

She looked so small compared to the house. It was a giant estate, complete with horse stables, in an older part of Henderson lovingly called Hendertucky. The houses were older, and you might find a dilapidated car in the front yard. But not at Sarina's parent's house, which was continuously updated. Her mom needed a hobby.

"They left you alone?" Roxy asked.

"Yeah, they needed to run errands. I have my phone next to me and have been sworn to contact them with any issues."

"So, how are you feeling?"

"I'm okay." Sarina's lips played with a smile. She looked tired. But then again, who wouldn't be after all she'd been through. "I'm glad to be done with all this. Now I have time to actually process everything that happened."

"How's that going?" It sounded like a nightmare to Roxy. After all Sarina had been through, oblivious sounded like a better idea.

Heck, after Roxy's day, she would give anything for oblivious.

"I've cried a lot, but mostly because I just feel dumb. I put up with so much and he didn't deserve it. I shouldn't have put up with any of it." Sarina shook her head. "I don't want to think about it anymore. How are you?"

"It's not about me. It's about you."

"Please don't make it about me. I'm so sick of me." Sarina smiled, but her lips drooped as she watched Roxy. "What's wrong?"

"Rafe is married." The words stuck in her throat, as well as the tears that wanted to fall, but she refused to cry.

"What do mean 'married'?" Sarina's eyes popped open.

"Not single. Has a wife. There aren't many different options for marriage."

"Oh, honey. Maybe it's a misunderstanding."

Roxy shook her head. "It doesn't matter. He swore he wouldn't keep things from me."

"Honey." Sarina frowned as she rested her hand on Roxy's. "What do you need? Do we think he can make this right? Do you want a pep talk? Or do we hate him?"

Roxy didn't want to hate him, but it was so hard. All her emotions were swirling inside. "I'm not sure."

"It's okay. You take your time and whatever you decide, I'll be here to support you."

She was so glad that she was with her best friend. Her day somehow went from fearing for her life, to "I love you", to her boyfriend had a wife. Quite the rollercoaster.

Personally, she was ready to get off.

EXTRAS

Thank you for supporting an independent author. It would be great if you could leave a review or a rating wherever you purchased this book, or on Goodreads.

Would you like to know when my next book is available? You can sign up for my new release email list at http://www.vanessamknight.com or like my Facebook page at http://facebook.com/vanessamknightauthor.

ABOUT THE AUTHOR

Vanessa M. Knight has always enjoyed writing, and once she found mystery and romance, she was addicted. She props her laptop in the suburbs of Chicago with her family and menagerie of four-pawed claw-babies (AKA cats and dogs.) That laptop has partnered-in-crime to write contemporary romances with a dash of humor and splash of snark.

When she has a few moments to spare, you can find her singing off-key (but she assures everyone it's still considered singing), reading, kickboxing, or killing a few brain cells as she stares at the many sitcoms and dramas available through the Internet and TV.

For more information on Vanessa, including her Internet haunts, contest updates, and details on her upcoming novels, please visit her website at www.-vanessamknight.com.

OTHER BOOKS BY THIS AUTHOR

MYSTERY

Swing Into Murder

Roxy Horne Series

Strangers in the Knight - Novella

Come Die with Me

Luck be Fatal Tonight

Straighten up and Die Right

Vegas Victory FC Novels

Deadly. Set. Vegas.

ROMANTIC SUSPENSE

Chicago's Finest Series

Second Time's the Charm

Stark Raving Mad

Stealing Vegas

Final Strike

Busted Series

Busting In

Busting Out

Busting Through

Busting Loose

CONTEMPORARY NEW ADULT

Ritter University Series

Major Renovations

What Happens in College...

Christmas Breakdown

Rushing In

Sophomore Slump

The Make-up Test

www.ingramcontent.com/pod-product-compliance
Lightning Source LLC
LaVergne TN
LVHW032007070526
838202LV00059B/6336